BLUSH

THE CRESCENT LAKE WINERY SERIES

LUCINDA RACE

MC TWO PRESS

BOOK 3

Blush
The Crescent Lake Winery Series
Book 3

By
Lucinda Race

Manufactured in the United States of America
First Edition August 2021

Print Edition ISBN 978-1-7331616-5-7
E-book Edition ISBN 978-1-7331616-4-0

INSPIRATION

Wine enters through the mouth, Love, the eyes.
I raise the glass to my mouth, I look at you, I sigh.
Willian Butler Yeats

"Peyton, are you in here?" Kate Price walked through the door that connected the Crescent Lake Winery tasting room and Kay-Dee's Bistro.

Peyton Brien looked up at her best friend. "Over here." She paused unpacking the box of glasses at the bar. "Look at you in your chef coat. Hard at work this morning?" There were a few stains on Kate's usually pristine coat that she wore over her slender prepregnancy figure.

"I'm trying some new recipes and knocked a bowl over." Kate's gaze took in the stack of boxes on the long wooden bar and on the floor. "What's all this?"

"The Finger Lakes wine trail spring season kicks off April fifteenth, which is less than two weeks away, and I ordered new logo wineglasses." Peyton held one up. "What do you think? I went with a new style for a new season—shake things up a bit." Spring was her favorite time of year, when she believed anything was possible, and she was excited to discover what was next in her life.

Kate took one out of the open box. "Nice, and I like that they're stemless. Classy. But you ordered a ton."

Peyton flashed her a grin. "You forget people come in droves to eat in a certain restaurant here at CLW and ever since you got back in the kitchen from having the twins, the tasting room is busier than ever."

Kate perched on a barstool. "Which brings me to the reason I stopped in. Any chance you want to try some of the new menu items?"

Peyton thought of the peanut butter sandwich in her bag. There was no contest. Lunch with Kate definitely had much more appeal.

Before she could answer, the back door to the tasting room opened and Jack Price strode in. "Did I hear someone say lunch?"

His tall, muscular body, blond hair, and golden-hazel eyes used to make Peyton's heart pound, but that was ten years ago when they were a couple. Now they were just coworkers and he was Kate's brother-in-law.

"Hey, Jack." Peyton returned to unpacking glasses.

"I didn't expect to see you today, Jack," Kate said. "Don mentioned you'd be in the fields all day, pruning vines."

He looked around the spacious room filled with small tables and wine displays. "Where is my brother?"

"He had a meeting at the bank about the new fermenting tanks you want to install this year."

Jack rubbed his hands together, and his smile crinkled the corners of his eyes. "Good. That means more food for me." He quirked an eyebrow. "That's if you don't mind me joining you ladies."

Peyton said, "No problem here." Thankfully, they had finally gotten past that awkward stage when they were in the same room. At one time, they had been friends, then lovers, and finally friends again years after he'd broken her heart. He'd asked her out a couple of times, but she'd turned him down. She doubted the feelings of renewal that came every spring would affect her and Jack.

Working for the Price family was more than a job to Peyton; it was her passion. And given how busy they'd been the past tourist seasons, that was a good thing. She was hoping for another successful season and maybe at the end of it, she'd talk to Don and ask for a raise.

Kate got up. "Give me five minutes and I'll meet you in the dining room."

"I'll give you a hand." Peyton stepped from behind the bar.

Jack held up his dirt-covered hands and gave Peyton a wink and smile. "I'll need to wash up."

Unaffected by his charms, Peyton walked with Kate through the inviting dining room. Small tables with two and four chairs filled the space. The large windows overlooking the vineyard allowed the warm sun to flood the room. Adding to the allure of the space, the French doors were propped open to the gazebo area, letting in the crisp spring air.

"This is one of my favorite views of the property. I'm glad you decided to build the bistro here."

Kate held open the swinging kitchen door for them. "I almost didn't. Sam was way too pushy and dangled my dream as a bribe just to get Don to take over the winery business. But it turned out to be a win for us. I have a wonderful husband, three healthy kids, and my own business."

"You're a lucky woman. I have one of the three."

"How is Owen?" Kate began to plate their lunch as Peyton watched.

"A typical almost eight-year-old. He's always on the

move. His new love is fishing; it's all he talks about—well, except his birthday at the end of August."

"And how are things with Jerry?"

Peyton slashed her hand across her throat. "Dead. Turns out he was just another loser. I can't seem to pick a good guy who wants to take things at a slower pace."

"What about going out with Jack? He's a good guy and hasn't dated much since he moved back from Napa a couple of years ago." Kate set an overfilled plate on the shelf between the prep area and Peyton.

Slowly shaking her head, Peyton said, "That ship sailed a long time ago. When he took that job in Napa, it broke my heart. He left without even a conversation."

Kate paused. "I'm sorry. I had no idea he left that way."

Peyton gave her a smile. "Ancient history." She felt a pang of regret for what might have been. Back then, she had thought they had a forever kind of love. Life would have been very different if he hadn't left. But then, she wouldn't have Owen, who was the light of her life.

Kate filled two more plates. "Hungry?"

"Starved." Peyton balanced two plates and walked through the swinging door backside first. Jack was on the other side of the room, looking at his cell phone.

Peyton said, "Lunch is ready."

*J*ack scanned his email. There was a forwarded email from the winery customer service team to his attention. The subject line: *Urgent. Please call me.* He dismissed it as a mistake and slipped the phone into his back pocket; he'd let them know later.

He flashed a wide smile at Peyton and made sure it

included Kate. He didn't want to come off as being single-minded, but a very pretty petite brunette with soulful deep brown eyes was always on his mind. The biggest regret in his life was letting Peyton break up with him all those years ago, even if going to Napa was the best course of action for him and his father.

He took the chair next to her. "So, Katie, should I just eat and tell you what I like the best, or is this where I need to give a grade to each individual dish?" His fork was poised as he waited to dive in.

"Tell me as you go, please."

Peyton looked up from her plate. "I don't know if I can eat all of this food. But I'll do my best."

The trio enjoyed lunch and lighthearted conversation.

Jack said, "Peyton, I swung by the Little League practice the other night and saw you were helping out some kids."

"They lost one of the coaches; he broke a leg, I think. The league director asked if I'd lend a hand for a couple of practices until they get a new coach."

"Yeah, Liza filled me in. I was thinking of volunteering. I could spend time with Johnny and George."

"I'm sure they'd love it." She took a drink of her water. "I'm not sure if Liza told you, but there's another practice tonight if you're serious about pitching in. The kids have been improving over the last couple of weeks."

"I'll swing by. Is it at the middle school again?"

"Yes, and there's only six weeks left, except for the final playoff game."

He thought, *That will give me six weeks to see her outside of work.* "Would you happen to have the director's phone number? I could give him a call this afternoon."

"If you're serious, swing by the tasting room before

you head back out into the fields and I'll write the number down. But to be an official coach, you'd have to get a background check." Peyton gave him a side-look. "That takes a week, usually more to get back."

"I should be in good shape; I coached the boys' basketball team last winter." He patted his stomach. "Kate, best lunch I've had in quite some time. Thanks for letting me crash the party." He jabbed a piece of frittata before he got up and popped it in his mouth. "This is a keeper. What wine would you pair it with?"

It didn't take Kate but a moment to turn the question around. "Peyton, what would you suggest?"

She took a bite and seemed to let the flavors mingle on her tongue. "The Pinot Gris. Unless you decide to add some heavier ingredients like sausage."

"There you go, Jack. Our tasting room guru has made her selection."

Peyton's cheeks flushed a sweet shade of pink. Jack was pleased to see that some things hadn't changed. He picked up the now empty plates. "I'll leave these in the kitchen and I'm going to see if Don's back yet." He looked at Peyton. "I'll stop back for that number."

"Sure. I'll be here until four."

Damn. She's completely unfazed by my presence. Is there any hope she might still have lingering feelings for me? He walked out of the dining room with the plates, leaving Peyton and Kate to enjoy the rest of their lunch.

*K*ate leaned back and crossed her arms. "That didn't stir up old feelings at all, did it?"

Peyton lifted her eyes. "What, having lunch with Jack? No. Why? Should it?"

"You loved him once and…" Her voice trailed off. "Huh."

"I've had years to get Jackson Price out of my system. As far as I'm concerned, we're coworkers and now, possibly, he might be Owen's baseball coach but really, it's no big deal. No sparks or embers here."

"I don't think I could be as chill around my ex as you are being around yours." Kate wiped her mouth on the napkin. "Especially a Price. When they get under your skin, they tend to stay there. I know from personal experience."

Peyton drank the last of her water before responding. How could anyone really understand that when she and Jack had dated, they were both different people than they were now? But she had loved him with all her heart. Did it even matter? "Who knows, Kate. Maybe it was because we were young, and life has taken us down very different roads. Besides, we agreed when he moved back that the past was just that, the past, and no sense dwelling on it."

Jack jogged into the dining room. "Excuse me, ladies. Kate, I didn't find Don. Will you tell him I'll catch up with him later? I need to get back outside."

"Sure."

He looked at Peyton. "Any chance you could get me that phone number now? I'd like to call the director this afternoon."

"I'll be right back." Peyton followed him into the tasting room. "Jack, it's really nice that you're going to help out. I wish more adults had the time to volunteer. It means so much to the kids."

She wrote down the phone number and handed it to him. "Here you go."

He stuffed the slip of paper into his shirt pocket. "I'm glad we can work together like this, for the kids."

She could feel her forehead crinkle. "Me too."

"Well," he hemmed, "I thought, given our history—"

"We should live in the present, Jack. The past doesn't matter." Peyton walked behind the bar. "I need to get back to work."

A flash of confusion hovered in his eyes. "Alright. See you around."

She went back to unpacking glasses, but her eyes followed him as he walked out the door.

2

*P*eyton called down the hall to her son. "Come on, pokey! We're going to be late for practice."

She thought Owen mumbled that he couldn't find his glove. She stuck her head into his bedroom. It was like a small tornado had hit sometime in the last half hour. She could see two long, skinny legs sticking out from underneath the twin-sized bed with the Superman bedspread half on the floor.

"O, your glove is in the middle of your bed."

The spread flew up and over the end of the bed and he crawled crablike out from underneath it. His blond hair was sticking up everywhere, and his grin warmed his deep brown eyes. "Thanks, Mom."

"You need to change into your uniform. Coach said you're having team pictures tonight too."

"But I can't find my shirt." He whirled around.

"Everything is on the top of your dresser."

He pulled his T-shirt off and dropped it on the floor. She pointed to it. "Hamper, please."

"Do you think Jack will come to practice again?" His

eyes lit up every time he talked about Johnny and George's uncle. "Or maybe even a game? He always builds forts with us when I'm over at their house."

"We'll have to see. Now get ready; we need to leave."

She went into the kitchen to pack water and a snack for them both. She wasn't going to mention that Jack was a new coach, just in case he changed his mind. In reality, he was doing this for his nephews. It had nothing to do with Owen or, for that matter, her. She couldn't help but wonder if he was dating anyone. *Not that it matters to me.* At any time, Jack could fade into the background, just like he had done years ago when he left. She wouldn't mind watching him work with the kids, though; he was easy on the eyes and it stirred long-dormant feelings.

There was a time when she got to do more than just look at him. She sighed with regret. Those days were long gone. He had been a great kisser too; probably still was. She closed her eyes for just a moment to remember what it had felt like to be held in his arms. Her blood hummed just from the memory.

"Ready to go, Mom."

Her eyes fluttered open and she tossed Owen the small insulated snack bag, attempting to cover for being caught daydreaming. "Let's go, champ."

Peyton didn't see Jack's pickup truck in the ballfield's parking lot. She tried not to be disappointed and reminded herself that if he had volunteered to coach, he'd come. If nothing else, he was a man of his word when it came to his nephews.

Sometimes, when she thought of him, it was like she was in high school all over again, waiting to catch a glimpse of him when she was at the Prices' house. Jackson Price had been her first love, and in her fantasy life, she'd thought he would be her only love. But that was when she was in high school, before her life changed and she had Owen.

"Mommy."

She parked and looked in the rearview mirror. "Owen." She added the same urgent tone in her voice as he did. She bit back a grin. "What?"

"We gotta go to the dugout."

She half turned in her seat and noticed a dark pickup pulling up next to her. Jack.

"Look out the window."

A grin split Owen's cheek and he waved frantically. "Hi, Jack!"

He got out and leaned into the open passenger window. "Hi, Owen. I brought a couple of your teammates with me." He pointed to the back door. "Johnny and George."

Owen popped the buckle on his booster seat and grabbed his glove. "Really? Cool." He slid toward the door and Jack opened it so Owen could hop out. "Come on, Mom."

The back door of his truck opened and his nephews tumbled out, giving Owen a high five. Then they said hi to Peyton.

Johnny said, "Come on, Owen, let's go play."

The grin on Jack's face widened. "Yeah, come on, Mom. It's time to play ball."

Her stomach clenched. She was happy he showed up for the kids' sake, but it was disconcerting being this close to him. Those old feelings poked at the shell over her heart. "I'm right behind you."

Jack and the boys were headed for the grassy area just beyond the blacktop. The kids were talking about how far they were going to hit the ball and what position they wanted to play tonight.

"Owen, you and the boys can run ahead. We'll be right behind you." Before the words had even left her mouth, they were off and running.

Jack and Peyton strolled through the grass, side by side. She gave him a sidelong look. "It was nice of you to volunteer."

"I wanted to help out the kids and Liza. It's like you said a while back. Sometimes a mom just needs a break. The boys have been a handful lately, pushing her buttons."

"I know how that is. Owen does it too."

He nodded as if he really did understand. "This will be fun and something to get me out of the house at night. It seems for the last six months, all I've done since I bought that old farmhouse is work. I haven't even taken the boat out yet for the first trip of the season."

"I'm surprised—you love being on the water. I remember even when I was still in high school and you'd come home from college, we'd go canoeing or borrow a rowboat so you could get your fix." She looked at her sneakers and wished she hadn't brought up the past.

"We used to have a lot of fun, getting the gang together and paddling out to one of the small islands."

She looked straight ahead. "It was. I've been thinking about getting a two-person kayak for me and Owen. I'm currently in research mode, but I still haven't decided."

"You do love your research." He gave her an easy smile.

She stopped before they entered the field. The three boys huddled with the rest of the team. She pointed to a tall guy wearing a red baseball cap. "There's Head Coach Barrett."

Jack looked where she was pointing. "I need to check in and see where he needs me tonight."

She stuck an old Mickey Mouse baseball hat on her head and tucked the ends of her chin-length bob underneath the cap and brushed her bangs off her face.

Jack's eyes sparked with appreciation as he took in her outfit: jean shorts, baseball-style T-shirt, sneakers, and now the hat. "I like the hat."

"Thanks."

"I hope the team appreciates how good you were when you played shortstop back in high school. You had a great arm."

"Allow me to correct you on a few important points." She playfully wagged a finger in his direction. "I had a great arm and wheels on my feet. And no, there is no reason for me to be modest. Our team was good and that's why we made it to the state championship my junior and senior year."

He nodded.

"We won the finals my senior year, not that you would know. You weren't there." She turned away and stalked toward the infield.

*J*ack was surprised at the hurt in her voice and jogged after her. When he caught up with her, he touched her shoulder. "I was there. For every game."

She slowed and, with a shake of her head, said, "Not for the last one. I wanted to celebrate with you, but you were nowhere to be found. And then a few weeks later, poof before I graduated from high school." She waved her arm and her voice ratcheted up. "You made the decision to move to California without so much as a conversation with me, forgetting about your plans for graduate school." She tapped her chest and blinked away tears. "I would have understood, but you didn't have the courtesy to even tell me. I found out when I stopped by your parents' house and saw your bags packed. That wasn't cool." She stopped short of saying it had crushed her.

His eyes grew wide. They had gone from a friendly conversation to her fighting tears; was she still hurting from what had happened? "I saw the last out you threw, and then my buddy needed help. He had a flat tire and he was my ride to school. When I came back to the field, you were gone."

He didn't address the rest of her point. She was right.

She thrust her chin up. "I call BS. You should have talked to me before you left. Well, I'm glad you told me, but it doesn't change the rest. For right now, I need to get in gear. I promised to help one of the kids with his batting and he's waiting for me."

Jack couldn't believe Peyton turned her back on him again. He'd be damned if he would apologize for helping a friend, and it had been twelve years. She should have had more faith in him. The whole idea behind the change in his plans was to get away from Crescent Lake Winery and his father, not her. He wasn't going to follow along on the path his father had chosen for him—to work in an office or be a salesman. He had wanted to work with the land. Surely Peyton understood it was his passion.

He walked in the direction of the coach, but his thoughts were with her. He wanted to ask her to have dinner with him, see if they could get back to a better place and then maybe even start dating again.

He did a one-eighty and walked over to where she was

showing a boy how to choke up on the bat. He waited while the boy propped the bat on his shoulder and eyed the ball.

She positioned him away from the tee. "Practice swinging the bat and stay choked up on it. Okay?"

She jumped back just as the bat came slicing through the air. Jack pulled her into his body before the aluminum bat could connect with her midsection. The zing he felt being this close to her jolted him body and soul. What could he do to get them back to where they might have been if they had stayed together? He had been trying to ease toward spending time with Peyton, alone, for months. Someone was always around when they were together.

"Are you okay?" His lips hovered near her ear. He could feel the shiver race through her. Was it nerves or, could he hope, being close to him?

She pulled away. "I'm fine." She straightened her hat even though it wasn't askew. Her mouth tipped down- ward. "What did you want to talk about?"

He pushed ahead despite her chilly look. "I know this isn't the best time to ask but I'd like to take you to dinner, the two of us."

She gave him a wary look. "Like a date?"

He couldn't help but keep his smile sliding from one side of his face to the other. "It's a thing people do when they want to spend time with someone they like."

She chewed her bottom lip and looked everywhere but at Jack.

He remembered this habit. It wasn't necessarily a good sign.

With a slow shake of her head, she said, "I don't think that's a good idea. I'm really busy with Owen and, well, you know. Our history would make things awkward. We should keep our relationship in the friend zone."

He felt like a deflated balloon. "Oh." He hadn't expected her to say no; he thought things were changing between them. "Well, um, okay then. I'll go see the coach." The silence was awkward.

She jerked a thumb toward the boy still swinging the bat. "I'm going to get back to this." She kicked the ground in front of her. "Thanks anyway."

3

"**W**elcome." Peyton smiled at the three couples who approached the bar. "Is this your first time at our Spring Fling event?" She placed six stemless wineglasses on the wooden bartop.

One of the women picked up a glass. "Yes, it's the first time we've been to the Finger Lakes, and I love these glasses." Her voice had a distinctive Southern drawl.

"Have you taken the behind-the-scenes tour?"

"No. What does it cover?" The woman looked at her companions.

"You'll be escorted from the vineyard to the crush and aging rooms and then back here, where you can select five wines to taste. Or you're welcome to enjoy a bite to eat in our bistro"—she gestured to the doors behind them—"which is right through those French doors."

The woman turned to the other ladies like she was confident the men would just go along with the plan. "I'd love to do the tour and then the tasting. What do y'all think?"

The others murmured their agreement. She asked Peyton, "Where do we go to sign up?"

Peyton looked across the room and caught Jack's attention. He had just come back with a group. He came right over, smiling at everyone.

"This is Jack Price, one of the family members who owns the winery. He'll be happy to give you the tour."

"Thank you, Peyton." He clasped his hands together low, just at his waist. "If you'll follow me, we'll start in the vineyard." He pointed to his right.

The group followed him as he began his spiel about his great-grandfather, Samuel Price, who was a farmer and had encouraged his son Donald to plant grapes and make wine. His words grew faint as the group left the tasting room. By the time Jack brought them back, they'd be ready to sample—and, more importantly, buy wine.

Peyton turned her attention to a group of people who had just come from the bistro. They were ready to purchase hopefully at least a case. After she rang them up, the throngs of people were never-ending. This had to be one of their best events yet.

*J*ack walked the group from the vines through the process of how CLW wines were crafted. He stopped in front of Anna's lab. "My sister, Anna, is our enologist, but she's currently working in France. However, she's not just an award-winning winemaker but has an uncanny knack for creating specialty blends. In her absence, our father Sam has stepped in to help out."

Jack smiled when one of the men looked at his wife and asked, "What's an enologist?"

Jack continued. "An expert in making wines. They work very closely with me in monitoring the growing season right up to harvest."

"Isn't that a sommelier?" the same man asked.

"A sommelier will select and manage a wine cellar, perhaps in a restaurant. They're an expert in wines and how to pair it with food. It's all about the experience for the diner."

"Huh," the man said. "So this is quite the family affair. What's your favorite wine out of all the wines here?"

Jack made a show of thinking, but he didn't need to. "I'm a steak kind of a guy so the Cabernet Sauvignon would be my first choice." He tapped the stainless-steel tank next to him. "However, if I was thinking seafood…"

The woman grinned. "Wait. What if you were going to have Indian butter chicken?"

"Ah, trying to throw me off my practiced speech." Jack gave her a warm smile. But he was ready for her. "We have a very nice Riesling that's perfect. I'm sure you'll be able to taste it when I return you to Peyton, and if you want to have some fun, toss out a few dinner ideas and ask her what she'd suggest."

After thirty minutes, he returned the group to the tasting room, but Peyton had several people at the bar and wine was flowing as she explained the different varieties. It looked like she needed a hand with cashing out purchases. She handled each customer with finesse, as if each one had her undivided attention. She smiled, answering questions and making recommendations for pairings from appetizers to dessert.

He was pleased when he noticed his brother Leo walking through the back of the room and waved him over.

"Leo, would you be able to carry a few cases out for these folks?"

His younger brother stacked the two cases on a small dolly and turned to an older couple. "If you're ready, I'll follow you to your car." Leo pushed the door with his backside and held it open as they preceded him out.

After a couple more hours, the crowd had finally thinned. The last few customers were walking out the door when Jack leaned against the bar and smacked her a high five. Peyton poured a glass of water and, without asking, handed him one too. "Thanks for pitching in this afternoon. Things went from steady to a zoo in a blink of an eye." She took a long drink and pushed her bangs off her forehead. "What about the tours?"

"Dad and Don took over. They saw the controlled chaos out here and knew you needed an extra set of hands." He held his up. "Mine."

She frowned. "I don't want them to think I can't handle the traffic."

"You're kidding, right? Don't take that the wrong way. People were four and five deep in front of the bar. There's no way you would have finished everyone by closing time and given each one the personal attention you're famous for." He held up his hand. "With the number of people here today, I'd say this was the best opening weekend we've ever had."

Kate came out of the bistro. She was wiping her hands and still wearing her chef coat with black-and-white-checked pants. She made a beeline for the bar and dropped to a stool.

Peyton handed her a glass of water. "Good day?"

"Better than I had hoped. I ran out of the special within ninety minutes. I'm going to be prepping for a while before I can call it a day so I'll be ready for tomorrow. The final day is always the busiest during Spring Fling and I sent Stan home since he's going to come in early tomorrow."

It was nice of Kate to send her assistant chef home. Today had been so insane. Peyton looked at Jack. "I'll help. I can chop."

"I'll help too," Jack said, "and I'm sure Don will pitch in too if Mom and Dad can go over to your place and take over for the nanny."

"How's Jessie working out?" Peyton asked Kate.

"She's great with the kids. I swear she has an extra set of hands and eyes in the back of her head to take care of Ben and the babies."

"That's good to hear." Peyton had to wonder if she should have volunteered to help. With Jack around, it would be hard to remain aloof.

Kate laid a hand on Peyton's. "Don't you need to get home to Owen?"

"I'll call Mom to make sure they don't have plans, but I'm sure I have time."

"Thanks, Peyton. I appreciate the help."

Peyton hoped this wouldn't be a mistake. She gave Jack a tight smile. "What are friends for."

Side by side, Peyton and Jack chopped vegetables, making short work of the mounds of peppers, onions, and mushrooms while Don sautéed onions and Kate rolled out crust for quiche. The kitchen had a lingering aroma that made Peyton's mouth water; she realized she was hungry.

"Kate, would you mind if I made some sandwiches for us? They won't be chef caliber but they'll fill the void."

Jack said, "I'll lend a hand."

Peyton found it oddly disconcerting to be working this close to Jack. In some ways, it felt like old times. When they dated, they had often worked together on opening day. Surprisingly, it felt good to be more at ease when she was around him.

Kate glanced over her shoulder. "I can't remember when I ate last either. Sandwiches sound great. Grab whatever looks good from the walk-in."

Don kissed his wife's cheek. "If I were to guess, it was probably breakfast. Once you get to work, you tend to forget about yourself and focus on taking care of your customers."

Peyton watched them and wished she had a great guy in her life. One who, like Don, would move heaven and earth for their happiness as a couple. Unlike Jack, who took off without a backward glance or a decent explanation of why he chose to take a job three thousand miles away right after his senior year of college. She hadn't even known he was thinking about it. Her mood began to sour and she had to shake off the dark cloud that was beginning to cast a pall over what had been a good day.

*J*ack stood in the open door of the walk-in refrigerator. "What's everyone in the mood for? There's some chicken salad, or I could whip up omelets if you don't need the eggs for quiche."

"I vote for eggs, and I ordered plenty," Kate said.

He handed Peyton a bowl of eggs and gathered other ingredients to be mixed in. "Can you break six eggs into each of these smaller bowls and whisk them up?" He took two skillets from the pot rack and added butter, then handfuls of freshly chopped onions, peppers, and mushrooms. He made it look effortless; she'd still be dicing peppers if it were her job. "Could you grate some cheese for these? I saw some cheddar on the right side of the fridge."

"I'll grab a bag for you." She could hear Kate laugh softly and looked around the kitchen. "Did I say something wrong?"

"I'm a bit of a purist when it comes to cheese, Peyton. I don't purchase pre-shredded to use in the bistro. In my opinion, block cheese retains its flavors better."

"Oh, I had no idea. I hate to sound dumb, but I've never grated cheese before."

Jack took her by the hand and pulled her to the workstation. "I'll show you where the grater is."

She gave him a cautious look. Did he have a hidden agenda? But it didn't matter; she knew where she stood.

His spicy cologne teased her senses. It smelled like the same one she had bought him for his last birthday when they were together. It was something she'd never forget.

"Peyton, is something wrong?" he asked.

"No. Just wondering how quickly I'll get the gist on using the food processor. Remember, I don't cook."

He handed her a metal box-looking thing that was covered with sharp holes. "You're going to use this." His eyes twinkled with laughter. "It's called a cheese grater."

"Hmm, I've seen them in the store but didn't realize people still used manual tools. Are you sure we just can't toss the block into the food processor and press the *on* button?" She was teasing at this point, and it was fun to poke at him.

He handed her a wedge of cheese. "Just run the cheese over the face of the grater and it will pile up inside the box."

"Well, I kinda figured that." She took it and made short work of the cheese. She dumped it all in a bowl as the egg mixture sizzled in the hot pan.

"Give me five minutes and we'll be ready to eat."

She gave him a light pat on the back. Working together had been fun, but it had caused the scab over her heart to crack open. It had taken years to build that scab up. "I can't wait."

*B*efore she left for the day, she stopped back in the kitchen in search of Jack. He was drinking a cup of coffee and talking to Don.

"Hey, Jack, I just wanted to say thanks again for your help in the tasting room this afternoon."

"You're welcome. It was fun. Like old times."

She said, "Alright, we'll see you Tuesday for the game?"

"That's the plan."

He gave her a smile that sent a ripple through her. She shook off the old familiar feeling. "Okay. Bye, Don." She called out, "Kate, see you tomorrow."

Kate popped her head out of the back room. "Hold on; I'll walk you out."

The two women crossed the tasting room and through the side door, emerging into the early evening. The air was cool and Peyton shivered. She wished she had a coat.

"I'm going to cut to the chase. Can I just say that for

someone who says she's over her old love, the sparks were bouncing all over the place in my kitchen? Are you sure there's not a chance you would consider going out with him if he asked?"

"He already did, the other day at baseball practice, and I turned him down." She opened the driver's door and tossed her bag inside. "We're better off as friends."

"I think you should reconsider." Kate gave her a hug. "But I appreciate the help tonight. See you tomorrow?"

"Yes, I'll be here." Peyton got into her car and Kate went back inside to her handsome husband who waited for her. She was lucky. Too bad Jack couldn't be more like Don.

4

It was time for ball practice, and it had been two days since Jack had seen Peyton. He couldn't hang out around the tasting room on Sunday until she needed help, so he kept busy with tours, and then yesterday had been a much-deserved day off for her.

He caught up to her at the ballfield. "Hi, Peyton." She was watching the kids warm up. "Ready for the big game tonight?"

She flashed him an easy smile. "I think we all are. Owen and your nephews are so excited." She waved to Liza over his shoulder.

Jack's cell phone rang but he ignored it. He'd rather talk to the beautiful woman standing in front of him.

The umpire gave his whistle two short bursts and the kids ran to their respective benches.

"Um, before things get crazy, I was going to grab a pizza with Liza and the boys after the game. Would you and Owen want to join us?"

She raised her eyebrows. "You do know the team will go for ice cream after the game? It's tradition."

"Oh, yeah. I knew that." But obviously, they both knew he hadn't.

His phone pinged, indicating a new voicemail. He pulled it from his pocket, glanced at the number, and recognized the California area code. He'd listen to it later.

"We should get back to the kids." Peyton scanned the team; was she looking for Owen?

He walked over to the kids and clapped his hands together to get their attention. "Everyone gather around."

After jostling for position with the shorter kids in front, the head coach said, "Okay, team, does everyone know where you should be in the batting lineup tonight, and do you have your gloves ready?"

Several of the boys nodded and held up their mitts for him to see. Jack covered his mouth with his hand to hide a smile. At this age, the kids were so comical, some missing a front tooth and others just looking around like they didn't have a care in the world and the rest ready for action. The most important lessons he hoped they took away from this experience were working together and being kind to one another. The final outcome of the game didn't matter.

Jack said, "We're in the field first since we're the home team tonight."

"Ms. P?" A boy who seemed small for the age group was standing next to Owen. He held up his hand.

Peyton squatted down. "Yes, Joey?"

"What happens if I miss the ball? Should I still run to first base?" He twirled his glove and dropped it on the ground. With a snicker, he said, "Oops."

"When you hit the ball, run as fast as you can. If you miss it, you'll have three tries."

"But I haven't hit it ever."

Owen placed a hand on his shoulder. "It's okay, Joey. My mom says to try your best, that's all." He looked up at Peyton. "Right, Mom?"

"That's right for all of you. Do your best and we'll work on anything you have trouble with at our next practice."

Jack loved Peyton's encouragement to all the kids. "But have fun out there," he said.

The kids gathered into a huddle and placed their hands in the middle of the circle, hands piled one on top of each other. "On three, everyone say, *Go Bobcats!*"

The kids grinned and Peyton smiled over their heads at Jack. It was easy to see she was in her element around the kids and he liked how they responded to her.

The game was slow as molasses in winter, with each kid getting a turn at bat and other kids either playing or like the little boy she had worked with on hitting. He was actually looking everywhere but the action of the game, like he was bored silly.

Peyton joined Liza in the bleachers, one eye on Jack and the other on the game, not wanting to hover over the kids; they had Coach Barrett and Jack. He was pacing up and down in front of the bench, calling to the kids, encouraging them. Patience laced his voice and his body language. She wondered what kind of a dad he'd be someday when he met the right woman. A pang of regret washed over her. Once, she thought he might be her future. If they had gotten together, they might be married by now and have a few kids of their own.

She sighed and Liza gave her a side-look. "You okay?"

"Yeah, just thinking." She watched as Jack jumped in

the air when Owen hit the ball, then ran along the sidelines, encouraging the boy to run fast.

The smile on her son's face was priceless. If things had worked out differently, she wouldn't have Owen in her life, and that was something she wouldn't have wanted to miss.

After the game, Owen said, "Did you see me hit the ball, Mom?" He looked up at Jack. "What did you think? Was it good?"

"It was great." He ruffled the boy's hair.

"Can I walk to the car with Johnny and George?"

"Go ahead, but wait for me in front of the car, okay?" The words were barely out of Peyton's mouth before Owen was running to catch up to his buddies.

"He's got a lot of energy even after a game," Jack said. The sun had begun its slow descent toward the horizon and the air was getting cool.

"He goes at full speed until he drops, and then it's like a light switch. On and off are the only two modes he has." Families swarmed around them. Most times, it didn't bother her to see happy couples at a game, but walking next to Jack was a sharp reminder they weren't a couple. This was the second time tonight she had gone down that path. She wasn't going to dwell on regrets.

Peyton adjusted her shoulder bag. "It was a good game. I think the kids have learned a lot about being part of a team."

"When I was a kid, my dad never volunteered for our sporting events. Mom was always there in the cheering section or helping in the concession stand. In those days, he worked eighteen-hour days." Jack kicked a pinecone.

"When I knew my nephews needed more support, the decision was easy." He looked her way. "It's been fun as well as eye-opening."

"I know exactly what you mean." Her gaze came to rest on Owen, who was standing next to her car just as she had asked. Jack's truck was parked next to her car. "Are you going for ice cream?"

They stopped walking and Jack smiled. "Are you kidding? I wouldn't miss it. After all, it's tradition." He pointed at his nephews. "Are you riding with me or your mom?"

Liza waved her hand. "Ride with Uncle Jack but wait in the truck until I get there, understand?"

The boys asked, "Can Owen ride with us too?"

Peyton shook her head. "Sorry, O, but we haven't tried to get three seats in Jack's truck, and let's save that for a day when ice cream's not waiting for us, okay?"

He kicked the ground. "Alright, Mom."

"Hop in the car and buckle up."

Jack held open the rear doors on his truck and her car so the boys could get in.

Liza said, "I'm sure Jack would have let Owen move his seat if it was okay with you."

"I'm sure there's room in his truck, but I'm not in the mood to screw around right now. It's been a long day. Besides, it's less than a ten-minute drive." Peyton gave Liza a quick hug. "I'm glad you came tonight. It was fun having company in the stands, and the boys played well."

"They like baseball, but their real love is soccer. I'm not sure why they didn't have a spring league this year." She tilted her head. "Are you thinking about Owen playing soccer this fall? He'd have a great time and I know with my boys, it actually makes them tired."

"I'll ask him and see what he wants to do." She rested her hand on the car door handle. "See you at the ice cream stand."

After they finished their ice cream, Owen waved to his friends, who were walking to Jack's truck. He took Peyton's hand as they crossed the parking lot to her car. "Isn't Jack cool, Mom? Like, he's coaching our team and drives that cool truck." He was bouncing as they walked. "And did you know that he has a boat and he likes to fish!"

"You don't say. Did he tell you that?"

He shook his head and waited for Peyton to unlock the car door. "Nope. George said that he takes them fishing all the time and sometimes they go on his boat. At the big lake too, not the one we go to for swimming."

She wanted to laugh, but he was very serious in sharing the information.

"Maybe sometime he'll take me fishing and you can come too."

That did sound fun for Owen, but it wasn't going to happen. "You didn't ask Jack to take you on his boat, did you?"

"Well…" He got in the back seat and clicked the buckle while Peyton watched to make sure it was secured. "Johnny asked if I could go with them the next time Jack had a fishing day and he said that I had to ask you first, so can I? Can I go fishing with Jack sometime?" He clasped his hands together and his eyes pleaded with her. "I'll bet he'll ask you to come too. Won't that be fun, Mom?"

"Son, we don't invite ourselves places. We have to wait to be included."

His eyes grew wide. "So that means when Jack asks us, we can go on his boat *and* go fishing?"

She had walked right into that one. Hopefully Jack wouldn't mention it to her when Owen was around and box her into a corner. Baseball practice and ice cream with the team were one thing, but being on Jack's boat in the middle of the lake was an entirely different matter.

"I'll think about it."

Owen pumped his fist in the air. "Yes!"

Jack sat on the steps of his front porch. The moon was coming up and this was his favorite time of day, between the crazy part of his day and the loneliness of the night. He looked at his phone and saw there was a voicemail waiting for him.

"Hi, Jack, it's me. Corine. It's been a long time and I'm hoping you'll give me a call back. We need to talk. And if you're wondering how I got your cell number, I was finally able to convince your office manager that I was the wife of an old friend from Napa, trying to plan a surprise for my husband, so no worries. I didn't say who I was. I can't wait to hear from you. Call me soon."

His heart stopped when the message ended. He listened to it a second time. What the hell did his ex-wife really want? They had been divorced for almost seven years and there was nothing left to talk about. He tossed the phone aside. Now if Peyton had called him, he would have hit redial, just to hear her voice.

Something George had mentioned crossed his mind. The boys wanted to go fishing and asked if Owen could come with them. That was a good reason to call Peyton.

Should he call her tonight or wait until he saw her at the winery? Instead of waiting, he dialed her number.

She answered on the second ring, but when he identified himself, he could hear the hesitancy that entered her voice.

"Listen, I'm thinking of taking the boys fishing next week one day after school and I was wondering if Owen would like to go with us."

"On the boat or from the dock?"

"Whichever makes you the most comfortable." He could picture the look on her face as she tried to pick the lesser of the two evils. "The boys will have fun and you can come too if that makes you more comfortable."

She cleared her throat. "I guess the boat would be best and yes, I'll come just to make sure you've got an extra set of eyes on them. Three boys are a lot to handle."

He expected Peyton would be surprised to discover how strict he was with his boating rules for the boys, but he was happy she'd said yes. "I'll check with Liza and the weather and we can firm up a time in the next couple of days."

"Sure, sounds good. And Jack? Don't mention this to the kids until we can work out the details."

He took that to mean in case she changed her mind. But he didn't care. It was a chance to be with her, and he'd play by her rules.

"Not to worry. I won't say a thing."

"Good night, Jack." She disconnected before he could continue the conversation.

5

---

ack didn't get to his door before thinking he
might as well call Corine and get this conversation over with before he went inside. Talking
to her had hung over him all day, but the three-hour time
difference had made it difficult to call her from work. He
thought it was going to voicemail when she answered.

"Corine, it's Jack. I got your message."

"Thanks for calling me back. I wasn't sure if you'd
respond."

He rubbed his neck. "What's up? I don't have a lot of
time."

"Can you spare a few minutes for an old friend?"

"And ex-wife."

"That's what I wanted to talk to you about. I was
wondering if I could come out to Crescent Lake and see
you at the winery."

"For what purpose?"

"There's something we need to discuss."

He could hear the catch in her voice. Corine had been

more than happy to sign the divorce papers that ended their brief marriage. Not that he had cared; as long as they were divorced, it was good enough for him.

"We both know our marriage was a mistake from the start. If it hadn't been, wouldn't we have told our families?" Jack waited half a beat. "There's nothing left to talk about."

"I didn't like how things ended between us and I still care about you, which is why I'm calling. I'd like to say we're friends. This is important to me."

He felt like a jerk for being borderline rude. "Corine, our marriage has been over for a long time. Let's not rehash the past." Before she had a chance to say anything more, he said, "Take care of yourself."

He set his phone on the porch floor and muted the ringer when her number popped back up on the screen. He was going to have to figure out a way to tell Peyton that he had been married once, but he'd better start with his family.

wen yelled, "Mom, hurry! Jack's here."

It had been a week since Peyton had agreed to go fishing with Jack and the boys. She threw an extra bottle of sunscreen and another sun hoodie for Owen in her tote bag, just in case. Even with his easy-to-tan skin, he needed sun protection. She hoped this fishing trip wasn't a bad idea and wouldn't give people, namely Jack, a mixed message.

The screen door banged and Owen burst into the kitchen. He had a Spider-Man ball cap perched on his head and wore a matching T-shirt with dinosaur swim trunks.

"I showed Jack where the cooler was and he already loaded it in the back of the truck for us and I got my booster seat out of our car for him and Jack said three seats will fit no prob."

"Well, that is good news." She gave him a once-over. "Have you gone to the bathroom?"

He stomped his bare feet down the hallway, mumbling about life not being fair and something about fish. Holding back a chuckle, she called after him, "I can hear you."

The bathroom door closed with a thud.

"Peyton?" It was Jack.

"Come on in." She poked her head out of the kitchen. "Just adding a few last-minute things to my tote." She pulled the drawstring tight and smiled at him.

His warm hazel eyes held a hint of mischief. "Did you pack the entire house?" He took the oversized bag from her.

"With boys, there is bound to be something I forgot to pack. Owen'll either stab himself with a fish hook, fall in, or—" She stopped midsentence. "He doesn't have a life jacket."

He touched her arm. It reassured her. "I've already got one in the truck and before we even step onto the dock, he's putting it on."

"Where are Johnny and George?"

"We're picking them up on the way."

She could feel herself relax, just a little. "Good. And thanks, Jack, for getting the life jacket too."

"It wasn't a big deal. I picked one up at the marina."

Owen came running down the hall, wiping his wet

hands across the front of his tee. "Hey, Jack, I'm ready to go on the boat." He grinned. "Mom, can we go *now*?"

Jack pointed to his feet. "Hold on, sport. You need to put on a pair of sneakers first, or water shoes if you have them."

He held up a finger. "Be right back."

Jack asked, "Does it always take this long to get out the door?"

She shook her head. "You have no idea."

Owen hopped into the doorway. "Okay, now I'm really, really ready." He stuck a foot out to show off his water shoes. "Ta-da."

He took the bag from Jack and slung it over his shoulder like a peddler, almost losing his balance before he zipped to the door. "Come on."

"We're right behind you." Peyton took one last look around the room and picked up her purse.

He touched her arm again. "You're not worried about today, are you?"

She gave him a sidelong look. "Boys, a boat, and water." She threw up her hands. "What's to be worried about?"

As he opened the screen door, he said, "I've planned a little safety overview when we get out there and before we leave the dock."

With a small grin, she said, "You have no idea what you've gotten yourself into."

He laid his hand across his chest in mock fear. "I've done the kids and boat thing before. Do I need eyes in the back of my head?"

"Stop teasing me, Price, and let's hit the road."

• • •

rue to his word, Jack buckled the life vest on Owen, and checked Johnny and George to make sure the jackets were snug enough as soon as they got out of the truck.

"Uncle Jack," Johnny said, "I don't wanna wear a vest today. Can't we skip 'em?"

He wasn't prepared for the test of wills with the boys. "No vest, no boat." Finally the kids relented.

"Mom, I'm not a baby," Owen protested as she tried to hold his hand down the dock. "And not in front of Johnny and George. No one is holding their hands."

She bent down to look him square in the eye. "No running. Got it?"

"Yes." Owen beamed as he carried the bag down the dock and joined the boys, who stood next to Jack's boat.

Owen's eyes were wide as he took in the silver metal rails and navy-blue stripes of the bowrider. "Is this really yours? It's huge." He cocked his head and scrunched up his face. "Why does it say...*Just JP*?"

Jack nodded. "They're my initials: JP for Jackson Price. Lots of people name their boats. Do you like it?"

"More than anything." Owen looked at his mom. "Can we get a boat like this?"

Before she could answer, Jack placed his hand on Owen's shoulder. "Tell you what. You can come with me on my boat anytime you want, just like Johnny and George do."

"I can?" He looked at Peyton with his brown eyes as big as saucers. "Did ya hear that? We can go on the boat all the time."

Peyton placed a firm but gentle hand on her son's arm. "Owen, you can go only when you're invited."

"But Mommy, Jack said..." He looked at his mom and then Jack. His face fell. "Sorry."

Not wanting to step on toes, Jack said, "Don't worry, Owen. We're going to have plenty of time this summer to go on the boat and fish."

The dock rocked in the wake of a large boat as it passed by. The kids laughed and Owen pretended to surf with the rise and fall of the dock. Peyton reached for him, but Jack held out a hand and touched hers. "They're fine."

He pumped his hand down to the other boat. "But they should be crawling."

"Whoa!" the boys exclaimed with a laugh. "That was fun."

"Ready to climb aboard?"

His nephews scrambled on, but Owen looked at the space between the dock and the boat as another boat passed. The wake had the boat and dock bobbing out of sync. He looked at Jack, his mom, and then Jack again. "How do I get on?"

Jack put one foot on the swim platform and the other on the dock. He held out his hand to Owen. "Take my hand and step. Don't worry; I won't let you fall."

Owen looked up with trusting eyes. "Promise?"

"You have my word."

Owen leaped before Jack was ready, but he took a big step and it was so effortless, there wasn't any issue. Jack tucked the cooler on the boat and Peyton handed him the last bag.

"We have a lot of stuff for a couple hours." She slipped her sunglasses on.

"Better to be prepared and not need something than need it and not have it." He offered her his outstretched hand.

She laughed. "You remember that famous three-hour tour? Those people were marooned on the desert island for three television seasons."

"Good thing we're only on a lake, but being marooned with you on an island isn't a bad idea, especially since you have enough stuff to last days."

Without saying a word, she lowered her glasses and looked at him over the lenses. She took his hand even though she had been on and off boats all her life. His touch sent a zing through her body. She stepped on the platform and onto the dark-blue indoor/outdoor carpeting that covered the deck. The matching blue canvas was up to offer protection from the bright afternoon sun. "What can I do to help?"

He pointed to the cooler and bag. "Can you stow them under the canvas?"

As she was arranging things, Jack called for the boys to join him next to the captain's chair. He gave them a stern look. "A couple of simple rules." Owen started to groan and George rolled his eyes, but Jack said, in a firm but gentle voice, "Everyone has to follow the rules. Mom too."

"Even you?"

"Yes, even me."

Owen nodded. "Okay."

"There's no running across the deck of the boat. Never take your life jacket off, and if I ask you to sit down, I need for you to do it without question."

Looking up at Jack, Owen said, "I'll be good, Jack." He held out his small hand.

Jack wanted to chuckle, but Owen was so serious, he

gave the boy's hand a shake. "One final rule of the afternoon."

The three boys looked at him, crestfallen.

"Let's have lots of fun."

Owen's face split into a huge grin. "You got it, Jack!" He turned to his mom. "Did you hear that, Mom? Jack said we're gonna have lots of fun." He gave Jack a high five before he sat on one of the bench seats with his friends.

Jack looked at Peyton. Had he overstepped talking to her son? "Ready to cast off?"

"Just give the word and I'll take care of the lines." She looked so pretty standing on his boat. The sun gave her dark hair a golden glow. She had a hat ready to plop on her head.

He noticed there was a streak of lotion on her forehead so he reached out and smoothed it away. "You missed a spot."

Peyton relaxed as Jack towed the boys on a huge tube behind the boat. He was careful not to toss them into the water. She even took a turn despite the water still being a little chilly.

When they were done tubing, Jack secured the tube onto the boat's swim platform. She was surprised and pleased he had jumped right in to share the chores with Owen; he really was good with the kids.

Peyton said, "Jack, I can't remember the last time I had so much fun."

The boys sat cross-legged on the deck while they ate a light dinner. Jack and Peyton sat on the bench seats. When he was done eating, Owen held up a wriggling worm.

Each time he tried to wrap it around the metal hook, it would curl in the opposite direction. "Mom, will you help me?"

"After I finish my sandwich." She gave Jack a pointed look. She did not do worms.

"Owen, after we finish eating, would you like to help me drive the boat to my secret fishing spot?"

Worm forgotten, Owen's eyes lit up. "Can I?"

"Sure, and Johnny and George will have turns too."

Over Owen's head, Peyton mouthed *thank you*. Jack gave her a mischievous wink.

When they were done, she cleaned up the dinner containers and stored them in the cooler.

Jack waved Owen over. He plopped the boy in his lap on the captain's seat. "Peyton, care to take the co-captain spot and the boys can sit close to you?"

She eased back in the comfortable seat to enjoy the view while she kept a close eye on the other boys. Owen was first to drive. They both had blond hair, dimples, and a square jawline. After spending time together, Owen had picked up on some of Jack's mannerisms. Even the way Owen looked at Jack held the same intensity that Jack gave to everything he did. The sight of them together tugged at her heart and she wished he were Jack's son. He was a good man and she was happy their friendship was less complicated than when he first came back to town, and Owen certainly had a big case of hero worship.

Jack looked at Owen. "Are you ready to get underway?"

He grinned at Jack. "Can I hold the wheel?"

Jack placed Owen's hands at approximately four and eight, then placed one hand on top of Owen's and the other on the throttle. They worked together, driving the boat. Jack had endless patience with all of Owen's questions. As Jack pointed to where they were headed, Owen remained quiet, taking in each detail and nodding like he was understanding every subtlety of the process of navigating the lake.

The boat skimmed across the open water. The wind caught the edge of Owen's baseball cap, but before she could reach it, Jack grabbed it in one smooth movement and tucked it alongside his leg in the seat. Her boy was oblivious and clenched the steering wheel with all his might. The grin that split his cute face melted her heart.

She pulled her phone from her pocket and snapped a few pics. She couldn't wait to share them with Kate, and then she did selfies with Johnny and George. Today was too much fun to not capture it all.

As if he sensed her thoughts, Jack flashed her a grin and his head bobbed in Owen's direction. She gave him a thumbs-up. The only downside was that Owen was going to expect to drive the boat again, and soon.

6

"Hey, Kate," Peyton called through the open French door into the bistro. "Are you up for a glass of wine after we close today?"

Kate smiled at her from across the room. "I'll have a seltzer and hang out for a bit. I don't have to get back home until six. Nanny Jessie has everything under control."

Peyton gave her a thumbs-up and Kate winked. She couldn't wait to tell Kate about the fishing adventure with Jack and the boys.

Weekends were always busy at the winery, especially when tourist season was in full swing. Kay-Dee's had been a hit since the grand opening and customers were raving about the new menu this year.

Peyton had been skeptical the bistro would have helped sales all that much, but people wandered from the dining room to the tasting room and vice versa. And when the bistro was open on Friday through Sunday, sales soared by at least another twenty-five percent, even on a slow day.

Peyton turned her attention to the group of customers who needed her expertise. She lined up tastings and sold cases of wine with ease. Her assistant, Tony, was a huge help on the weekends while he was in college, and this summer, he was coming back full-time for his third year working at CLW. He hurried about, carrying cases of wine out to customers' cars, always with a smile. Today was definitely shaping up to be one of the extra-busy days.

*J*ack leaned against the doorjamb, his arms folded across his chest, and watched as Peyton smiled and chatted up customers. He loved watching her work, but he didn't want to get caught looking like some lovesick teenager.

She poured wine and explained what was special and different about each variety, right down to giving suggestions on what to serve with each. Invariably, she knew just what to do or say so that each customer left happy, toting bottles of wines and with a promise they'd return when they were in the area again.

She looked toward the back of the bar and then walked the full length, scanning under the counter. She was obviously looking for something that wasn't there. He crossed the room before she could catch Tony's eye. And then her gaze settled on him.

She smiled. "Hey there. Weren't you supposed to have the day off?"

He shrugged. "I didn't have much going on so I thought I'd stop in."

She cocked an eyebrow. "In that case, can you watch the bar? I seem to be out of Chardonnay."

"How much do you need?"

"Two cases—it's selling well. Kate's serving an Indian platter and it pairs perfectly with it."

He pulled a set of keys from his jeans and sorted through them until he held one up. "I've got a key and will be right back."

"Thanks." She turned her attention back to her customers.

Peyton was too busy to talk when Jack returned. He ended up pitching in, getting additional stock and helping people carry case after case of wine out the door. They made a good team. When the clock finally approached four, things slowed. The bistro closed at three, which was a good way to thin the crowds who had been enjoying themselves in the air-conditioned room. Peyton locked the door after the final two customers left. She sagged against the bar and wiped her forehead with the back of her hand.

Speaking to no one in particular, she sighed. "What a day."

Still full of energy, Tony grabbed the cleaner and paper towels and repeated the process of wiping down all the tables and chairs.

She held out a hand and wriggled her fingers in his direction. "I'll help."

Tony shook his head with a laugh. "Did you look behind the bar? The shelves are empty. You've got your work cut out for you."

She pushed herself to a standing position as Jack leaned at the other end of the bar. He gave her a crooked grin. "You're a fantastic salesperson. Ever think about hitting the road? I'm sure Don would be happy to have you on the sales team."

She loaded dirty glasses in the dishwasher rack. "No. I love being here. The interaction with the customers and watching their faces as they try a wine, fall in love, and then make the purchase. That's what makes me happy."

"Too bad. You'd clean up in commissions."

She glanced his way and her brow arched. "Are you trying to get rid of me?"

"Not at all. Just stating the truth." He eased open the refrigerator and pulled out a half-gallon jug of water. "I'm pouring—who wants a glass?"

Both Peyton and Tony stuck a hand in the air. Jack poured three large glasses and handed one to her. Tony grabbed his and went back to cleaning tables.

"Oh, that is refreshing." She wiped her lips with her hand. "Thanks!"

Setting the half-empty glass on the bar, she started checking bottles for what needed to be recorked, what was empty or unopened. She worked silently and efficiently. Without having to ask, Jack took cases of empty bottles out back.

When she had tallied up her inventory, she had a long list of items to backfill. "Tony," she called, "I'm going to restock—can you wash down the floor behind the bar?"

"Sure thing."

She grabbed the keys from the hook underneath the bar. Jack was coming back from the recycling room. "Care to lend some muscle?"

"I thought you would never ask." The gleam in his eyes indicated he had more than work on his mind.

Without a second thought, she admonished, "It's time to work, mister."

His laughter followed her as she left the room. She could feel his eyes on her back and she smiled to herself.

He said, "This could be fun. You and me in a closet."

She frowned.

"Pey, I'm sorry. I was teasing."

The moment fractured. A closet? Did she want to be in a small space with Jack? Would he think she was weird if she asked to stay close to the door while he helped get the wine?

"I know." Flustered, she ran her hand over her hair. "I need to finish up. I'm having a cool drink with Kate when I'm done."

She watched as a flash of disappointment flitted across his face. "I was hoping we could grab a bite to eat."

"Some other time? I promised Owen we'd have a fire tonight and cook s'mores."

He asked, "Would it be presumptuous for me to invite myself over, just as an old friend?"

"Probably." She softened. "But I was thinking of asking you to join us."

"I can pick up pizza for everyone."

"It's just me and the kiddo. Mom and Dad are going to a friend's house after I get home." She glanced at her watch.

He took the inventory list from her hand. "You go and relax with Kate. I'll finish up."

She protested, "I can't let you finish my work."

"You didn't ask. I volunteered." He turned her toward the door. "Go and enjoy your time with my sweet sister-in-law and I will see you at six thirty with pizza."

Peyton allowed herself to be propelled out the door. Over her shoulder, she called, "Half cheese, half special."

He grinned. "You got it."

Peyton gave him a broad wave and a smile as she disappeared around the corner with a quick stop at the bar to pour one glass of wine and a glass of seltzer.

· · ·

*J*ack couldn't help but grin as he carefully stowed another case of wine on the dolly. He was glad Kate and Peyton were friends. It was good for both of them. After consulting the list, he realized it would take more than one trip to backfill the bar. She really was an outstanding salesperson. He had to wonder if Don knew about her sales prowess. She needed a raise or a commission or both.

After making two more trips, he locked the storage room, did one last sweep of the tasting room, and said goodbye to Tony as he headed out the side door. Jack had snapped off the overhead lights when Don came strolling in.

"Hey, big brother." Jack looked around. "Did you forget a couple of little ones?"

"Do you mean my sons and adorable daughter? Mom and Dad called dibs on the kids for an overnight stay. Mom's going to swing by the house and take over for Jessie soon and give her the rest of the day off. I thought I'd whisk my beautiful wife out for a romantic dinner." He glanced around. "I know she and Peyton are together. Any idea where?"

Jack perched on a tabletop and folded his arms across his chest. "I do. They're having some girl time in the gazebo."

Don playfully punched him in the arm. "What are we doing in here?"

Before he could take a step, Jack asked, "Do you know how much wine Peyton actually sells in the course of an afternoon like today?"

"I don't have the specific numbers off the top of my head, but I'm pretty sure business is brisk."

"Do you have any idea why the sales numbers are up?"

Don gave him a quizzical glance. "What are you getting at?"

"Peyton does an unbelievable job talking up each type of wine and what to serve it with, and she basically draws the customer in until they feel they have to buy it. I've never seen anything like it. She has a knack for sales."

Thoughtfully, Don said, "Does she want to move into an outside sales position?"

"No, she enjoys being right where she is, and I don't think she'd want to be away from Owen for days at a time, but maybe you could give her a commission or a raise. Between what Kate is doing in the bistro and Peyton, we've struck liquid gold."

"All right, let me run the numbers and see what I can come up with." He paused. "Are you sure this isn't because you've got a thing for the girl?"

Jack frowned. "You know me better than that. I'm not the crazy guy who lets feelings for a woman get in the way of the family business. That's your department. You're the one who took off and followed Kate to her hometown. And then you took a job cutting down trees with her brother, just to be close."

Don held up his hand. "In my defense, look at how everything turned out. I got the girl *and*, three years ago, the job I was born to do."

"It just took longer than everyone expected for you to move home."

Don looked at Jack. "What's going on with you and Peyton? Still in the friend zone?"

Slowly Jack nodded. "Yeah."

"Are you seriously interested in her?"

"I am. I never really stopped caring about her."

"And Owen?"

"What about him? I really like him. He's spunky, funny, and a really good kid."

Don nodded in agreement.

"If things develop between the two of us and we take this to a committed level, I'll be the best role model I can for Owen. The boy needs a dad."

"I like the confidence." Don clapped him on the back. "Let's go find the girls and see if they're ready to spend time with the dashing and handsome Price brothers."

Peyton slipped her cell phone into her back pocket as she and Kate laughed over how cute Owen looked driving the boat.

"And Jack just went with the flow with the three boys?" Kate took a sip of her seltzer. "Well, I'm not surprised—he's always been good with kids. I was a little worried when he used to carry Ben around under one arm like a football, but that was more about new mother nerves than his ability." She peered over the rim of her glass. "So how does my friend feel about Jack?"

"He's a great guy. I'll confess I was concerned about spending time with him, but it was okay even though we dated for a while. Our lives went in different directions. The end." She swirled the wine in her glass. "We've come a long way over the last couple of years and I think we've become friends again." She sipped her wine. "You were a good friend when I needed one."

Kate's eyes widened. "Me? I didn't do much."

She lifted her eyes to meet Kate's. "You listened. You were the first person I told about the assault. You stood by my side and propped me up when I needed extra support."

Kate placed her hand on Peyton's arm. "I'm glad I was there for you. But you did the hard work; therapy is tough. You would have done the same for me." She leaned back in her chair. "And now look! We're the best of friends."

"In some ways, I feel you're like the sister I never had but always wanted." She could feel her lips twitch as she contained a grin. "Even if I think you're subtly encouraging me to date the handsome Jack Price."

Kate chuckled. "So you admit he's handsome. That's a good first start."

She felt color creep into her cheeks. "Stop. That doesn't mean I want to be in a relationship with him." She sipped her wine. "He's coming over tonight and bringing pizza for me and Owen."

"What? How did that happen?" Kate sat up straight and grinned. "Details."

With a small shrug, Peyton said, "I'm not sure. The invitation sorta slipped out."

"Girl, you need to tell me everything that happens, and I mean *all* the details."

Peyton sipped her wine and smiled over the rim. "It's not a big deal, really." But she had to wonder, *Wasn't it?*

O wen came careening around the corner into the kitchen a couple of hours later, tugging his sweatshirt over his head. "Mom, is Jack here?"

She glanced out the front window. "Not yet." She pointed to the paper plates and napkins. "Would you take those out to the picnic table for me?"

"Sure." As he picked up the plates, the napkins floated to the floor. "Sorry, Mom."

"It's okay. Just pick them up and get new ones from the cabinet."

"They're not dirty," he said. "Grammie keeps the floors washed all the time."

Peyton laughed. "I know she does, but let's just throw them out and get new ones."

He shrugged and started for the cabinet. A honking from the driveway interrupted his task. His eyes lit up. "He's here." He dropped the plates on the table and took off racing through the living room and out the front door.

The screen door banged shut and Peyton could hear him yelling, "Jack! Hey, Jack!"

She wondered how Jack would respond if she did the same thing. She peeked out the window, curious to overhear the conversation between them.

Jack held the top to the pizza box open just enough for Owen to peek inside. And then, as was typical, Owen stuck his hand in to sneak a glop of gooey cheese. Jack chuckled and playfully popped the top on the back of Owen's hand. "Hey, I think we're supposed to wait for dinner."

"It's okay. Mom won't get mad."

"Can I quote you?" Jack caught her watching them and smirked.

Owen turned and looked at him, his face squished up, looking confused. "Why?"

"I don't want to get in trouble with your mom." He placed a hand on Owen's shoulder and turned him toward the stairs. "Let's go have dinner. I'm starving."

With a quick grin, Owen said, "Me too." He hurried up

the stairs. She wondered where he found the energy to keep going when all he ever did was go at top speed.

She propped open the screen door. Jack stepped in and touched her hand briefly.

"Come on." Owen tugged on Jack's arm. "We're eating outside and cooking s'mores. Isn't that cool?"

Jack winked at Peyton over his shoulder as they walked out the back door. "Very."

Trailing behind the guys, she picked up the tray with paper plates, napkins, and their drinks. She stopped to throw the napkins out too. Once outside, she discovered Owen was talking Jack into lighting the fire. With one look, she realized it hadn't taken much convincing; he seemed to be having just as much fun as Owen.

She crossed to the deck railing. "Hey, guys. We can eat now and then play with the fire."

Owen's eyes grew round. They held a solemn look. "Mom, we don't play with fire."

"That's right." Jack straightened. "We can keep an eye on it from the table, and when it's time, you can help me pull up the chairs."

She watched as the two of them stared intently at the firepit. She smothered a grin at the way Owen kept saying Jack's name. It was almost as if he couldn't believe Jack was at their house. In a way, she couldn't believe it either.

Owen hopped up the couple of steps to the deck. He scrambled up onto the picnic bench, his legs dangling. He waited for his mom to pass him a plate with a slice of pizza and he turned to the fire and then to his mom and Jack.

Jack sat on the other bench next to Peyton and took the plate she passed to him, her hand grazing his. He held her eyes for a fraction of a minute. The intensity sent a shiver up her arm. Being in close proximity to this man made her think about doing things with him that hadn't crossed her mind in a very long time. She thought about it for half a second. On her last date, the idea of anything physical caused her heart to race, but it was totally different with Jack. It was nice to have that zing.

To no one in particular, she said, "Let's eat."

7

"Hey, Don." Peyton paused while wiping down the bartop. "What brings you down here today?" When he had stopped in the gazebo last night, he hadn't indicated he wanted to talk with her. Was something wrong? She continued wiping down the wine bottles on display behind the bar even though Don stopped in the middle of the room. She knew from her long association with the Price family that he was taking in every detail, no matter how big or small.

He perched on a barstool and gave her a friendly smile. "I've been looking over the sales numbers and comparing them to last year at this same time. We're up thirty percent. Do you have any idea why?"

She set aside the damp cloth she was using. "People are raving about the bistro. They say the food is amazing and they really like how Kate's menu enhances different wines, usually in ways they hadn't thought of."

"We have seen a spike in the last few weeks, which I can attribute to the bistro being open again and the Spring

Fling event, but there's been a consistent and steady increase of thirty percent before that."

"Marketing's been doing a great job on social media for a while now too. Promotion for the bistro and the tasting room has been a huge draw. Liza's brought more people by to check out the gazebo for weddings and anniversary parties. I think that has attributed to another small spike. When they're here looking around, they usually buy a bottle or two."

He seemed to consider what she said. "Do you think we need to add additional help? It seems with the increase, you and Tony might not have enough hands on deck, so to speak."

Peyton considered how hard last Sunday had been before Jack stopped by. "Maybe having another person to help carry out cases and fill in for tastings would be good, sort of a floater."

"All right then. You did a great job hiring staff for the bistro, so go ahead. One or two people, if that's what it takes." He held out a paper.

"I'll set up interviews for you as soon as I can." She took the paper from him.

"I won't be involved in the interviews, and the new hire will report directly to you."

She was taken aback. This was the first time she had been given complete autonomy when it came to hiring. She scanned the paper. A range was listed for a starting hourly rate.

Confused, she said, "How do I know what to offer?" She set the paper aside.

He gave her an encouraging smile. "Go with what you think is best."

"But, Don, I haven't hired anyone without you, Sam, or Kate weighing in. Ever."

"You can handle it." He got to his feet. "Oh, and Tony reports to you now too, so you might want to think about a raise for him. I would suggest fifty cents an hour. I've already given him the good news that you're his boss." He tapped the bartop and flashed her a smile. "Thanks for your hard work, Peyton." He strode from the room without waiting for her to respond.

She leaned against the oak counter. What had just happened? All of a sudden, she went from an employee to a manager. But he didn't mention a raise. Did that mean she was taking on additional responsibility without compensation? What about a discussion of his expectations?

"Busting my butt must be paying off if the numbers were that good compared to last year." Absentmindedly, she picked up the damp cloth and began to wipe down the already clean bottles, pleased to be a trusted member of the team, but it left her with many questions—like why did Tony get a raise, but she didn't?

She picked up the paper and scanned it again. It was a job description for a part-time person for weekends and holidays during the season. "At least this will make it easier to interview someone." The tasting room phone rang and she answered it.

A female voice said, "Hello. I saw a posting online for a part-time job in the tasting room. Is the position still available?"

Peyton grinned. Sneaky devil, he had this all planned. It was a good thing Don came when he did; otherwise, she would have turned away a potential candidate. "Why yes, it is. Who is this, please?"

"Lily Peters, and I've recently moved to the area."

She certainly sounded energetic over the phone. "Do you have any questions about the job, or would you like to schedule an interview?"

"I don't have any questions. The posting was pretty detailed."

"Would one o'clock tomorrow be okay?" Peyton hoped she could come in soon. Maybe if she worked out, she could start this weekend.

"I'll be there."

"Do you need directions?"

"No, thanks. I've already looked them up. See you tomorrow."

The line disconnected. It would be nice if she had a few applicants to choose from. Before she could get back to work, the phone rang three more times. She had her wish: a total of four interviews for the next day.

*P*eyton dressed for work in a tan skort and a deep-purple polo with the winery logo, and matching purple tennis shoes. She didn't want to look formal for the interviews, and this was what she wore when the tasting room was open, so it would set the tone.

She got to the winery at ten o'clock. Her first interview was in a half hour. She flicked on the spotlights and saw a small glass vase of wildflowers sitting on the bar. Next to them was an envelope. Her name was printed across the front in large bold letters. Nose to blooms, she inhaled the faint sweet smell of anise from the black-eyed Susans, which were mixed with wild lavender.

She pulled a card from the envelope and recognized the handwriting. *Have fun interviewing today, Boss Lady.*

Peyton laughed. "Jack."

From the shadow of the hallway, she heard, "Did I hear my name?" He crossed the room. "I see you got my card and flowers."

"You shouldn't sneak up on me." She turned with a laugh. "Thank you for the flowers. It wasn't necessary." His brow arched and that familiar twinkle appeared in his eyes. "But it's a sweet surprise." She touched his arm. "What brings you to my little corner of the vineyard today?"

"I was on my way out to check the vines when I saw your car coming down the drive. I wanted to swing by and wish you good luck."

She tucked the card into her bag and stashed it all in a cabinet. "I was surprised when Don promoted me and told me to hire someone." She leaned against the bar. "He must have confidence in me. But he didn't give me any specifics about what exactly he'd like me to do different. I'm going to see if he has a few minutes later to discuss the details."

"I'm sure he'll make time for you." Jack grabbed a jug of water from the fridge. "We all think you're amazing." He poured a glass and drained it. "It's thirsty work out there."

"Oh really? I couldn't have guessed." Peyton smothered a laugh. "And I'm sure I've been the topic of conversation at every board meeting."

Jack grew serious. "You're doing a great job here and the family appreciates your hard work."

A flash of worry washed over her. *Did I get the promotion because Jack told Don to give it to me? I bust my butt every day. Please don't let it be that he pulled strings.*

"I just realized my first interviewee will be here soon." She didn't look at him while she straightened a small stack of flyers with CLW specials.

"Oh. Well. Why don't I take off and you can tell me about your day later? I can swing by with a pizza or subs."

She didn't look up. "Not tonight. I promised Owen we'd watch a movie."

*I*f he didn't know better, he'd think she was giving him the brush-off. It had to be nerves about the day ahead. "I'll see you later, and good luck."

"Thanks, Jack, and don't worry. I'll hire a great person."

He could hear a strain in her voice that hadn't been there when he first arrived. "Peyton, really, we're not worried. I'm not; that's for sure." He walked toward the door and turned. "Are you upset with something I said?"

Her voice was curt. "No."

He hesitated. "If you want to talk later, call my cell."

She nodded and turned her back toward him.

Instead of going to the maintenance building, he took the back stairs, two at a time. Without knocking, he pushed open the door to Don's office. He was on the phone and pointed to the chair opposite the large desk.

It was the desk that, up until three years ago, his father had sat behind every day for over forty years. After Sam Price had a mild heart attack, Don had taken over as president and CEO of the family business, a role Jack had to admit Don was born to do.

He waited as his brother wrapped up the conversation. Setting the phone in the cradle, Don looked at him with mild curiosity. "What's up?"

Jack drummed his fingers on the arm of the wooden chair. "I was just in the tasting room with Peyton."

"Okay." Don shrugged. "That's nice. But what does that have to do with me?"

"Well, I wondered what might have gone on between the two of you regarding her new position."

Don leaned back in the chair. "I'm not sure where you're going with this, Jack. Spit it out."

"We were talking about the interviews today. I told her how the family thinks she does a great job and we have complete faith in her hiring just the right person."

"Again, not sure where this is going." Don shook his head. "Am I missing something?"

"I don't know. She got all quiet and distant, like she was upset." Jack jumped up and crossed to the large window that overlooked acres of vines. "I offered to bring dinner over to her place to celebrate and she blew me off."

"Maybe she thinks you two have been spending too much time together lately and wants to keep things friendly."

He shook his head. "Nah, she was distant before I mentioned anything about dinner."

"Are you sure you didn't say anything else? You're known for not being very smooth with the ladies."

"Yeah, I don't think it's me." He replayed the conversation in his head. "Ya know, I may be reading too much into it." He turned from the window. "She wanted to talk to you, so maybe check in with her. Give her a shot of moral support."

"I'll drop down later." Don grinned. "Kate's bringing the kids over and we're going to have lunch in the gazebo."

"Got enough for me?"

With a laugh, he said, "Nope, it's lunch for two and a half since the twins will be all set."

Leaving the office door open when he went out, he called over his shoulder, "Have fun."

*P*eyton bent at the waist and shook out her arms. Her shoulders were so tight. She couldn't help but worry that her fourth interview might be a bust too.

She straightened up right as Don walked into the room. She felt her cheeks grow warm. "Hi. I thought I was alone."

He crossed the room and gestured for her to join him at a small table. "How are the interviews going?"

She slipped into the chair and tidied the papers in front of her. "Let's just say the first three interviews were awful." Her shoulders sagged. "Maybe I'm not any good at this." Don waited patiently while she continued to talk. "One girl came in the outfit she wore last night, and her makeup was smudged. I wondered if she had gone to bed yet. And the other, well, let's just say his command of English was limited except for expletives."

"And the third?"

She shrugged and held up her hands. "No show."

Calmly he said, "You just need one good applicant."

"I'm hoping my last one today will be a good fit. I like how she sounded on the phone: perky and pleasant." She looked at him. "Are you sure you don't want to do this instead of me?"

Don folded his hands in his lap. His deep brown eyes were kind. "Peyton, I've promoted you to be the manager of the tasting room. You've embraced every challenge and found ways to grow the business. You earned this job. I'm confident you will hire the best staff. You understand every facet of this business: inventory, swag items, right down to the specials you run."

Peyton sat up straighter. "But, Don, isn't that really something marketing does?"

"You're the person on the front lines, and remember, I've analyzed the numbers. Our sales have steadily increased over the last year. You've played a significant role in that success."

"I, I don't know what to say."

Don stood up. "I forgot to mention this job comes with a twenty-five percent pay raise."

"Don." She swallowed hard. "That's very…"

"And as an additional incentive, if you increase and maintain sales ten percent over last year, there'll be a year-end bonus. We'll assess that on a quarterly basis retroactive to January 1st."

She was glad she was still sitting. This would mean she could give Owen some of the things she wanted him to have, and save for a small house. Money had been tight since she gave up the hostess job at Sawyers. Owen had been having issues with separation anxiety. "I don't know what to say—that is very generous."

"It's long overdue and earned." Don pulled his cell phone from his pocket and glanced at the screen. "It seems Kate and my children are waiting for me in the gazebo."

"Thanks again. I really appreciate everything."

"I should be thanking you. Keep up the exceptional work."

Peyton did some quick math. With that kind of a raise, someday maybe she could even get a house near one of the smaller lakes in the area. Not on it, but maybe within biking distance. That would be something Owen would love. Heck, they'd both love it.

She blinked away tears of happiness. She had gotten the promotion on her own.

few hours later, Peyton wandered up to Don's office. She tapped on the door and poked her head in. "Hi. Do you have a minute?"

Don was a few years older than Jack, with similar coloring except their eyes. Jack had golden hazel eyes and Don's were dark brown, but both men were blond and looked alike. Sitting behind a large monitor, he was intently studying the computer screen. Without looking up, he said, "Come on in." He tapped a couple of keys on the keyboard, then stood up and stretched his arms in front of him. "How can I help you?" He gestured to the chair across from his desk.

Peyton sat down and crossed her legs. It wasn't normal for her to be in Don's office, but he was warm and welcoming. "I've hired someone for the tasting room and potentially for special events too. Her name is Lily and she'll graduate from the University of Buffalo with dual degrees in business and marketing in a couple of weeks. So, for the short term she'll be here to train when not in finals and on the weekends."

Don nodded. "Good school and program."

"She wants the job as a possible entrance into an apprenticeship at the winery."

"Now that's very interesting."

"There's something about her that I really like."

"Let me give it some thought. Have her work with you

for a couple of weeks. I'll pop in over the weekend, casual-like, and see what my first impression is and we can go from there."

"That's great. Thanks." Peyton stood. "I need to get back downstairs."

"You have great instincts and are a valuable member of the team and a part of our extended family." He gave her a wide smile. "And my door is always open."

"Thanks, Don."

8

Peyton settled Owen in a tub full of bubbles and a mountain of toys. Thank goodness he still had fun playing in the tub. She left the bathroom door open so she could hear him and she joined her parents in the den.

She relaxed into the sofa and looked between her parents. "I got some great news at work today." She paused. "Don gave me a promotion to oversee all aspects of the tasting room. As of now, I have two people working for me, a really nice raise, and if sales exceed projections, I will receive a year-end bonus."

Dad beamed and nodded. "Good for you, Peyton. Congratulations. I knew your hard work would pay off, and now it has."

Mom beamed. "That's great news, sweetie."

"Thanks." She sat up a little straighter, excited to share the news.

"What are you going to do with the extra money?" Mom asked.

Without hesitation, she said, "I think it's time I buy a house and give you some much deserved privacy."

Mom's face fell. "No, Peyton. We love having you here. It's like families used to be: several generations living under one roof."

Dad glanced at Mom before settling back on Peyton. He gave her an understanding nod.

Softly she said, "I wanted to tell you first before I talk to the bank."

Before she could get their reactions, she heard, "Mom, I need help."

She had started to get up when Mom stopped her. "I'll go. You talk to Dad."

He looked at her and nodded in the direction of the hall. "This is the only home he's ever had. Do you really want to leave?"

"I never meant to live here indefinitely. Being out on my—our own would be a good thing for all of us."

Dad's face drooped. "Peyton, Mom and I love that you're here with us. We get to spend time with our grandson and you."

"You'll still see us a lot, but don't you ever wish you had some quiet time?"

His eyes sparkled. "That sounds dull."

"Don't talk that way. You both have so many things you enjoy." Peyton shook her head and gave him a small smile.

Dad chuckled. "I understand why you feel like you want to move, and I support you and the idea of home ownership." He winked. "Besides, when you get married someday, you'll want to move and take Owen, so I'm going to enjoy you both for the foreseeable future until you find your forever home."

She laughed with a snort. "I don't think you need to worry about me getting married anytime soon. I'd have to be actively dating and find someone I'd want to marry, but I've made up my mind. I'm going to talk with the bank and see what it takes to get a mortgage and then start saving for a down payment."

He nodded. "Just do me one favor. Don't buy the first house you see. Take your time and look around."

She flashed him a grateful smile. "You know me. I move at a turtle pace when it comes to money matters. Who knows? I might even find a place that needs a little TLC and try my hand at home repairs."

"When the time comes, if there is anything Mom or I can do to help, just ask. In regard to getting married, that ship hasn't sailed yet."

She frowned. "Well, I'd need to find a good man first, and one who would understand about my past."

"What about Jack Price?"

"Dad. He's an amazing guy, but we had our chance." She could feel her shoulders slump.

"From what I remember, he was always quite interested in you and you always had a smile on your face when you were together. You're still that same smart, funny, beautiful, and fun-to-be-with girl."

"You have to say that kind of stuff—you're my dad. But we both know the circumstances of Owen's conception. It took me years to deal with being date-raped. I wouldn't want anyone to think less of my son because of that."

"A good man won't let that change anything, and your son is an amazing kid."

The sound of tires crunching gravel drifted through the

open window. Peyton looked at Dad. "Are you expecting someone?"

"No."

She got up and looked out the window. Jack was taking the porch stairs two at a time with a grin on his face and brown shopping bags in both hands.

She answered the door before he could knock.

"Hi, Peyton. I hope you don't mind I just dropped by." A sexy grin graced his mouth.

She turned and looked at Dad, who gave her an exaggerated wink, as if to say *I told you so.*

She held open the door and, with a plastered-on, cheerful smile said, "Come on in. This is a nice surprise." But what was he doing here really?

*J*ack came through the door. "Hey, Ken. Good to see you again." He held up the two bags. "I brought dessert."

Peyton said, "That's very nice, but it wasn't necessary."

"I was hanging out at Mom's with Liza and the boys. They've been giving Liza a run for her money today and she needed backup. Mom kept them busy baking cupcakes and I thought your family might enjoy some." He gave a one-shoulder shrug and held up the other bag. "And cake needs ice cream, so here I am."

Ken got up from his recliner. "I'll take those from you. Have a seat, Jack."

He handed Ken the bags. "Thanks." So far, his idea hadn't tanked. At least not yet. His main mission was to ask Peyton for a date again, and maybe she wouldn't refuse if he asked her in person.

He looked toward Ken's retreating back and touched her hand. "You're not upset that I dropped by?"

She gave him a tentative smile. "It's fine, and thank you for the cupcakes and ice cream. But I *am* surprised to see you tonight."

Did he hear a gentle reproach in her voice? The sound of Owen laughing drifted down the hallway. "Can we go outside and talk for a few minutes. Alone?"

She seemed to vacillate between saying yes and staying within the comfort of the house. "Let me tell Dad we're taking a short walk."

Jack waited while she left the room. He could hear the sound of their voices but not what was being said; hopefully Ken was in his corner. He looked around the cozy room. The walls were covered with photos of Peyton in various stages of growing up. She had been cute as a baby, with a mass of dark curls and a little bow for her mouth. He stopped when he saw her high school graduation portrait. He'd loved that girl with all his heart, and he loved the woman she had become.

He moved around the room, looking at more photos of Owen, from his first picture with Peyton up to his last school picture. He was a good-looking kid.

"Ready?" She pulled a cardigan sweater on and stood in the doorway.

"Right behind you." Jack reached around Peyton to push the screen door open. "Good thing you put a sweater on over your T-shirt—it's cooled off quite a bit now that the sun is setting." Why did he say that? He sounded like an old lady fretting over the weather.

Her voice was low. "Thank you."

He wanted to slip his hand in hers as they strolled down the wide front steps but the vibe rolling off her reminded him to go slow, like a turtle if necessary. When they got to the bottom, he tipped his head back and looked up. "The stars are going to be stunning tonight. There's not a cloud in the sky." He could feel the tension in her body. "Rumor has it you received some good news today."

She gave him a sideways look. "I have to ask, does everything that happens at CLW get discussed around the boardroom table?"

He laughed out loud. "No. My parents' kitchen table is where all the important decisions are made. Why do you ask?"

"Curiosity," she said softly. "Don stopped down today and gave me a raise."

"You've earned it." Jack couldn't keep the pride he felt from his voice, and he hoped she could hear it.

"With the raise, I can talk with the bank and see what I need for a down payment on a house. Nothing huge, but big enough for me and Owen and who knows, maybe a dog. If I get real lucky, I might find something near a lake."

He was taken aback. "I never thought you'd want to buy a house."

"Why? Single moms do it all the time." He could hear the hurt in her voice.

"You're more than capable. It's just that I know how much my parents love having the boys around. After Steve died, they asked Liza to move in. I assumed your parents would feel the same about their grandson."

"But she didn't pack up and move home. She's forging her path on her own terms, and that's all I want too." Peyton grew quiet and he knew, once again, he'd put his foot in his mouth.

"What are you going to do?" His heart flipped. He had been having this crazy fantasy of them buying a house together someday. It never occurred to him that she'd be planning to get her own place. *You're just a jughead. Of course she wants to have her own home—isn't that why you bought the Simmons place? To prepare for your future and give you the capital to buy a bigger house?*

"Since this is all new to me, I'm going to plan, look around, and take my time."

She stepped away from him, and the loss of her warmth felt like part of him was missing. Taking a deep breath, he said, "The reason I stopped by tonight was I wanted to ask you to have dinner with me. I really like you and I'm not the same guy I was twelve years ago. I've grown up."

*P*eyton gave him a sharp look. "What are you saying? You want to turn back the clock and pick up where we left off?"

"I want to see if there is a spark of the feelings we had for each other before I left." He took a step toward her and touched her hand. "I don't want to pick up where we left off. I want a fresh start. We've both changed, but my feelings for you are stronger today than they were more than a decade ago."

"But, Jack..." There was a part of her that wanted to say yes; she wanted to see if there was more than this undeniable connection to him, but she needed to be careful. Just having him touch her hand made her feel like she was safe. "It's not just about you and me. I have a son to think about. Not that I'm asking for a declaration of undying love, but I can't let him get hurt. He has pain about not having a dad in his life. Hell, he already thinks the sun rises and sets on you." She turned away from him and wrapped her arms around her body. "We should just stay good friends. That way, no one gets hurt."

Jack gently turned her around so she was facing him. His steady gaze willed her to look into his eyes. She tipped her chin up.

He said, "I can't see what the future holds, but I want to spend time with you and your son. You're both important to me."

She grew thoughtful and walked a short distance to a painted wooden bench near the front flowerbed. She patted the space next to her. *I want to just throw caution to the wind and see where this is going, but what if Jack breaks my heart? Can I take a chance on him again? When we're together, those old feelings surface, reminding me of what it was like when he was by my side. But this time, it's not just about me. I have to think about my son.* She needed to understand how he saw Owen before she could make her decision.

He sat down. "Talk to me."

"When you look at my son, what do you see?"

*H*e wasn't sure if he understood the question. "A smart, active little boy who is the light of his mother's life."

"What else?"

Jack balled his fist and rested it on his leg. He knew what she meant now. "Your son, Peyton. It's not that I don't ever think about what happened to you, but it doesn't define who you are or who Owen is."

Slowly she nodded and looked at him, her gaze steady. "Thank you."

"You have nothing to thank me for. It's how I feel. I would do anything for either of you."

Peyton took his hand.

"Can I consider that a yes? Are you ready to go out with me?"

"Yes, but can I ask you one question?"

"Of course. Anything."

"When Don told me about the changes for the tasting room, I wondered if I got the promotion because you pulled some strings."

"Peyton…" He waited until she looked into his eyes. "You've been around my family's business a long time. Have you ever seen anyone be handed a promotion just because? Everyone earns their place in the organization, even if you're a Price."

She grasped his hands tighter. "I really did get it because sales are up over thirty percent?"

He beamed. "Yes, you nut. You're a natural salesperson and shame on Don for taking so long to tell you." He brushed her hair from her face. "Besides, if push came to shove, Don might choose you over me. You're much prettier and you can sell sand in the desert."

She sighed. "You say the sweetest things." She leaned into the crook of his arm and rested the back of her head against his chest, gazing up at the stars. "This brings back memories of sitting on this bench, doing this very same thing a long time ago."

He dropped his voice. "Those nights always ended with a good-night kiss."

She eased away and turned her head so that she could look in his eyes. "A spark is not a fire, Jack."

"Understood."

She settled back into his arms. "But this is nice." As far as she was concerned, they could sit like this all night. It was just about perfect. "So you haven't said. When do you want to have dinner?"

"Is tomorrow night too soon?" he asked.

"I think that can be arranged."

She could hear the smile in his voice. They were falling back into an easiness that she'd missed but wasn't going to take for granted. Not this time.

9

"Shoot." Peyton fished her pearl earring out of the sink and tried to stick the post through the hole in her earlobe. Last night, sitting under the stars, it had been a great idea to have dinner with Jack, but tonight her hand was shaking with nerves, making it tough to line up the earring and the hole. Thank heavens she'd closed the drain before fussing with her earrings.

She shouldn't be nervous. Jack had agreed they would take things slow. She'd offer to pay for her own meal just to keep them in an easy-breezy kind of relationship. But it didn't make her nerves lessen. After all, this was Jack.

"Damn it!" She finally pushed the post through the hole and secured the back.

"Mom?" The door to the bathroom creaked open.

The sad hitch in her little boy's voice made her heart skip and she dropped to one knee and pulled the door wide open. "Hey, Owen. I thought you were helping Grammie make a salad."

His lower lip quivered. He covered his eyes with the

back of his hand. Softly he asked, "How come I can't go out with you and Jack tonight?"

She eased his hand away from his eyes and tilted his chin up. She brushed a lock of blond hair off his forehead, mentally adding the barber to her never-ending list of to-do items. "Buddy, it's grown-up time tonight."

His deep brown eyes locked on hers. "I promise I'll be good. I won't even ask for dessert."

Peyton smothered a laugh. He was so darn cute that she wanted to say yes, but this was the first time she had been on an important date in years. He had never known when she dated anyone else. And much to her surprise, she was looking forward to having dinner with Jack. Just Jack. He had been one of her best friends since childhood, her first love, and he'd been angling to take her on a date for the last couple of years. He had been moving slowly just to get her comfortable with him as a friend; it had taken all this time. But recently something had changed. Was it seeing him help out with the kids' baseball team?

"The next time Jack and I go someplace fun, you can go too." She tousled his hair. "Okay?"

He nodded as she studied his face. Kicking at the area rug with his bright-blue sneakers, he asked in a small voice laced with hope, "Is Jack gonna be my dad?"

She sank to the floor, heedless of her dark-blue pencil skirt, and pulled him into her lap. Kissing his cheek and holding him close, she said, "Jack and I are good friends."

Solemnly, he said, "But all my friends at school have a dad and I don't, and Jack is fun and he likes kids. I can tell."

She turned so she could look into his eyes. So far, she had been lucky. Her little boy hadn't pushed the issue of having a dad, but heck, she knew it would only be a matter of time until the subject came up.

"Owen, I have a lot of fun with Jack, like you do with your school friends. Do you understand what I'm saying?"

He nodded and dropped his chin. "I guess so," he mumbled into his chest.

Peyton eased him into a standing position and got up to her feet. She hugged him tight against her body. "You're going to have a lot of fun tonight with Grammie and Grampy, and you won't even know I'm gone."

He brightened. "I'm going to ask Grammie if we can have ice cream for dessert." He dashed from the room before Peyton could respond.

She straightened her skirt. Looking in the mirror, she shook her head. *This outfit is all wrong. I look like I'm going into an office rather than out for dinner with a handsome blond man with golden-hazel eyes that make my knees weak.*

She marched into her bedroom and flung open the closet doors. After pushing garments across the rod, she pulled out a purple floral dress with a scoop neckline. It was a simple A-line style that flowed over her curves. Being petite never bothered her; she could wear heels whenever she wanted to. With a laugh, she thought, who was she kidding? She never had a reason to wear high-heeled strappy sandals. Tonight was an exception.

She shimmied out of the skirt and blouse, tossed them aside, and slipped the dress over her head. She looked in the mirror and was satisfied. Now she looked like she was going on a date.

. . .

*J*ack parked his truck in Peyton's parents' driveway. He felt like a bumbling teenager all over again. Thank heavens he hadn't got a zit or some other weird flashback. His jangling nerves reminded him of the first time he picked her up for a date, a guy who hadn't grown into his arms and legs. He'd had braces and yes, a zit smack-dab in the middle of his forehead. Peyton was the only girl who had captured his heart. Finally, he was getting a second chance to take her out again, just the two of them.

He checked the rearview mirror to make sure his hair had stayed in place. He wanted to get a haircut, but a few weeks ago in passing, Peyton had mentioned she liked it a little longer, so he had bought some hairspray to keep it under control. He smiled to himself. Who would have thought he'd voluntarily use a haircare product? There had to be a better way to control it or maybe he'd just cut it off again; it was cooler working in the vines.

He closed the truck door. Owen was standing on the top step of the porch. It was wide and wrapped around three sides of the old white farmhouse. Jack held up his hand in greeting. "Hey, sport."

Owen came hopping down the steps, making sure his feet thudded on each one as he made his way to the driveway. "Hi, Jack." Owen squinted up at him. "Mom's still in the bathroom."

Jack smiled. "She is?" He couldn't help but wonder if she was as nervous as he was.

"Uh-huh."

"Well, I'm sure she'll be out soon."

"Mom said that maybe next time you take her someplace fun, I can come too."

Jack knelt down to the boy's level. "I'll talk to her tonight and we'll make definite plans. Maybe you'd like to go fishing on my boat again, just the three of us. How does that sound?"

To see Owen's face light up made him happy. He was a good kid. He had his grandfather, but he needed someone else to do guy things with. "Remember Mom doesn't like to put worms on the hook?"

"I can help your mom while you catch the big one."

The sound of a throat clearing caused Jack and Owen to look up.

Jack's mouth went dry. Peyton was standing on the porch. His gaze drank her in like a man thirsty from time spent in a desert: high-heeled sandals, knee-grazing dress… He stopped at her face, framed by deep-brown hair highlighted with streaks of reddish gold. If she was nervous, it didn't show in her soft brown eyes.

"Mommy, you look so pretty." Owen looked up at Jack, his eyes shining.

"Peyton." He took a step forward. "You're beautiful."

Her musical laugh ratcheted up the pounding of his heart. "Thanks, Jack. You clean up pretty good yourself. The last time I saw you at work, you were covered in grease."

He shrugged with a grin. "The joys of being head of operations and maintenance. You tend to wear the job some days."

Peyton pointed to the door. "Son, time to go inside."

He dashed up the stairs, stopping midway, and turned to Jack. "You won't forget about going fishing again, will you?"

"Not a chance, sport."

He gave Jack a little wave. "See you later."

Peyton bent over to kiss Owen's cheek and then held open the screen door. She looked him in the eye. "You be good for Grammie, okay?"

He flung his arms around her neck. She whispered in his ear and he nodded.

As if on cue, Peyton's mom stepped into the doorway. "Hi, Jack. I didn't hear your truck pull in."

"Hi, Mary. It's good to see you again." He smiled at the boy. "Owen must have been watching for me. He was outside the moment I pulled in."

Mary smiled and mussed Owen's hair. "You're all he's talked about for the last half hour." She grinned at Jack. "You've got quite the fan."

"Bye, Mom." Owen zipped inside.

"I'd better go. There's no telling what mischief he'll get into." Mary kissed Peyton's cheek. "Have fun, you two, and don't worry about a thing." She winked at Peyton. "Stay out as late as you want." She let the door bang behind her.

Jack watched as color flushed Peyton's cheeks. He thought it was cute her mother could still embarrass her. "Thanks," he called after her.

Peyton shook her head. A smile twitched her lips. "I'm sorry about that."

"Don't be. My mom would have said something similar if the shoe was on the other foot."

"I need to grab my purse. Two seconds." She went inside.

Jack took the stairs two at a time. He thought it might be a good idea if he held her hand while she came down the stairs in those shoes. *Heck, who am I kidding? It's just a good excuse to hold her hand.*

Peyton came outside and gave him a heart-stopping smile. "I'm ready."

If she was surprised he'd met her at the door, she didn't indicate. He held out his hand and she placed hers in his callused one.

"What's the plan for the evening?" She glanced down. "Am I dressed okay?"

"You look fantastic." They made their way down the stairs, holding hands like it was the most natural thing in the world. "I thought we'd have dinner in town at La Fontaine's and then go out by the lake and sit and talk. There's supposed to be a full moon tonight."

She tensed momentarily. "That sounds nice." Her voice was soft.

"We can do something else after dinner if you'd prefer." He knew she loved the lake. She had taken Owen swimming a couple of times last summer with his family. But her low-key reaction wasn't what he had expected.

She straightened her shoulders. "We can go to the lake. It's fine."

He heard the hesitation in her voice. "If you're worried you'll be cold…"

She wouldn't look at him. "No, not at all. It's just that, well, I try not to be at the lake after dark."

Jack could sense her withdrawal. What the hell had he said? "No, it's fine. Let's just go for a drive and have a drink somewhere." What was wrong with him? He had just put a damper on their date before they even pulled out of the driveway.

She placed her hand on his arm before he could open the passenger door. "Jack, I haven't been at the lake after dark in nine years."

His heart dropped. He was an idiot. "We'll find something else to do after dinner." He gave her a half-hearted smile and opened the truck door. After helping her in, he walked around to the driver's side, berating himself for reminding her of the worst moment of her life. He got in and buckled up.

As the truck rumbled, she said, "Jack?"

He swung his gaze to her. He loved the curve of her cheek and the dimples that appeared when she smiled.

"You know I hid what happened to me, from everyone, for a long time. It has taken years to come to terms with being drugged and raped. But after a lot of hard work with my therapist, I'm good." She tipped her head slightly. "Maybe tonight would be a good time to drive to the lake. As long as you're with me, I know there's nothing out there that will hurt me."

She stretched out her hand and he took it. He held on and hoped to reassure her she was safe. "Peyton, I'm never going to ask you to do anything you don't want to do. Not tonight, not ever."

She dropped her eyes to his lips before giving him a small smile. "I've known you my entire life and I trust you. Which is why tonight may be the right time to lay a ghost to rest."

He lifted her hand to his lips and grazed her soft skin. "We don't have to talk about what happens after dinner. Let's just enjoy a leisurely meal and see where the night takes us."

Peyton's dimples slowly emerged. "That sounds nice."

Out of the corner of her eye, Peyton watched the sinking sun highlight Jack's profile. His high cheekbones and strong jawline were softened by his hazel eyes, and those deep killer dimples caused her heart to quicken when he grinned. Tonight, he had a dusting of whiskers. She preferred him clean shaven. But if she were being honest, he was smoking hot and still made her pulse race. It had been this way since she was sixteen.

She wanted to pinch herself. After all these years, they were actually on a date again. He had been so supportive when she finally told him what had happened that summer eight years ago. Since sharing her nightmare, something good had come from it all. She had kept it a secret for so long but when the truth had come out, she had the never-ending support of her parents and friends.

"Look at the vines." Jack interrupted her train of thought as if he sensed she was going to a grim place. "They're loaded with clusters of flowers. It should be a good harvest as long as the weather holds."

"That old saying holds true; April showers bring May

flowers." They drove past acre after acre of Price family land planted with grape vines, old and new.

"Has Anna told you about the new blended wine she's working on in France?" she asked.

Peyton admired Anna. She knew grapes better than anyone she had ever met and seemed to have the magic touch when it came to blending juices for fun, unpretentious wines as well as the classics. Even now, she and her fiancé Colin were living in France to create two new blends as a joint venture with Marchand Winery.

"She definitely has a knack. Her last summer blend sold out before we had even finished bottling it."

Peyton laughed. "That's a slight exaggeration. But as soon as the tasting room opened in February, we were out."

He gave her a sidelong glance. "You had something to do with that. Kate knew what she was doing when she asked you to organize the Valentine-themed tasting. Setting it up outside next to the bonfire was a great idea and a huge hit."

"I'm not a real event coordinator. Liza is, and she'll handle future events." She could feel her cheeks grow warm under his praise. "Besides, it was Kate's food. All I did was set up a table, pour wine, and of course light the kindling. Thank goodness it was a sunny day; people were happy to be outside after the deep-freeze cold snap we had."

"You're being modest." He took her hand from the console. "You planned, advertised, and consulted with our resident chef to select just the right appetizers. I'd say you did more than *just* pour wine."

"Well, thank you." She laced her fingers with his. "You're pretty good at boosting morale, boss."

"Now, there is only one boss at CLW, and that's Don." She could see his eyes sparkle.

"Is he really thinking of changing the name from Crescent Lake Winery to CL Winery?"

"Nah. He just says that kind of stuff to get Dad riled up. You know how the old man gets. The Price kids messing with his real baby, the winery."

"Speaking of your dad, how's he feeling? Has he had any more issues with his heart?" Peyton didn't let go of Jack's hand as they entered the charming town of Crescent Lake.

He slowed and put on his blinker. "Are you kidding? Mom keeps after him about what he eats, drinks, and how much he exercises, and even goes with him to doctor appointments. There's no way he would even think of getting sick again." He eased into an open parking space a short distance from the restaurant. "After all, Mom would kill him if he did."

She squeezed his hand before she released it. "Your mom is a sweet lady and she really loves your dad."

"Did you know they went to grade school all through high school together? But it was after college that they started dating. The rest is history." He grew serious. "When we came close to losing him, I was more worried about Mom than Dad. He's her world, and to lose him would be the one thing she just wasn't ready to deal with." His finger slid down Peyton's arm. "Someday I hope to have that kind of a relationship. After watching my parents, I know what it takes to make a marriage work for the long haul."

He turned in the driver's seat and held her eyes captive. "I know that when the time comes, I'll be all in.

The woman I choose to spend my life with will be the one woman I won't be able to live without."

The intensity of his gaze caused Peyton to think about things she might never have, but longed for. Would anyone want to marry her and be a father to Owen? They were a package deal.

She paused and waited for him to either elaborate on his comment or change the subject, but when he didn't, she said, "I'm starving. Shall we have dinner?"

*J*ack planned to take this budding relationship slow and steady. Tonight was just the beginning of his plan to court her, the old-fashioned way. He didn't care about what had happened in their past. She was perfect for him.

Standing by the front of the truck, Peyton waited for him to come around. Hand in hand, they strolled down the wide, flower-lined sidewalk. The spring air held a hint of summer. As they approached the deep-red ornate door to La Fontaine's, he asked, "Do you mind if we eat on the patio?"

She flashed him a heart-stopping smile as he pulled open the door. "I was hoping we would. It is a beautiful night, perfect for dining alfresco."

A short, stocky man was headed in their direction. He greeted them with a warm smile and a hug for Peyton. "Jack, my old friend, I wondered when you would wander in. I know you have one of the best chefs in the eastern half of the country at the winery, but it's been, what, over a year since you've graced my restaurant?" He took

Peyton's hand. "And you, I don't think I've seen you, since…well, I don't know when."

She laughed. "Joseph, you're such a charmer. It wasn't that long ago I was in with my parents for their wedding anniversary."

He waved his hand. "That's not the same thing as a date." He looked from Peyton to Jack. "This is a date, right?"

Jack slipped his arm around Peyton's waist and pulled her close. She relaxed after a moment. This was Jack, and he'd never do anything to push her too fast. "It is. We would like a romantic table for two on the patio."

"I can always guess when a couple is dating. It's a gift." Joseph winked and picked up the menus and wine list. "Follow me."

She stepped onto the slate floor and looked around. The white twinkle lights were artfully draped around the perimeter and woven through the climbing roses that were just beginning to flower; they were early for mid-May. The air was perfumed with their fragrance. She squeezed Jack's hand and grinned.

"Owen wouldn't have appreciated this setting at all."

He pulled out a wicker-backed chair. "But I do." His voice was for her ears alone.

She sat down and looked up at him through her dark lashes. "It's been a long time since we've been alone and on a date."

"How am I doing?" He tried to keep his tone light, but he was serious. He wanted everything to be perfect.

She smiled. "You're doing just fine."

Joseph set the menus down and discreetly eased away.

Jack took the seat across from her and passed her the wine list. "Are you in the mood for wine tonight?"

"I am." She glanced down and then handed it back to him. "You're the expert. You choose."

"No, go ahead." He gently pushed it back to her. "Red or white. I'm easy."

She glanced his way and then scanned the list. Her cheeks flushed a charming shade of pink. He loved that he could make her blush so easily.

"Chardonnay, then." She set the list aside and smiled as Joseph approached with a pitcher of water.

He looked between the couple. "Have you decided on a wine for the evening?"

"Yes," Peyton's brow shot up as if to give Jack one last chance before she ordered. "We'll have a bottle of Sand Creek's new Chardonnay."

"Excellent choice." He glanced at Jack.

A flash of surprise slipped over his face. Was he disappointed with the wine she selected? "Whatever the lady wants is fine with me."

"I will bring you a special plate of appetizers."

Joseph left and Jack leaned forward, taking her hand. "I thought he'd never leave."

"Shush. He might hear you and I wouldn't want to offend him."

"I'm curious why you picked the Sand Creek wine." He continued to hold her hand lightly in his.

"I like it. It has notes of melon and pineapple." Peyton eased her hand away and placed her napkin in her lap. Maybe she should have ordered a CLW variety. "Would you have preferred one of your wines?"

"Not at all. I like that we can support Tessa and Max." He took a sip of water. "I've been rooting for them, and the business is beginning to grow as it should. At the last wine association meeting, Tessa and Max made it known their business is thriving and put to rest any thoughts of them selling. But enough about my sister and her husband."

Joseph came back to the table with the wine and poured Peyton a small sample. Jack was content to let her take the lead. She swirled the wine, inhaled the bouquet, and then took a small taste. Her eyes sparkled in the twinkling lights. "Delicious."

Joseph poured them both a glass and left the bottle in its chilled granite sleeve. She took note and smiled at Jack. "I'm sure you prefer it at room temp."

"It does exude the best flavor that way." He took a small sip and nodded at her. "Excellent choice."

Before Jack could say anything more, Joseph appeared with a small plate of appetizers. They ordered dinner and finally they were alone.

Jack nibbled on a slice of prosciutto and melon.

A comfortable silence surrounded the couple as she looked at him. "I was a little surprised you asked me to dinner since we're just friends. After all, we've been down this dating path once before."

"Friends is a good place to start." He leaned forward, his eyes locked on hers. "Besides, I was young and dumb in college, and back then, I didn't realize what I had until it was gone."

She didn't respond to his statement. "We've both changed since then." She shifted in her seat and he waited, as if he could sense she had something on her mind. "I haven't been on a date in a while, and it's usually hard for me." Her eyes bore into his. "I still struggle to be the girl I was before the night of the bonfire."

"You're who I want to be with now, not the eighteen-year-old. What happened that night hasn't changed how I see you. Smart, witty, beautiful are just a few words to describe you."

She blinked back a tear.

He squeezed her hands a little tighter. "I care about you and Owen. I want to spend time with you, have fun outings, have adventures, and take Owen along too. You never have to worry about anything other than being honest with me."

If it had been anyone but Jack, the touch of his hand would have set her nerves jangling, but it was familiar and even gave her a little tingle, in a good way. Her eyes never left his. "Jack, I care about you too and I'm glad you understand I'm different."

"In some ways, we both are." He leaned across the table and his finger gently touched her cheek. "Don't ever forget I'm here for you. Always."

*D*inner had been delicious and Jack kept her laughing, but now Peyton steeled herself on the drive out to the lake. She wiped her damp palms on the skirt of her dress and shivered despite the warm air in the truck.

Jack glanced her way. "Are you okay?" He took her hand. "We don't have to do this."

She thrust her chin out and rolled her shoulders back and exhaled, steeling herself to control the fear that threatened to clutch her heart. "I want to do this, and I need to talk about it."

He applied gentle pressure to her hand. The truck slowed and its tires crunched over the gravel as he pulled into the small parking area. The moonlight reflected off the glass-like surface of the lake. With the truck off, the sounds of the water gently lapping the shore reached her ears and the darkness enveloped the truck, but not in an oppressive way. It soothed her jagged nerves, just a little. She had loved the lake at night.

Jack didn't move to open his door. She wasn't sure if he

was waiting for her to do or say something. She eased her hand away but immediately missed the strength that flowed from him to her. She needed to tell him more about that night and somehow it was easier if they weren't connected.

Softly she began, "I loved the lake—it didn't matter season or time of day—from the time I was a little rug rat." She smiled into the dark. "Mom swore I had lake water in my veins." She glanced at Jack. "I remember you and your brothers would race to the waterslide to see who could get down it first."

Jack was nodding as she talked. "Good times."

"When we got older, you know there were always parties out here. The last one I came to was the summer after college." She stared out the side window and propped her elbow on the door, resting her cheek in the palm of her hand. "That night"—her voice quivered—"I wanted Tessa and Anna to come with me, but they had something else going on. There was a guy I liked, and Don was at loose ends from the breakup with Kate, so he drove me."

"I was in Napa at the time."

She could hear the sadness in his voice as he stated the fact. She sighed. "Everyone was a lot younger than Don and when he decided it was time to leave, I said I'd catch a ride."

"It was something you had done before."

She put her hand on the door handle. "Can we go for a short walk?"

He didn't hesitate. "Sure." He pushed open his door and grabbed a lightweight coat from behind the seat. He passed it to her. "You might need this; it's getting cool."

"Thanks." She took it and wrapped it around her

before getting out of the truck. She could smell a different cologne on it, citrus and musk mingled with a hint of vanilla. The heels of her sandals sunk into the soft gravel. Peyton was grateful he didn't push her to continue the story.

"Did you get your lifeguard certificate here?" he asked.

"Didn't all the kids in town?" Her laugh was strained. "Not that I ever wanted to be a lifeguard. My dad had said it would look good on college applications."

They reached the picnic table. She wiped off a few pine needles from the top before she sat on it and patted the space next to her. "Have a seat."

He sat close and slung his arm around her shoulders. "Warm enough?"

"I'm fine." She scanned the area and pointed to the large open firepit. "That doesn't look like it's been used in a few days."

He looked around. "It's the perfect night for a fire. I suspect the younger set will be along later."

She cocked her head and looked at him under her lashes. "Are you saying I'm old at thirty?"

He chuckled. "I've got a few years on you, but we're just experienced."

They both grew quiet. Listening to the sounds of crickets and peepers relaxed her. She looked up at the star-filled sky. "Look! A shooting star."

They watched as it streaked toward the horizon.

"I never even gave it a second thought when the paper cups were passed out. I was among old friends; what could happen?" Jack didn't need all the details. She skipped to the end of the story. "The last thing I remember before waking up at my parents' was a hand helping me off a log."

He took her hand. "Pey, I wish I had been there for you."

She didn't want him to think what happened had crippled her permanently. Her voice was strong. "What happened that night doesn't define me. It's a part of my past." She took a deep breath and whispered, "I'd like a new memory from the lake. Kiss me in the moonlight?"

Jack brushed his lips across hers. "I've wanted to kiss you for ages."

She felt him pour his heart into the long, slow, sweet kiss. Peyton pulled back and looked into his eyes. "Now this is what I call a sweet memory."

*

*J*ack pulled up in front of his house. A shot of pride flashed through him when he looked at the restored front façade. "Ready for the nickel tour?" A grin slipped over his face. "A lot of it is still the original, but I think you'll be able to see my ideas starting to take shape."

"I didn't realize you bought the old Simmons place. I mean, I knew you bought a house to flip, but I had no idea it was this one. I guess I haven't been paying attention when Kate talked about it. It's been what, six months?"

"It has, and I'm not so sure I want to sell now. After living out here, I'm enjoying the quiet, and the place came with ten acres. Someday when I have kids, it'll be a great place for tree forts and who knows what else. Maybe I'll even clear a spot for a pool."

"It sounds nice."

He could hear the wistful tone in her voice. "Have you given any more thought to buying a house?"

"I have an appointment at the bank next week to see what I would need for a down payment and how much I'd qualify to borrow. Details." She flashed him a grin. "But enough about my plans. Show me around Casa de Price."

She opened the truck door and he took her hand as they crossed the damp grass and walked up the wooden steps.

He turned her around. "Close your eyes and picture flowers lining the stone walkway."

She laughed. "The imaginary one?"

"Shush. Just do it and tell me what you see."

"Split-rail fence draped in trailing roses looking like they've taken over, and in the spring before they get green and full of flowers, daffodils in bloom, the kind that spread on their own as if they're welcoming spring."

"You're right, and maybe plant a few trees on either side of the driveway?"

"Exactly." Peyton looked at the wide front porch. "This space needs color and a couple of rocking chairs. Maybe a porch swing at that end." She pointed to the opposite side. "Have it run almost the width of the space and on the other side of the rail, more flowers and greenery."

"I'll make a note of it all." He tugged at her hand. "Come inside."

Jack could see it all taking shape. This is what she would do with her house—make the outside as inviting as the inside.

He pushed open the old wood door with its panels of inset leaded glass. "I was going to replace this, but instead, I'm making a custom storm door to help with heat preservation and maintain the beauty of the original front."

He guided her into the main hallway. "All I've done in here is install new windows and gut the plaster so I can insulate. You'd be surprised how these old houses have almost nothing for insulation."

She looked around the center hall. "The huge living and dining rooms will be spacious enough for you to host family events here. I didn't realize the house was so big; from the road, it's deceptive."

"Wait until you see the back half of the house, and upstairs there are four good-sized bedrooms, but I think I'm going to take one that is adjacent to what will be the master bedroom and convert it to a walk-in closet and bathroom."

"Another good selling point if you were to put it on the market."

He could read her expression. She didn't look or sound bored. "Want to see the rest of the house, and then we can sit out back and have a fire? Unless you're in a hurry to get home?"

"Not at all. This is fun." They walked into the old-fashioned open kitchen and family room area and she stopped. "This is an amazing space."

"Most of it's still the original, but I was able to take down the walls and make it one huge space. Nothing a few supporting beams couldn't handle." He gestured to the new glass patio doors. "This way."

She glanced over her shoulder at the space. "This will be a real family kitchen. The heart of the home."

"Someday." He held her hand as they crossed the patio. It still needed a ton of work, but it was another good reason to hold her hand. "Careful. Some of the stones are loose."

"I bet you'd say that even if they weren't." She looked at him. "You can just hold my hand."

"I'm trying to be a gentleman and besides, I don't lie. They really are loose."

She stumbled and gripped his hand tighter. "I see that now."

"Easy. I've got you." He guided her to the old bench in front of the firepit, which he had gotten ready earlier in hopes she'd agree to come back. There was so much he wanted to tell her, and being with her was something he had dreamed about, but the reality was even better.

He pulled a book of matches from his pocket and lit the kindling. It took off and he sat next to her on the bench. "Are you warm enough?"

Once he slipped his arm around her, holding her close to his body, she said, "I am now."

For a few minutes, they sat and watched as the logs caught, enjoying the silence.

She said, "Will you tell me about Napa? Was it all you had wanted it to be?"

"It was a good experience. Working for a different business gave me perspective on how Dad ran CLW, and now Don has followed the same path, but at least he's open to trying new ways to increase the harvest—organic methods for the new fields we cultivate, which is something Dad wouldn't have allowed me to take the lead on." He tried to keep the bitterness from his voice but some things still annoyed him.

"If you had it do over again, would you go?" She didn't look at him but continued to watch the flames dance.

He thought about that answer and how so many things would have been different if he knew now what mistakes he would make.

"I would, but I would have asked you to go with me. If I could do that, both of our lives would be so different." He would never have made the stupid mistake of marrying Corine and if Peyton had a child, he would be its father.

Softly she said, "We can't change the past. We have to own it and move forward."

He bent his head so their lips met. "I want to change our future, Peyton. Give me another chance. I promise I won't break your heart a second time."

She looked into his eyes. "We aren't the same people this time, Jack."

"I know. I hope you'll see I'm a better man." He kissed her tenderly and with her return kiss, he decided to take that as her answer for now.

In the early morning hour, Peyton lingered in Owen's bedroom doorway, watching her little guy sleep. His arm had been flung across his Spider-Man pillowcase, his legs askew on top of the covers. She noticed the room was cool from the open windows, but she suppressed the urge to pull the blankets over him. He was always a hot sleeper.

Talking about the assault with Jack hadn't brought back the nightmares as she had feared; she actually felt lighter than she could remember. Last night had been good for her in many ways and when he kissed her, the thrill that raced through her veins had only happened once before, when she had loved him so long ago.

She walked into the kitchen and leaned against the pale-blue tile kitchen counter as the intoxicating scent of coffee wafted through the room.

Peyton traced the outline of her lips with her fingers. Should the dormant feelings she had for Jack, which she had done her best to bury, stay that way? It hadn't been easy when they ended their relationship. Was it wrong for her to let this budding relationship continue? What if she did and it withered on the vine like an under-ripe grape and they hurt each other again—or worse, Owen?

The sputtering sound from the coffeemaker indicated it was time for her first cup of the day. Just as she finished pouring, her mom wandered into the kitchen wearing a pale-lilac bathrobe, her dark curls perfectly arranged.

Peyton handed her a full mug. Mom opened the refrigerator, added a splash of cream, and handed the carton to Peyton. She added cream to her mug, took a sip and then smiled over the rim. Mom's hazel eyes sparkled as she sat down. Without saying good morning, she said, "Tell me all about last night. Where did Jack take you and what did you do after dinner?"

Peyton sat down. She propped her elbows on the table, mug between her hands, and took her first sip, making her mother wait while she gathered her thoughts. "It was romantic and intense and one of the best nights I've had since we dated the first time." She closed her eyes and sighed.

"Does this mean you'll be going out with him again?"

"I don't know. Maybe. I need to really think about what's best for me and Owen." Peyton let the words dangle in the air for a moment, knowing Mom would continue to pepper her with questions if she didn't keep talking. "We went to La Fontaine's. The food was amazing."

Mom scooted her chair closer to the table. "Now, that is very romantic and fancy."

"After dinner, we went for a drive out to the lake, and then he took me to his new house for the grand tour."

"That sounds very nice." She laid a hand over her heart. "How was it at the lake? Difficult?"

Peyton tipped her head from side to side. "Not too bad. My therapist and I have talked a lot about it, going out there at night. I think I finally found closure." She softly slapped her hand on the table. "But his house…man, is it amazing. He bought the Simmons place. I'd love to have a house like that someday. He's going to fix it up and flip it, but I'm not so sure he'll be able to. Even though the house needs a ton of work, he bought it with ten acres of land. Everything outside needs attention—the yard, the porch, and back deck."

"And what happened after the tour?" Mom's eyes gleamed over the rim of her coffee.

Peyton toyed with her mug and looked out the window. "He has a firepit in the backyard and we sat out there for a while, listening to music and talking about old times. It was relaxing and I would say a very successful first date."

"Pey, it's hardly the first date. You have been down this road before with Jack. And I know the last time, he broke your heart."

"In all fairness, we were too young to be that serious. Besides, I didn't say I was going to run out and get married tomorrow. It felt awesome to get dressed up and go out to dinner with a very handsome man who I happen to like, a lot."

"What's next? If he asks you out again today, will you go?"

"It's still one tiny step at a time, but if he asks, yes. I'll definitely accept." She glanced over her shoulder toward the hallway. She made sure her sweet boy wasn't coming into the kitchen before saying, "What should I tell Owen? Last night, he asked if Jack was going to be his daddy because the other kids in school all have dads."

Mom gave her a sympathetic nod. "How did you answer him?"

"I told him Jack and I were very good friends, and it seemed to pacify him for the moment. But it won't be the last time he brings up the subject."

"Did you happen to mention that to Jack?"

"You're kidding, right? That sounds like I'm looking for a father for Owen."

"Your son's best friends are Jack's nephews and they all hang out together, and Owen definitely has a case of hero worship. The last time you came back from Kate and Don's, all he could talk about was Jack playing catch with him and the boys. It might come up, and out of fairness to everyone, maybe you should tell him."

Peyton groaned. "I know. I like that he has a man other than Dad to look up to. Maybe he doesn't think of Jack any differently than he does Don."

Mom's eyebrow arched. "Owen knows Don is your boss. They're brothers but that doesn't mean Owen sees them in the same way. Owen spends a lot more time with Jack. He's even talked about going fishing again."

"I heard them mention something about fishing, but I wasn't really paying attention and we didn't talk about it."

"Owen told us all about it last night. He even asked if we'd come too."

Peyton set her cup down. "You're right. I need to talk to Jack."

"You and I both know he wouldn't have mentioned anything to Owen about fishing if he didn't want to spend more time with him." Mom finished the last of her coffee. "As much as Jack is interested in you, I know he genuinely likes Owen."

Peyton let the idea roll around her brain. "He does

make an effort to talk to Owen. You know, really talk to him, ask questions, and focus on his answers."

Mom nodded. "He's a great kid."

Peyton couldn't contain her grin. "Of course he is."

"Mom?"

She got up from her chair as Owen stumbled into the kitchen. Rubbing the sleep from his eyes, he asked, "Did you and Jack talk about our next date?"

Mom hid a smile behind her hand.

Peyton wasn't surprised that was his first question and then realized they hadn't made plans to take Owen on the boat. She fibbed, "Jack wanted to check on the grapes to make sure he didn't have to work before we firmed things up."

His face scrunched up as if confused. "What's wrong with the grapes?"

"You remember Jack is in charge of all the vines at work. And we'll be harvesting them in the fall. He needs to make sure they're on schedule."

She looked between Mom and Owen. Could her explanation get any worse?

Owen opened his mouth to ask another question, but she said, "You must be hungry. How about I whip up some pancakes for us?"

His face brightened. "With blueberries?"

She ruffled his hair and turned him to the door. "Absolutely. Now go wake up Grampy and let him know we're having panny-cakes for breakfast and we still need to get you to school on time."

He ran off down the hall and Peyton sank into the chair. "See what I mean? There aren't any flies landing on that kid."

"Then I would suggest you make plans with Jack today

to alleviate any additional questions over dinner."

"Since I just committed to cooking breakfast, I'd best get started." She took Mom's coffee mug from the table. "You're on bacon duty."

"The pancake mix is in the pantry." Mom laughed and pushed her chair back across the tile floor. "And when are you going to suggest to Jack that you go on a family date?"

Peyton grimaced. "I'm not sure. But if we go fishing again, I intend to make it crystal clear to Jack that I am *not* baiting a hook."

Jack came up behind Peyton at the wine bar in the tasting room. He hadn't intended on making her scream and drop two glasses, but that was her reaction. Laughing, she swatted at him. "It's a good thing we're closed or the customers would wonder what's going on."

Her cheeks flamed bright red as he stepped over the glass and trailed his finger down her cheek.

"Hello." Her voice was like velvet to his ears.

He wanted his lips to do the talking, but he took a step back. He wasn't about to pressure her. "I had a great time last night." He watched as her eyes flickered with something unreadable. "Did you enjoy yourself?"

She looked at the floor. "You need to clean up this mess."

He wanted to laugh at her serious expression. "I will in a couple of minutes. Did you have fun?"

She nodded. "Dinner was wonderful." She dropped her eyes to avoid looking directly at him. "Thanks for the house tour too."

He waited to see if she wanted to talk about how they had spent most of their time by the fire, kissing.

"Mom told me Owen mentioned he's excited to go on the boat again and fish."

He easily adapted to her change of topic, but he would have preferred to kiss her. "He's a great kid and it'll be fun. Owen can fish and you can either drop a line or just relax, and of course your parents are more than welcome." He didn't confess that when he bought the bigger boat, family events were on his mind. That might freak her out.

"Sure, that sounds fun. I know Owen would have a blast. When do you want to go?"

Jack pulled out his phone. "I'll check to see what the weather forecast is for early next week." He tapped the screen and then turned it around so she could see it too.

"How's Monday after Owen gets off the bus? Hopefully we'll be recovered from a busy weekend."

He studied the screen again. "Monday's good."

"Sounds like a…" She paused. "…plan." Obviously, she wasn't ready to say the word *date*. Not yet.

"Let's make a deal. I'll take care of the boat, bait, and beverages, and you can take care of the picnic."

Her pretty mouth formed a small bow. "Jack?"

He gave her a crooked smile, hoping to make her relax. "Peyton?"

She landed a light punch on his arm. "Be serious for a minute."

He wiped the smile from his lips but continued to beam inside. "I'm totally serious. What's going on behind those pretty brown eyes of yours?"

"Well…"

"Yes."

"I wanted to give you a heads-up about something

Owen said in case it comes up. He asked me if you were going to be his daddy. You know kids; they say the darndest things."

"And what did you tell him?" He took a step closer.

"I told him that you were our very good friend and dodged the rest of the question." She held up her hands. "But I know my son, and I wouldn't put it past him to ask you directly."

"And what should I say if he does?"

"Stay on the friend angle and avoid the rest."

"Like a boxer who bobs and weaves as a defense mechanism?" He was glad Owen was thinking along those lines. Now to get Peyton headed down the same path.

She pushed her bangs off her face. It was one of her tells whenever she was nervous, and one he knew well.

"Jack." He could hear the mild exasperation in her voice. "It's hardly a defense anything—it's the truth."

"It is. We are very good friends and I hope someday to be more than friends. But for now, Owen will understand he and I are good buddies too. I enjoy spending time with him."

"Good." She wiped the palms of her hands on her slacks. "Now we need to get back to work." She gave his chest a playful shove. "And I need to clean up this mess."

"I've got it. After all, I'm the reason you dropped the glasses in the first place." He stepped around her. Before he disappeared into the stockroom, he said, "The next time, I'll make sure your hands are empty."

"You should. I could have been holding a couple of bottles of wine."

Her laughter followed him down the hallway. He jogged back to the tasting room.

She glanced up as he reappeared. "No broom?"

"I'll get it in a second, but what time do you want to go fishing?"

"Whenever. It is totally up to you."

"I was thinking—let's pick Owen up at school. Do a tour of the lake on the boat, maybe a little swimming or tubing, and then in the early evening, the fish will be biting again. We can have dinner on the water and come in around dusk."

"Owen would sleep like a log when we got home."

Jack could feel a smile spread across his face. "Now it's a date!"

"And you still need a broom." She gestured to the shards of glass.

He tapped two fingers to his brow. "I'm on it."

"Hey, do you want to come over for s'mores tonight?"

He wanted to do a fist pump but he played it cool. "Sure, and pizza, too? Say, six?"

"Perfect. Owen will be happy to see you."

"Hopefully he's not the only one."

After enjoying pizza, Peyton and Jack were sitting in front of the firepit with Owen, who was suspending a long-handled marshmallow stick barely into the flame. It licked at the two white puffs, which suddenly caught fire. "Mommy, help!" He waved it through the air.

Jack hopped up and grabbed the stick from his hand before the small fireball could take flight. "Hey, hold on there." He blew out the fire and flashed a goofy smile at Owen, who was visibly upset. "Can I eat this one? I love them super toasted."

Peyton moved to comfort her son, but Jack's gaze stopped her. She paused, waiting to see what would happen next.

"It's burned and yucky." Owen stuck out his lower lip.

Jack's eyebrow shot up. "So then I can eat it? This is my favorite kind."

Peyton wondered why he seemed so excited over a burnt marshmallow but given Jack's enthusiasm, it sure seemed to be his favorite.

Owen eyed him suspiciously. "Yeah." He watched as

Jack gingerly slid it from the stick and popped it in his mouth in one bite.

He licked the sticky bits from his fingers. "That's so good."

She hid her smile as Owen's mouth gaped open and eyes widened at someone actually eating all the char. She handed Jack the bag, and he popped a fresh marshmallow on the stick before handing it back to Owen. "Here you go."

Owen cocked his head to one side. "Was it really good or are you just foolin' me?"

Jack sat back down and gave him a sly wink. "It's the only way I eat them. I like the crunchy sound from the outside, and the inside is super gooey and messy too." He held up his fingers, showing the little sticky bits left. He licked them off and Owen looked at Peyton.

"Mom, can I try that? But still put it on the graham cracker and chocolate?"

And then it clicked. Jack was pretty sly in getting Owen to step outside his comfort zone. She scooted forward on her chair. "Sure, and I can help you."

His gaze moved to study Jack. "No, I can do it myself."

Jack smiled at her, and the way he did was for her eyes only.

"How about Jack helps you blow it out and then you can slide it onto the cracker?"

Owen hesitantly stuck the marshmallow into the fire and quickly pulled it out. He frowned again. He repeated this action two more times before it actually began to burn. Without looking up, he asked, "Should I blow it out?"

"Go for it." Jack leaned in and took the stick just as Owen puffed his cheeks and blew. Only one side was black. He turned the stick and Owen burned it again and then blew it out.

He beamed. "Can I have a big piece of chocolate on this one?"

Peyton held out a cracker with a square of chocolate and, using the other cracker, slid the marshmallow free. Owen stood at her knee, waiting impatiently to wrap his hands around the treat.

"I'll make you one next." He put a fresh marshmallow on the stick and Jack took it from him.

"You can eat yours and I'll toast this one."

Over his head, she looked at Jack watching them. She wondered what he was thinking, as his expression was unreadable. Was he bored to tears?

"This is nice," he said softly.

"It *is* nice out tonight." Peyton wasn't sure if he was just commenting on the weather, so she chose to not read into it.

He made a circle with his finger from Peyton and Owen to himself. The look in his eyes was filled with tenderness. She was getting accustomed to the sweet things he said and did.

"It's a little mundane compared to what you're probably used to." She wasn't fishing for a compliment, but she thought it was nice to be sitting fireside, enjoying a quiet late spring evening with her son and Jack.

"Hanging drywall or being with you." He shook his head. "But being serious for a moment, I never knew how much fun this could be until I started spending time with you and Owen."

"We do it pretty regularly. S'mores are one of my weaknesses."

Jack pulled the marshmallow from the stick and waited

for Owen to slide off his mom's lap. Instead, he looked up at her. "Jack can make it for you, Mom. He's good at it too."

Owen looked at the back door.

"Do you want to go inside?"

He nodded. "Can I watch the *Lego Batman* movie?"

"No, you have school tomorrow, and then I'll pick you up. We're going fishing with Jack."

"Really?" He looked at Jack and then back to her.

"Really. Now march." She glanced at her watch to check the time and then smiled at Jack. "If you want to stay a little longer, I'll tuck him in and we can enjoy the fire."

He set the stick on the table and leaned back in the chair. "That sounds great. Need any help?"

She stood up. "No, thanks. I'll be right back." She followed Owen inside and hovered in the family room door. "Go put your pj's on and brush your teeth and I'll meet you in your room."

He raced down the hallway and called over his shoulder, "I'll be right back."

Within minutes, Owen was tucked into bed with his cozy blanket and stuffed dog. She checked his nightlight was on and said, "I'll be right outside if you need me."

He nodded. "Are we really going fishing tomorrow?"

"We are, but you need to get to sleep now."

He closed his eyes. "I'm gonna dream of catching the big one."

She kissed the top of his head. "Good night, son."

With one final look, she closed his bedroom door and went back out to the backyard and Jack.

He held out a hand and pulled her into his lap, then asked, "Is this okay?"

She laid her head on his shoulder. "This is nice." He wrapped his arms around her and held her close to his chest. "You're really good with him."

Jack took her hand. "He's a good kid and it's easy to see why—you're a great mom."

"Thanks."

He toyed with a lock of her hair. "I like spending time with you, too. When do you think we can go out again to the movies or something? Alone."

She moved closer to kiss his lips. Her arms slid around his neck and she shifted in his lap. "You know Owen will want to go with us. He thinks dates should be for three, not two."

He pushed her hair back and cupped her face in his hands. "Movies Saturday night for the adults and then on Sunday, we can go play mini-golf after you close the tasting room."

"That sounds like fun." She tilted her chin down and lifted her eyes. She murmured, "But before then, how about we spend a few minutes enjoying the peace and quiet?"

Her lips brushed over his. The kiss deepened and her pulse quickened. It felt like heaven on earth to be in Jack's arms. His lips began a slow trail behind her ear.

"Mom!"

She paused mid-sigh and pulled away. "Perfect timing." She pecked Jack's lips.

"I can wait." He helped her up from his lap and said, "I'm not going anywhere."

*J*ack watched Peyton go into the house, leaving him staring into the fire. His phone vibrated in his back pocket. He pulled it out and there was a text from Corine.

Jack, please stop blowing me off. I really do want to talk to you.

He could hear Peyton talking to Owen. Her voice was getting louder; she was coming back out. He put the phone back in his pocket. He'd deal with his ex-wife later, but it did make him wonder when he should tell Peyton about his very short-lived marriage.

She poked her head out the door. "Do you want something to drink? Beer, wine, coffee?"

"Is water an option?"

She laughed softly. "Yes."

He pushed the idea aside. He didn't want to spoil their evening. It had taken him almost three years to be able to spend time with Peyton away from the winery and not at a Price family picnic or CLW event. Bringing up Napa would ruin everything by talking about his failure, at least in this setting. It wasn't something he was proud of, but he had to face facts. He got married because he was lonely and estranged from the family and a friend needed his help. If he talked to a therapist, he was sure they would confirm he'd rushed into that relationship because of an emptiness inside of him. It hadn't been love. He was looking to take care of someone. But he knew all that, so no therapist was necessary.

Peyton closed the door behind her and handed him a glass of water. "Sorry that took so long. He wanted his favorite blanket, and then he was ready to settle down."

"It's fine. I understand; Liza's boys are the same way."

He patted the space next to him. "Why don't we sit and talk."

She sat close to him, and he slid an arm around the back of the chair, not quite touching her. He needed to tell her about Napa, but the words stuck in his throat.

"I saw the loan officer at the bank and basically he said I have excellent credit and he gave me a range of how much I could spend on a home, and then the news I'll need a twenty percent deposit to avoid paying mortgage insurance."

"How do you feel about that? Good or overwhelmed?"

She studied the flames. "It's exciting, but it's going to take me a solid year of saving every dollar I can. I'm going to put all of my raise and any bonuses into the house fund, along with what I've already saved."

"I'm happy to go with you when you start looking, to check things out for structural issues." The only place he thought she should live was his house, where there was plenty of room for Owen. He was even thinking of adding a bonus room above the garage which could be another bedroom or playroom, but that would push her way too hard and too fast. He smiled to himself, but it was the best solution.

"I appreciate that." She sipped her water. "Tell me why you didn't come back to CLW much when you lived on the coast. Not even for holidays."

And there it was, an opening. "Do you want the long version or short?"

"Whatever you want to tell me, but at first I thought you'd be gone a year, maybe two, and when that stretched into years, it didn't make any sense. The Prices have always been a strong family unit." She looked at him. "What kept you away so long?"

"I guess to really make sense of things, it goes back to my junior year of college. I wanted to take classes in biology and science to learn more about growing grapes, digging into the science more along the lines of what Anna was doing. Dad was determined I would get a business degree and run sales for CLW. We had a lot of arguments about my future and he just wouldn't listen to me. The closer I got to graduation, the more I knew I couldn't work in an office or sell wine for the rest of my life. It wasn't my passion, nor was I driven to be the best. Besides, Don had the salesman thing all wrapped up. He was doing great by comparison and it was good training for him to run the business at some point in the future."

"You never talked about this when we were dating. Well, I knew you and Sam had friction, but all parents do with their kids. It's normal."

"I started to think I didn't have choices until I was talking to Grandpa Jones, Mom's father, and he told me that when Mom graduated college, all she wanted to do was grow flowers when his plan for her was to become a CPA." With a snort, he said, "Can you imagine my mom going into an office every day wearing a suit and heels?"

She laughed. "Your mom loves to grow flowers and vegetables. Her gardens are the envy of most people in town."

"That is exactly my point. Yes, she was involved in the winery business part-time, but she was able to follow her dream, which happened to blend perfectly with Dad's. All I wanted was a chance to be who I wanted to be and he was too busy pushing me to be who he wanted. So I was left with no decent alternatives and I jumped at the first opportunity I came across." He pulled her close to his side and kissed her hair. "In the process, I made a mess of us."

"You should have talked to me. I would have understood instead of finding out when your bags were packed."

He could hear the hurt that still lingered. "If I could change one thing from my past, it would be that brief conversation between us when I had one foot out the door. It was the biggest mistake of my life and I'm sorry."

She turned on the seat and searched his face as if looking to read his mind. "That's in the past and I would like to leave it there. We don't need to talk about Napa again."

Relief washed over him even though there were still things she needed to know, but not tonight. Talking about Corine could wait.

"My feelings for you haven't changed, and I hope that we can keep dating and see what might develop."

She brushed her lips against his. "I'd like that."

1 4

*A*fter last night, Peyton was happier than she thought possible. When Jack told her he had strong feelings for her, she was on cloud nine.

Studying her reflection in the mirror, she thought, *I'm going to throw caution to the wind and let the relationship evolve. We aren't the same two kids we had been all those years ago. Mistakes were made on both sides.*

She started to brush her hair but paused. The breakup had really been more on Jack than her. They had plans and she had believed him when he said they would travel through Europe the summer after she graduated from college. So many dreams up in smoke.

Can I trust him this time? I'm not the naïve, lovestruck teenage girl I was back then, and I'm going into this with my eyes wide open. There's no way he could hurt me.

She finished brushing her hair into place, gave it a squirt of spray, and swished mascara over her lashes. Her train of thought turned to Lily, the new hire for the tasting room. Thank goodness they'd spend the day together, training. After a light lunch paired with various wines, she would show Lily how to present a tasting to a customer. Hopefully she would quickly catch the rhythm of the experience the winery was known for. Peyton was proud CLW had set a high standard for the tastings, which some of the other wineries emulated.

As an afterthought, she added a touch of petal-pink lipstick and was ready to seize the day.

hen she arrived at the winery, one of the CLW trucks was driving toward her. She waited next to her car and slid sunglasses over her eyes. She could tell by the bulk of the driver it was Jack. Her heart quickened and her breath caught when the truck lumbered to a stop. Small clouds of dust billowed up from the tires.

With a wide smile, he jumped out. "Hey." A subtle heat warmed his hazel eyes, the flecks of gold bright in the sunlight. "This is an unexpected treat."

His long legs made the distance between them evaporate. He slid an arm around her waist and pulled her close to his chest. Then he gave her a long, slow, simmering kind of kiss. Without a care if she got dirty, she stepped into him. Peyton had a fleeting thought about the kinds of things they might do behind closed doors, but then it was too soon for that, wasn't it?

"Hi." His voice was deep and husky.

"Hi, yourself." She kissed him again, surprised at the intensity of longing within her. Her body remembered what it felt like to be with him.

He searched her face. "Busy day?"

"Yes, and you?"

"The usual. I just came in to get a couple of five-gallon

water coolers. We're getting pretty parched out there; working in the vineyard is tiring." He eased out of her arms. "Sorry; I'm all sweaty and you don't need to work all day smelling like me."

She chuckled. "There are worse things." She ran a hand over her chin-length hair to tuck an escaping lock behind her ear. "It's important to stay hydrated." She laid a hand on his chest. His heart beat under her fingers. "It's Lily's first day of training."

"That's great." He took her hand and they strolled around the side of the building to the tasting room door. He opened it for her. "I'm going to head back out. You know vines wait for no man or woman." He pecked her lips. "I gotta run." A wicked gleam sparked in his eye. He leaned into her and gave her another one of those knee-weakening kisses that she really liked and said, "I'll call you later, okay?"

Feeling tingly all over, she said, "Sure. I'm here until four."

He started toward the other building and turned around. "It's going to be nice tonight—want to take Owen and go out for some twilight fishing?"

"Sounds like fun. I'll pack sandwiches but we can't be out too late. School night."

She watched as his face transformed into a boyish grin. "You got it, and you're good with sandwiches. I'll be over around five."

"Wait. Why don't we ask Don and Kate too? Owen was just asking about Ben the other day."

He walked backward and grinned. "I'll talk to Don."

Before she could respond, he hurried to the mainte-nance garage without another glance.

on, Kate, and Ben were waiting on the dock as Jack, Peyton, and an ever-talkative Owen arrived. He was already in his bright-red life jacket with frog-green sneakers, carrying his fishing pole and a small Superman tackle box. Peyton admired Jack's patience with him.

The wood dock creaked as it rocked slightly under their feet, and water lapped at the thick wooden posts. The marina was quiet. It looked as if they were the only people to venture out tonight.

"Jack, can I drive the boat tonight?" Without waiting for an answer, Owen grinned at the others. "Hi, Kate. Hey, Don." He bent down to tickle under Ben's chin. "Hi, Benny." He gazed up at Kate. "Hey, he's got the same color life jacket that I have."

Kate held on to his hand and tousled Owen's hair with the other. "It's like you boys are twins."

"Like brothers." He flashed his mom an angelic look. "Right, Mom?"

"That's right, Owen. Brothers from different mothers." Peyton smiled broadly and looked between Don and Kate. "Where are the twins?"

"Sherry and Sam volunteered to stay at the house with them so Ben can have some time with us."

"That's great, but I hope you're ready for tonight. Owen usually doesn't stop talking the entire time we're on the boat."

Jack unlocked the gate and stepped aboard. Don handed the cooler up, and he stowed it away from the steps. He held out his hand. "Owen, hand me your fishing gear and then come aboard."

As Jack asked, Owen passed it over and then scurried up the steps, jumping with a thud on the boat deck. Jack turned to Peyton. "Come on, beautiful."

Peyton took his hand. His fingers clasped hers and he gave her a slight squeeze. The pressure sent a zing through her. She smiled at the happiness on his face. Taking the boat out tonight was going to be fun. Kicking back with good friends was just what they all needed from time to time.

She easily stepped onto the boat and leaned over to double-check Owen's life jacket.

Kate stepped lightly up the stairs and turned to Ben. "Come on, kiddo."

Jack said, "We've got this." Stepping in front of Kate, he helped Ben step onto the boat.

Ben and Owen sat on a bench, clutching their fishing gear and talking about the fish they wanted to catch while Don untied the mooring lines. Jack crossed to the captain's seat and turned the ignition switch. Without a stutter, the engine sprang to life with a deep rumble. Owen's eyes lit up as Jack gestured for him to slide into the seat. "Are you ready to help get us out of the dock?"

His head bobbed and his grin was wide. Peyton was sure it couldn't get any bigger. Jack held the wheel with Owen, his large hands covering the small ones.

Peyton settled onto a bench seat and enjoyed the breeze as it teased her hair. The sun kissed her skin, keeping her warm as the air wafted around her.

Kate had Ben between her and Peyton. They fell into easy conversation as the Price boys and Owen were maneuvering leaving the marina.

Glancing at the cooler, Peyton said, "I see you packed something for us to munch on."

Kate laughed. "I see you did too. Some habits are hard to break. When I lived at home, I was always the one—well, Mom and me—to pack the coolers." Her smile widened.

Don took Ben up to the co-captain seat, leaving the girls to talk. The engine and the wind muffled their voices, and Kate dropped her voice even lower for Peyton's ears only. "So tell me, how are things with you and Jack? You seem to be spending more time together lately."

"We've talked and decided we want to date and see where things go."

"That's great news." She leaned in closer to Peyton. "I see Owen thinks Jack walks on water." She pointed to the pair sitting in the captain's chair. "It's plain to see the feeling goes both ways."

"It does, but what happens if this goes south and Owen gets hurt in the crossfire?" Peyton looked to Kate for reassurance. "I have heard some of the single moms at Owen's school say they never let their kids meet the guys they date."

"In this situation and given your history with Jack, it would be kind of hard to not spend time together. The Price family is entwined pretty tight, and Owen has known Jack for years. Your dating him has been a slow—well, turtle-pace process. I don't think it would implode so badly that you wouldn't have any sort of a relationship. Besides, even if the romance withers on the vine, Jack and Owen can still be close."

Peyton's gaze lingered on her two guys. "I guess you're right. Jack would never let something interfere with his relationship with Owen."

Kate waved a hand to draw her attention. "You need to stop thinking what might happen if this ends and concentrate on all the good stuff coming your way now. He's a terrific guy."

"I know he is." Could Kate hear the tiniest sound of doubt in her voice?

"Did I tell you the story about when Don and I broke it off?"

Peyton shook her head. "I know Don's version but not yours."

"It was right after I graduated from culinary school. It was the night before I was going for a job interview at a five-star restaurant in Boston. But Don expected me to pack up and move here and get a job at Sawyers as a chef. He even said not to worry about getting the job because he knew the owner." She smacked the vinyl seat cushion. "I was so mad, I broke it off with him. I ended up blowing the interview and went back home to Loudon with my chin to my chest to try and mend my broken heart. Within a few months, Don left CLW, moved to my hometown, and took a job with my brother, all in an attempt to win me back."

With a short laugh, Peyton said, "I remember it caused quite the uproar in the family."

"And it took over five years to get me to move here."

"Kate, you have the world by the tail."

"But my point is the Price boys have their faults and sometimes they don't think with their heads, but they love with their whole heart. When they make a mistake, even if it is a huge one, forgiving them only enriches your life even more."

"You mean like when Don suggested that you move to Crescent Lake and conveniently forgot about your dreams of working in Boston?"

She nodded. "Yeah, Don crushed my feelings with his

thoughtlessness and it took a while for me to forgive him. We eventually moved on with our life but now look where we are—happily married, with three adorable children and careers we both love."

"I'll remember that. Thanks, Kate."

She watched as Jack continued to encourage Owen as he navigated the wake from a speedboat that cruised by. She crossed the deck and rested her hand on Owen's shoulder. "How's it going over here?"

"We're just about ready to drop the anchor and get ready to eat." Jack ruffled Owen's hair and said, "And then we fish. Right, buddy?"

"Right, Jack." With a brisk nod, Owen's gaze never faltered from the water. He was all business.

Peyton masked the grin that threatened to slip out. She didn't want Owen to get the wrong idea, that she wasn't taking his driving skills seriously. "I'm going to get things ready for supper, and Owen?"

Without looking at her, he said, "Yeah, Mom?'

"There's hand sanitizer in my bag. Use it before you eat."

"Oh, Mom," he groaned.

Jack winked over his head. "Peyton, do you mind if I use some too?"

Owen whipped his head around to look at Jack and then his mom.

"Help yourself." She turned her back to the guys and her smile grew.

Kate was laying out their picnic. Ben was happily munching on chips while he sat in the middle of the deck. An inner peace settled over her. This is what it felt like to let good friends into her life and treasure the simple moments.

ack had settled Owen with his pole, reminding him to stay seated and wait until he had a firm tug on the line and then Jack would help him reel in his fish. "I'm going to be right here with your mom."

Owen gave a nod, but his focus was watching the water, waiting for the elusive fish.

Jack slung his arm around Peyton's shoulders. Don and Ben were at the end of the boat with a line dropped into the water while Kate sat watching them. After a while, Owen squealed, "Help! Jack!"

He took two giant steps and bent down on one knee to coax Owen through reeling in his fish. After a brief struggle, the prize was on the deck of the boat.

Peyton snapped a couple of pictures of the two of them with the fish before it was released back into the water. "Good job, kiddo."

Owen beamed and said, "Thanks, Mom. Can I do it again?"

The sun had begun its slow descent to the horizon. Jack shook his head. "We need to pack it in for today."

He groaned.

Peyton said firmly, "Owen, time to put away the fishing gear. We need to head in."

"Aw, Mom. We just got here."

She could see the pout forming. "Owen." She used her stern mom voice and he reeled in the line. She could feel Jack watching her. She glanced in his direction and gave him a nonchalant shrug.

Don finished stowing Ben's gear and piped up. "Owen, do you think you could finish up quick and then sit with

Ben as we head back to the dock? He's looking pretty sleepy, and if you could help keep him awake, Kate and I would really appreciate it."

Owen handed Don his pole and, in two short hops, plopped down next to Ben. He started a very serious conversation about fishing and how he reeled in "the big one," oblivious to the adults sharing a laugh.

Within about twenty minutes, they were back at the marina. The temperature was dipping and Kate had wrapped both boys in lightweight blankets to ward off the chilly air. As they approached the shore, Don held the line. He jumped to the dock and with a few efficient knots, the boat was secured. Ben was sound asleep, snuggled in Kate's arms. Owen was visibly drooping too.

Jack took Peyton's bag. "I'm going to run this and the cooler up to the truck, then come back and carry one tired little boy off the boat."

Kate handed Don her little boy. "He's like a floodlight. One minute on, and then the next off."

"I remember those days." Peyton could definitely empathize. "In fact, there are some days he's still like that."

Jack's long stride was eating up the dock as he came toward them. His eyes never left hers. She steered Owen to the steps. "Jack's going to carry you."

"I can walk." He was too tired to seriously protest.

Jack held out his arms as Owen dragged his feet down the steps. "Peyton, can you check that everything is off and grab the keys?"

She did a visual sweep of the boat and pulled the keys from the ignition. "All set." She secured the gate. "Ready."

Jack carried Owen up the dock, Peyton walking beside them. Don and Kate were in front of them and when they reached the vehicles, Peyton kissed Ben's cheek. "Drive safe, you guys."

Kate said, "This was fun—we need to do it again."

Jack chuckled. "If you and Peyton keep packing those delicious snacks, count me in."

Owen picked his head up from Jack's shoulder. In a sleepy voice, he asked, "Are we going fishing again?"

"Not tonight, buddy, but soon." Jack carefully set him on the back seat in his booster seat and Peyton buckled him in securely.

Before she could get in the front, Jack pulled her into his arms. "Some night, we should go out on the boat, just the two of us." He nuzzled her neck as they swayed together. "I'll show you how to find the constellations."

She pulled his face close to hers. "How about next week?" She was mildly surprised at herself, but the flutter of nerves resurfaced. She tamped them down, reminding herself she was safe and the past didn't affect today as much as it once had.

"Now that's what I like—a woman who plans ahead." He lowered his mouth to hers and brushed her lips. "Definitely soon."

15

This road wasn't a direct route to the tasting room, but Peyton hoped to bump into Jack and thank him again for last night. Going on the boat with Kate and Don had been fun. She made a mental note to call Kate too and see if she wanted to go shopping or something in the near future. She had amazing friends.

She hadn't gotten lucky and spotted Jack before she arrived at the winery, so she took a minute to sit in her car once she'd parked. She needed to compose herself, prepare for the day, and maybe stop thinking about Jack long enough to—

A knock on the window startled her. She slid the window down and there was Jack with that half-cocked grin and smoldering eyes. She gave him a sassy smile; her insides still quaked whenever she saw him.

He leaned on the door and kissed her through the open window. "Morning, sunshine. I didn't mean to startle you."

"I was lost in thought."

His easy smile caused her blood to warm as she

thought of being alone with Jack on the boat. "About a night under the stars with me?"

"Maybe." She gave him what she hoped was a sexy wink. "I was also thinking about how much has changed since Kate moved to town. Don's a lucky man."

"He certainly doesn't take her for granted. When they broke up and he left all of this"—Jack swept his arms over the landscape—"to move to Loudon, he changed."

It was funny he brought that up since she and Kate had just talked about it last night. Had he overheard their conversation? No, the wind had masked their words. "I remember thinking that was the single most romantic gesture I had ever witnessed."

"As with all things, they've come full circle. They're back and raising the next generation."

"Do you think they'll have a big family?"

Jack straightened and opened her car door, pulling her into his arms. "Three might be their limit, but I'd rather talk about us and when you want to take the boat out, just the two of us."

She laid a hand on his chest, aware of how her own heart quickened. "Right now, we both need to get to work. I have more to teach Lily about our wines before Friday. If the last few weekends are any indication, we will be slammed with customers."

He kissed her forehead, and then his lips trailed down the side of her face. She molded her body against his long, lean frame and savored the calm that cascaded over her and the smell of the subtle, earthy fragrance of hard work mixed with the scent of his woodsy body wash.

She gazed into his eyes. "How would you like to come for dinner tonight? Potluck on the grill."

He pecked her lips. "It's a date, and I'll pick up supplies for Owen's favorite fireside treat too."

***

"*B*en's daddy is super nice." Owen sunk his boat under the bubbles in the bathwater.

Peyton heard the unmistakable longing as each letter in *daddy* dragged out. At least he had wonderful grandparents. "Don's a good guy. Now please finish up your bath."

She listened outside the bathroom as he played with his boats, laughing when the battle kicked into full swing at the same moment she popped her head in and pointed to the bar of soap. "Son, a bath requires you use more than just water. Soap too." She couldn't help but shake her head at the dirt ring around the white porcelain. She'd have to clean the tub too. "Oh, and let me know when you're finished. I'd like to get ready too."

"But, Mom," he groaned. "Jack's gonna be here soon and if I do all that stuff, I'll miss *all* the fun."

Holding back a smile, she waved her hand. "Get moving."

She stepped into the hall and chuckled softly. He was such a character, albeit a dirty one at the moment.

Mom came down the hallway and nodded toward the bathroom. "How's he doing? Washing up or playing?"

"The latter." Leaning against the wall, Peyton said, "I was trying to get him to hurry. I need to put my makeup on."

"Use our bathroom and I'll take care of everything else." Mom turned and then said, "Wear the pink lipstick. It looks good on you."

A knock on the front door interrupted Peyton's response. "That must be Jack." She poked her head into the family room. "Dad, I'm not quite ready."

He waved her off as he got out of his recliner. "No problem. I'll keep him occupied until you make your grand entrance."

"Oh, Dad." Her steps were light as she hurried down the hall.

*J*ack had been sitting on the sofa when Peyton walked into the living room, a large bouquet of flowers and a tote bag on the coffee table in front of him. As soon as he saw her, he stood.

"Hey there." His eyes sparkled.

"Hi." He was heart-stoppingly handsome in jeans, a black T-shirt, and sneakers. His lips grazed hers, lingering there and sending her lips tingling. Peyton could feel the blush rise from her neck to her hairline. Dad had discreetly left the room.

"Thanks for inviting me." Jack handed her the flowers and she inhaled their subtle fragrance. He slung his arm around her shoulders and pulled her close, kissing her temple.

"I love wildflowers." She glanced up through her lashes. "Are you sure you don't mind hanging out with my parents?"

"As long as I'm with you, it doesn't matter, but I am looking forward to some alone time soon." He looked into her eyes. His were shining.

Squeezing him tight, she was interrupted by thundering feet racing down the hall.

"Jack! Jack! Jack!" Owen came flying down the hall and leaped up, expecting Jack to catch him.

With a smooth motion, he scooped Owen up with one arm. "Hi there. I heard you had a bath."

Owen wrinkled his nose. "Mom made me. Said we were having you over and I needed to smell good."

Jack gave Owen a serious smile, but Peyton could see the mirth lingering in his hazel eyes. "Sometimes we just need to get cleaned up, especially when our mom asks."

Owen's eyes grew wide. "Does your mom tell you when to take a bath too?"

With a half chuckle, he said, "Not anymore." He set Owen down and handed him the bag. "Would you carry this in the kitchen for me?"

The little boy peeked inside the bag. "Wow, look at all those marshmallows."

*P*eyton held Owen in her arms as he snored softly, an uneaten toasted marshmallow on his stick. She had been enjoying the warmth of his body snuggled into hers and conversation with Jack without realizing her son had slipped off to dreamland. She eased them both from the chair and whispered, "I'm going to tuck him in."

"Would you like me to carry him inside?"

She shook her head and moved to the door.

Jack slid the glass door open and followed them down the hall. The television in the family room was off and her parents' bedroom door was closed. There wasn't a light under their door. Jack eased open Owen's door and left them.

Peyton snapped on the bedside lamp. The room was washed in a soft, dim glow. She was happy he had changed into pajamas before they went outside. He flopped on the bed, his legs and arms everywhere like cooked spaghetti. It was hard to tuck him into bed, but she pulled the covers over him and tucked them around him.

His eyes fluttered open, locked on hers. "Mommy?"

She smoothed back his hair and kissed his forehead. "Yes, baby."

"Am I ever gonna have a real dad?"

Peyton's heart flipped in her chest. This was not what she expected tonight. What should she say? "Owen…"

"Ben has a daddy and so do all my friends, except me." He dropped his chin closer to his chest. "I really want a dad."

"Sometimes…" Hell, what could she say to make him understand? "Sometimes, mommies want to have a baby so much, they do it without a dad. And that's what happened with me. I really wanted to be your mom. And you are so lucky you have so many people who love you, like Grammie and Grampy and me."

"And Jack?" he asked.

*J*ack stood outside Owen's bedroom door while Peyton put him to bed. He froze when he heard him ask about a dad. How would she answer him? Then he heard Peyton say, "Jack is our very good friend."

"But he likes us a lot. I can tell."

The sound of his voice tore at Jack. He wanted to step into the room and pull mother and son in his arms and never let them go. Peyton deserved to have her happily ever after, and Owen would be the best son a man could ask for. He continued to eavesdrop.

"Mom, do you like Jack like Grammie likes Grampy?"

Jack held his breath. Would she confess her true feelings to her son?

Her voice was soft and he strained to hear her response. "It's complicated. But I do like Jack very much."

In the semi-darkness, he eased down the hall and back outside to the fire, which he poked at while he waited for Peyton. His brain was struggling to process what he had heard and decide what his next move should be. Who was he kidding—when it came to this girl, it wasn't about moves or lines. It was about just being with her, spending time with her and her son. Getting to know each and every gesture again, things that made her laugh or ticked her off. He wanted to know her better than she knew herself. This time, he wouldn't screw it up and would always put her needs first.

He looked up at the sound of the back door opening. Peyton looked weary. She sat down heavily in the chair next to him and leaned back. Covering her eyes with her hands, she exhaled and dropped her head toward her chest.

They sat together for a long time. His arm was around her, holding her close while she remained quiet. The flames in the pit had reduced to glowing embers when at last she looked up and gave him a small smile.

"Do you want to talk about it?"

With a shake of her head, she said, "I really don't."

He wrapped his arms around her and held her tight, his chin resting on top of her head. "I'm here if you change your mind."

She took a ragged breath and then exhaled. "I appreciate that. For now, can we add a log to the fire and stay wrapped up in each other's arms?"

He stood up and tossed in a log, then eased her onto his lap. "We can stay like this all night if you'd like."

"That sounds like heaven." She relaxed in his arms.

16

"*P*eyton, where are you?"

"In the storeroom, Jack." She descended the step stool but when she stepped on the final stair, it gave way under her weight and her ankle twisted as she fell to the ground.

"Son of a…" Tears sprang to her eyes.

Jack rushed over to her. "What happened? Are you hurt?" He slipped an arm around her waist and helped her up.

She gingerly put weight on her foot and was happy she could stand with only a minor twinge. "I'm fine. The last step cracked or something." She stretched out her leg and rolled her ankle in circles, checking for pain or, worse, lack of movement. Pleased to see it was okay even though it was tender, she gave him a small smile. "If you had been a few minutes later, you wouldn't have had to scoop me off the floor."

He helped her to a chair and pulled a wine box over for her to rest her leg on. "Let me take a look at your ankle, and then I'll check the step too."

"Stop fussing over me. I'm fine, really." She eased down to the seat and pointed to the steps. "But it's probably a good idea if you could check them out. I wouldn't want Lily or Tony to fall; someone could break an ankle."

Gently, he probed her foot and lower leg and watched her face for a reaction. She had minimal pain. "It's not even swelling up. I'm fine. Really."

"I'll take a look at the step."

She enjoyed the view of his backside as he tugged up and pushed down on the step.

"There's the problem." He tapped the lower board. "It's split near the ends. I'll get it fixed before I go back out." He flashed her a wide smile complete with dimples. "I got your voicemail. Rather than call you back, I thought I'd come in." He turned to face her and gave her a heart-skipping smile. "This is so much nicer than an impersonal phone call, don't you think?"

Her insides quivered. It was time to ask him out on a date She could do this. Jack wouldn't ever hurt her. "There are certain advantages." She licked her lips. "I was wondering, if you didn't have any plans like working on the house or something, but if you do, that's okay too…"

"Sweetheart, just ask me." Mischief hovered in his eyes. "I might say yes."

"Would you like to take the boat out for the night. Just you and me?"

"Why, Ms. Brien, are you asking me out on a date?"

She relaxed and laughed. "I am. Are you interested in spending an evening with me? Alone?"

"You don't have to ask me twice. Tonight?"

"Are you free on such short notice?"

He cocked his head and pretended to think. "Let me see… I could have dinner with a beautiful woman on the lake or I could hang drywall." He tapped his index finger to his chin. "I wonder…which one I should choose."

She gave him a playful push. "Maybe I should have put a time limit on your response."

He grinned. "So it wouldn't sit well if I said I needed to get back to you?"

"Jack Price. Do you want to go out with me or not?"

With a hearty chuckle, he said, "Yes, and I'll pick you up at four thirty." He gave her a quick kiss. "Now that my plans for the evening have changed, I need to take off." He pulled her to a standing position and looked at her ankle. "Good, you're bearing weight."

She placed a lingering kiss on his mouth. "Told you I was fine. Now take off—I have work to do to. And I've got a hot date tonight with this guy I kinda like."

"See you later." With one final quick kiss, he jogged down the hall and out the back door.

That wasn't too awkward. She picked up her clipboard and got back to work. She needed to finish so she could figure out what she was going to wear and pack their picnic supper.

Before she could get started again, her cell phone pinged with a text message.

Stay off the step until I can get it fixed, please! XO

There were few vehicles parked at the marina and most of the boats were docked when Peyton and Jack arrived. It would be quiet until the weekend, when the marina would become like a zoo. She was happy they had come midweek—it was as if they had the lake to themselves.

She could feel her cheeks go pink as she imagined what they might be doing in a small cove somewhere. She was ready to take their relationship to the next level. She had even talked to her therapist about it and how she was ready to be intimate with Jack. Her therapist had suggested Peyton tell Jack that he was the first man she had been close with since the night she was assaulted, just in case there were any residual emotions that unexpectedly bubbled up.

After giving that conversation a lot of thought, she decided she would talk to Jack over dinner. Hopefully it wouldn't make things uncomfortable and put a damper on the night. But he needed to know, and they had agreed to always be open and honest with each other.

The late afternoon mid-June weather was the perfect way to start their date. She grabbed the tote bag and Jack took the cooler. They strolled hand in hand down the wooden dock to the boat. The breeze was still warm as it caressed her skin, the sun still high in the deep blue sky, broken only by an occasional puffy cloud drifting by. She drank in the fresh air if for no other reason than to calm her nerves.

The water gently lapped the sides of the boat. She tossed the bag on board and Jack held out his hand to help her step up. A loud splash and a fish jumping out of the water caused Peyton to look and lose her footing. With a laugh, she fell into Jack's waiting arms.

He took the opportunity to plant a kiss that was so mind-bending, she felt it to the tips of her toes. She swore they curled inside her sneakers. She sighed and, placing both hands on either side of his face, she kissed him back with all she had.

His voice was low and smooth. "As much as I'd like to

keep you here in my arms, maybe we should cast off and find a more secluded place."

He set her back on the steps and she took the cooler from the dock. "Do you need help with the boat?"

"No, I've got it. If you want to set up dinner, we can eat as soon as we get farther out."

Things were going to get intense in a good way. It was all going to be okay.

As they puttered away from the dock, Peyton set two plastic wineglasses on the small round table next to the sofa behind Jack. She uncorked a bottle of something new and took the tops off the covered bowls that contained cheese, crackers, and various finger foods.

The boat slowed and Peyton crossed the deck and ran her fingers down Jack's back and across his shoulders. "This is really nice."

"It is." He glanced at her and then pointed to a small island in the middle of the lake. "We'll pull up over there." He expertly maneuvered the boat into a cove and dropped the anchor. "Did you bring wine?" He cocked an eyebrow "Or a beer, by chance?"

"I brought a bottle of Anna's still-to-be named blend." She flipped open the cooler. "And yes, I packed beer and water too."

"The perfect woman."

She handed him a bottle of pale ale and poured herself a glass of wine. She sat on the bench seat and took a sip. "This is amazing. Do you want to try it?"

He flashed her a smile. "I'm good with the beer, but thanks."

She thought of Anna taking off to work in France for a year to create new wines. She could certainly get through a tough conversation; after all, this was Jack. "Can we talk?"

He was relaxed, his arm around the back of the cushions, his hand twirling a lock of her hair. "Sure." The gentle tone in his voice encouraged her to continue.

She lifted her eyes and dove in. "Jack, I haven't been with anyone since you, before that night at the lake."

His gaze never left her face. The kindness in his eyes gave her the courage to continue. "You've dated but never wanted to…"

"No. It never felt right and when I talked to my therapist about us, she encouraged me to be up front. It's best if all my cards are on the table just in case I get sort of emotional."

"Peyton." He reached out and ran a finger tenderly down her cheek and kissed her lips. "We don't have to do anything until you're ready."

"That's just it; I *am* ready, but in some ways, I feel like this is the first time ever. Well, you know you were my first, but other than you, I've never made love to a man." She could feel the heat flush her cheeks. She wanted to look away, but his eyes held her hypnotized.

"Do you know what I admire about you?"

She shook her head.

"Your strength, your courage, and your unflinching honesty." He pulled her close and spoke softly. "You're in control." His lips trailed down her neck and back up to her mouth. "If you want me to stop, I will." He kissed his way down the other side of her face. "I respect you and will never ask you to do anything you're not ready to do."

Peyton laid her finger across his lips. "Less talking. More kissing."

• · •

*J*ack pulled Peyton deeper into his arms and his kiss. She tasted like sweet wine and smelled like raspberry. He savored the softness of her body as he held her close. He covered her face with featherlight kisses. His fingers trailed over her contours as he remembered every inch of her face.

She moaned softly as he teased her with light nibbles down her neck. Her head fell back, giving him full access. His blood was humming and his heart pounded in his chest like he had run a marathon. She fit perfectly against him, just as he remembered.

Her hands slid down his back. She tugged his shirttails free and slipped her cool hands underneath. Her nails lightly slid over his skin and made his nerve endings explode. He longed to touch her everywhere.

He paused in his exploration with his lips, teeth, and tongue. He didn't want to break the spell that had woven around them, but he pulled back. "Should we get more comfortable?"

She looked up through passion-filled eyes. Desire hovered there. With a single word, *yes*, she stood and took his hand. "I brought a blanket we can lay on the deck."

He wanted to slow things down, give her time to relax and enjoy their evening together. He said, "As much as I want this to continue, let's have supper, and then we can pick up from here." He nuzzled behind her ear.

She laughed, low and sexy. "Will you forget?"

"No." He claimed her lips again and she molded to him. When he released her, he smiled. "A picnic is very romantic."

"You know me; I love all things romance." She stood

on tiptoe and kissed his cheek. "You like to project a tough exterior, but I know there's a tender side too."

He looked into her eyes. "When it comes to you, I do." He placed a finger across her lips. "But don't tell anyone."

She gave him a sweet smile. "Your secret is safe with me."

She passed him a plate and he filled it, but he didn't taste what he was eating. All he wanted to do was get back to where they were all those years ago, but slowing things down was the right thing to do for her. So much wasted time. He wanted this to be a night they would both remember for years to come.

He longed to feel the beat of her heart in sync with his and her skin against his. To be one with the woman he loved.

He stopped midbite. He hadn't told her he had fallen in love with her, or maybe he had never stopped. But he didn't want her to think he was saying it because they were about to make love.

"Peyton, everything is delicious." Hell, that sounded lame. It was like pleasant dinner conversation with an acquaintance.

"The deli has great picnic packages." She gave him a quizzical look. "What's gotten into you?" She touched his hand. "Are you nervous?"

"Ha, not on your life. But there is something I wanted to tell you… I'm not sure how to say it."

She sipped her wine. Over the rim of the glass, she said, "Now you're having trouble talking."

"I've missed you. I've missed what we had together and I've wanted this for a long time. Longer than probably you realize."

She dropped her eyes. "I have a confession. When I

drive into the winery, I look around, wondering if I'll see your truck."

Hope soared. Could it be possible she was in love with him too? Even just a little bit? He grinned. "That's good to know."

She scooched across the blanket to his side and slipped her arms around his neck. "I'm happy that you're an important part of my life again." She kissed his lips and dinner was forgotten.

He eased her back onto the blanket as shadows were lengthening across the boat. Candles cast a small glow, just enough light so he could see her face. He slipped his hand under her blouse. Her skin was soft. Running his hand over her ribs and the underside of her bra, he let his finger trace the outline of the silky lace. He had to see it. He pushed her top up and over her head in one fluid motion.

His heart hammered in his throat—she was still stunning. The white lace was more of a turn-on than he imagined, ultra-feminine and silky soft at the same time. Peyton sucked in an audible breath. He paused. Pure pleasure washed over her face. But he had to ask. "Is this okay?"

She breathed, "Yes."

He continued his exploration, sliding his hand across her midsection, and stopped at the button on her shorts.

Peyton took that opportunity to pull his shirt off. She was taking control of the exploration. For the moment, he was in a holding pattern. But it felt good. He lay back and let her tease and tantalize his torso inch by inch. Her lips followed her fingers. He groaned.

He heard a phone ping. Peyton was oblivious. She continued her trail of kisses. It pinged again. And again. Whoever it was, they were persistent.

"Pey, we should see who that is."

She groaned and reached into her tote bag. "It's mine." She punched in the security code and said, "It's Mom. Let me just check her messages."

He toyed with her hair while she listened. She bolted up, her face draining of color. She punched a few numbers and while she waited, she cried, "Owen is sick!" She held up a finger. "Mom, what's going on?"

Jack wished he could hear the entire conversation but had to wait while Peyton said, "All right. We'll meet you there." She bit her lip. "We'll be there as soon as possible." She paused. "Tell Owen I love him very much and we're on our way." She disconnected and clutched the phone in her hand, holding it so tight, her knuckles turned white.

"We have to go. Mom and Dad are rushing Owen to the emergency room. They don't know what's wrong with him, but he's running a fever and is sick to his stomach and crying in agony." She jumped up, pulled her blouse on, and began to throw things in her bag and cooler.

She cried, "Jack, nothing can happen to him! He's my whole life!"

He took her in his arms and held her tight. "I'll haul in the anchor and we'll be there as fast as humanly possible."

"Thanks." She turned and finished cleaning up before he could start the engine. She tossed his shirt across the deck and he pushed the throttle forward while he shrugged it on. He reached for her hand. "Don't worry, love. We'll be there soon."

Peyton nodded. There were no words.

17

Jack's truck skidded to a stop at the emergency room door. Peyton pushed the truck door open and leaped down, at a dead run before Jack turned off the engine. She burst through the emergency room entrance and saw her father sitting alone on a wooden bench, his face drawn and pinched.

Breathless, she cried, "Dad! Where's Owen?"

He got up and hugged her tight. "It's okay, honey. He's with the doctor and Mom is with him. I wanted to wait for you."

"Does the doctor know what's wrong with him?"

"They think it's appendicitis. They're waiting for a few tests to come back, and if it is, they have a surgeon standing by, ready to operate before it bursts."

"I need to see him!"

Dad said, "Yes. Come with me."

Jack rushed in. She took a few steps but then turned to him. "Thanks, but you don't need to stay."

"I'm not going anywhere. I'll be here when you get back."

Peyton held out her hand. "Come with me?"

He opened the door to the exam room for her and the smell of antiseptic assaulted her senses. The sounds of beeping machines grated on her raw nerves. It had been almost an hour since Mom had called and she needed to put her eyes on Owen. She had to see him for herself.

As she reached the curtain, a hand flicked it back. An older man with salt-and-pepper hair and a dark mustache and beard, dressed in dark-blue scrubs that failed to conceal rounded shoulders asked, "Ms. Brien?"

She withdrew her hand. "Yes?"

"I'm Dr. Johnson. I've been looking after Owen since your parents brought him in."

"How is he?"

His voice was monotone. "It's appendicitis. The surgeon will be ready for him in less than thirty minutes. But I wanted to ask you a few questions and you need to sign a consent form for surgery. Can you come with me for just a moment?"

Her eyes slid to the curtain.

Dad said, "Peyton, talk to the doctor and I'll keep Mom and Owen company. You can see your son after you've spoken with the doctor."

"You're right, Dad." She looked at Jack. "Will you..." Her voice trailed off. "Come too?"

"Yes."

The doctor looked at Jack. "Are you Owen's father?"

"No, sir. A family friend."

"What papers do I need to sign?" Her voice was strained.

"First, is there anything we should be aware of? Any bleeding issues, allergies to any medications, anything at all?"

Her eyes never left the doctor. "No, not that I'm aware of. Now can I see my boy?"

He took the clipboard he had been holding and slid it to her. "If you'd sign the consent to treat form, and the next page is our ability to bill your insurance."

She scrawled her name on both lines. The doctor's chair scraped across the floor and he gestured to the closed door. "Thank you. Come with me."

In a few long strides, Peyton burst around the curtain. "Owen!"

He looked up and burst into tears. "Mommy!"

She drew him into her arms, crushing him to her chest while murmuring, "I'm here, baby." She smoothed his hair off his forehead and laid her lips on his warm cheek. "I'm here."

In the hours since Owen had come up from surgery recovery, Peyton's parents and Jack had gone home. In her pocket, her cell phone vibrated. She sat up in the chair and glanced at the screen. A text from Jack. *Hope you got a little sleep. How are you and how's our patient?*

She responded, *I'm fine and he's still sleeping. Thanks again for staying a while last night.*

No need for thanks. Keep me posted?

She wrote, *Sure thing. Bye.* She slipped the phone back into her pocket. After unfolding herself from the unforgiving hospital chair, Peyton tiptoed over to her son's bedside. She rested a hand on his forehead. No fever. Adjusting his blankets, she crossed the darkened room and stood next to the window overlooking the dark and empty street below. She wrapped her arms around her body and shuddered. There wasn't any way she could completely protect Owen from everything bad in life. She glanced at him over her shoulder. Sound asleep, as if he didn't have a care in the world.

The hands on the wall clock made their journey around the face. The first rays of a promising sunrise began to brighten the sky. On the horizon, subtle pink and orange streaks with violet and blue slowly grew in intensity. Around her, the hospital was still, as if all the world were waiting for the day to begin.

"Mommy?" Owen's voice was a whisper.

"Hey, O. How are you feeling?" She kept her voice low on the off chance he'd drift off again. She watched his eyelids flutter. He seemed to struggle to focus on her. "Go back to sleep. I'll be here when you wake up."

Owen sank into a peaceful slumber.

Peyton sat down in the chair and covered herself with the thin white blanket a nurse had given her, and closed her eyes.

*J*ack stood in the doorway. Would the smell of rich coffee gently wake her or should he let her sleep? He waited, unsure what to do. He didn't want to wake Owen.

Peyton struggled to sit up. "Jack, is that you?"

"Easy." He knelt down next to the chair. His voice was a whisper. "I brought you breakfast."

She pushed off the blanket and looked into his eyes. She looked much better than when he had left her just a few short hours ago.

"When did you get here?" she asked while her eyes drifted to Owen.

"About two minutes ago." He kissed her softly on the mouth. He glanced at Owen. "He looks like he's zonked. Want to stretch your legs?"

She nodded. "I don't think anything could wake him up. He's always been a very sound sleeper and with the residual anesthesia, he'll be out for a while longer." She took the travel mug from his hands and slid the top open. She took a small sip, and he smiled as she closed her eyes while enjoying the caffeine jolt.

"This is delicious. Thank you." She eyed the bag on the table at the end of the hospital bed. "You really brought food too?"

He held out his hand. "Come with me. I saw a waiting room at the end of the hall. We can have breakfast together."

She glanced at Owen, who was snoring softly, and then placed her hand in his. He grabbed the bag. The hall was empty. The small waiting room had a love seat and several chairs scattered around the perimeter. A television was bolted to the far wall and large curtainless windows over-looked the parking lot.

He kissed her. "Not a very romantic place for breakfast, but I'll take it."

They sat next to each other on the love seat, thigh to thigh. Peyton set her coffee on the table and held out her hand. "Food, please. The smell is making my stomach groan and taste buds weep."

With a small laugh, he withdrew a foil-wrapped sand-wich. "I made egg McJack." He folded back one side of the foil and handed it to her.

The look of confusion faded quickly and she laughed

quietly. "I get it. Eggs on an English muffin. Like Mickey D's."

"Yup, only better. It has *crispy* bacon and real cheddar cheese."

She took a bite and looked up. Her eyes widened in surprise. She covered her hand over her mouth and mumbled, "Did you actually make this?"

"I do know how to cook." He faked indignation. "I can clean up after myself too. And from what you said once a long time ago, it might be a good thing that if we're ever at my place, I'll do the cooking and you can clean up."

"A perfect partnership." She laughed.

He watched as she devoured the sandwich.

"That was delicious."

"You've got a little ketchup on your chin." He wiped it off with a napkin.

"Thanks for remembering I love ketchup on almost everything." She touched his hand. "Aren't you having one?"

"Nope, they're both for you."

A frown filled her face. "We'll share it."

He reached into the bag and held up three more. "Just kidding. We each have two." Jack handed her another one. "I know you'll forget about eating as soon as the little man opens his eyes." With a wave of his hand, he said, "*Mangia.*"

Peyton unwrapped her next sandwich and took a bite. Her eyes popped. "Jack, this is amazing—it has sausage."

"Stick with me, gorgeous, and I'll cook for you anytime." Jack saw a change of thought slide across her face.

Worry clouded her eyes. "What if something bad had happened to him? How would I have handled it?"

He set his sandwich aside and took her free hand. "I wish I could promise you that you'll never have another scare with him again. But I'll be here if you need me. For anything."

She laid her head on his shoulder. Jack wrapped his arms around her and held her close. He could stay like this all day, but that wasn't going to happen.

The sounds of the hospital coming to life drifted into the room. She tilted her head back, cupped his cheek, and kissed his lips. "You're a very special man. We should finish breakfast and get back to Owen's room."

A short time later, a nurse entered Owen's hospital room with a friendly smile, her attention on the patient. "Good morning, Owen. How are you feeling?"

"Good, but I'm hungry."

"I'm going to check your temperature and your heartbeat. Is that okay?"

He nodded.

Jack was beside the chair and Peyton hovered next to the hospital bed. "Is he okay?"

The nurse slung the stethoscope around her neck. In a soothing voice, she said, "His vitals are normal. Someone will bring his breakfast in shortly. We'll see how he does with Jell-O and clear liquids. The doctor will be in for rounds midmorning, and if all is going well, you should be going home later today."

Peyton turned to Jack and beamed. "Now that is good news."

"I'm sure you're both anxious to get your son home." The nurse finished adding notes to the whiteboard across from the foot of his bed and sailed out of the room.

Peyton pointed to the hallway and indicated Jack should follow her. When they got in the hallway, she said, "I'm sorry about that."

"About what?" Jack leaned against the wall. He knew what she was talking about but wondered where this conversation might go.

"The nurse thought you're Owen's dad. That must have been awkward for you."

Casually, Jack said, "Not at all."

Once again, he could see the faint rush of color brighten her cheeks. He wanted her to think about what it would be like to have him be a part of Owen's life permanently. "I'm going to head off to the winery for a little while, and then I'll be back around noon and I'll drive you both home. Any requests for lunch?"

She laughed. "You don't need to be our chauffer. Mom or Dad will pick us up." She dropped her eyes. "I wanted to say that I'm sorry about the way our date ended."

He crossed the small space between them and tipped her chin up. "There will be lots more dates."

She looked up through her lashes and it was almost his undoing. Right then and there, he wanted to declare his love for her. But now was not the time or place.

"I'll be back later. If Owen can eat something other than clear liquids, let me know." He gave her a slow, sweet kiss. "And if you need anything at all, or you just miss me before that, I'm just a call or text away."

"Thanks, Jack." She gazed into his eyes. "I mean it. For everything."

With a quick glance at Owen, who was now watching cartoons, he gave Peyton one last kiss and got on the elevator.

ack arrived at Owen's hospital room just after twelve carrying a soft-sided cooler that sported the winery logo. Peyton looked from the bag to Jack and then to Owen, who was coloring. "Guess who's definitely going home this afternoon?"

Jack's grin split his face. "Let me guess."

Owen looked up at Jack and squinted like he was staring into the sun. "Are you teasing? 'Cause it's me. As soon as stuff's done."

Peyton knew that look. Owen's wheels were turning. She wasn't surprised he had listened closely to the adult conversation. She perched on the edge of the bed and smoothed the covers down. "Yes, and Jack, we were hoping you could drive us home?"

Owen's face brightened. "Can we go on the boat today too?"

Jack chuckled. "I think the boat will have to wait for a few days, but I'm happy to be the chauffeur." He held up the bag. "Who wants lunch first?"

"Can I, Mom?"

"Sure, if you feel like eating something. The nurse said it was okay as long as you drink plenty of liquids."

Owen pushed the books and crayons aside. "What did ya bring?"

Jack set the bag on the table and unzipped it, pulling out cartons of fruit yogurt, peanut butter and jelly or ham sandwiches, sugar cookies, and juice boxes. "Owen, would you like a yogurt?"

He nodded, his enthusiasm growing at the sight of the small feast. "And a cookie?" He glanced at his mom.

She responded, "First some juice, yogurt, and then maybe half of a cookie if your tummy feels okay."

Without missing a beat, Jack handed him a container of strawberry yogurt and a spoon. "Pey?"

Suddenly ravenous, she held out her hand. "Ham sandwich, please."

Jack perched on the other side of the bed. "Things okay at the winery? Did you happen to check on Lily and Tony for me?" She nibbled on the thick sandwich.

"It was good. Nothing special." He polished off one sandwich and picked up another.

"I didn't ask. Do you need to get back and then pick us up?"

He tilted his head and gave her a long look. "Are you trying to get rid of me?"

"Mom, Jack really likes us and he wants to be the hero."

Jack's eyebrow arched. "Yeah, Peyton," he chuckled. "Every guy wants to be a hero."

She rolled her eyes. "Fine. Be Superman."

Owen poked Jack on the arm and with a knowing nod, said, "Mom's favorite is Superman."

1 8

It had been two weeks since Owen's surgery when Peyton slipped into a kitchen chair and added a dash of cream to the mug of coffee her mom handed her. "Thanks. I really need a jolt of caffeine."

"You had a nightmare." It wasn't a question, just a simple statement. "It's been a while."

Peyton blew on the coffee and then took a small sip. "I've had the same one for the last couple of weeks, since Owen got sick. In my dream, he's desperately ill and there's nothing the doctors can do and he dies."

Mom studied her thoughtfully. "That had to have been awful, but, sweetheart, it was just a dream."

"It scared the hell out of me. I wasn't home when he needed me. Thank heavens you were, but what if something had happened to him?" Peyton could feel the tears well up in her eyes. "He's my world."

Mom's tone was soft. "Of course he is, honey, and we all love him." She placed her hand on Peyton's. "He still would have gotten appendicitis even if you had been home."

A pregnant pause filled the room. With a slow shake of her head, she said, "I should have been here."

"You can't be with him twenty-four hours a day—that isn't healthy for either of you. He's a little boy and there will be trips to the emergency room for stitches, maybe a broken bone or two. You're a great mother, so stop beating yourself up for something you couldn't have prevented."

Slowly, Peyton said, "I guess." She rose and topped off her coffee. It gave her something to do as her mind raced. "I'm seeing my therapist today, and hopefully she'll give me some tips so I don't become a helicopter mom."

Mom's eyes twinkled. "Will Jack be a topic too?"

It was such a mom question, meant to divert Peyton's attention to something positive. She dropped back into her chair. "Jack is an amazing guy. I'm not sure I'm ready to have a serious relationship with him yet, but we have a lot of fun. I know I can't dwell on the past but sometimes..."

"In his defense, Sherry told me he hated the business side of the winery, and Sam was having huge fights with Jack about his future. Jack wanted to focus on the agricultural side and moved to the West Coast to learn and work. He didn't leave you; he wanted a different career path."

She shook her head. "I know his issues with Sam were part of it, but I think he changed his mind about me, about us, too. He should have talked to me instead of moving three thousand miles away with only the announcement he was leaving."

"You both were so young. I'm not taking his side, but maybe if you had really talked to him instead of letting your stubbornness take over, things might have been different."

Peyton ran a hand through her hair. "Can people change?"

"If you're asking me specifically about Jack, yes. He's matured into a good man and one who has strong feelings for you. You shouldn't doubt it. I see the way he looks at you."

"Jack is the only man I thought I'd ever love. But he broke my heart once. Even after all this time, I still love him." She thought about how close they had come to acting on those feelings. With a soft laugh, she said, "He's had to have developed patience. You know I've given him the cold shoulder for the last few years. I was only comfortable when we were in large groups of people until recently, when I started to see him in a new light."

"He's not a saint."

"I know he's not, which brings me full circle. What if—"

Mom interrupted her. "You're enjoying each other's company and having fun. What if you're blessed with a lifetime of love? Isn't that worth the risk?" She got up, picked Peyton's cell phone off the counter, and thrust it at her. "Why don't you call him and make plans?"

Peyton took the phone and set it down. She shook her head and firmly stated, "I can't possibly go on a date until Owen is fully recovered."

"Oh, Peyton, stop using your son as an excuse to avoid spending time with the man you're in love with. Other than way too much pent-up energy, he's fine. Make plans with Jack. You deserve to have some fun."

She picked up her cell and hesitated. "What should I say? He probably thinks I've disappeared, which wasn't my intention, but I needed to focus on my son."

"I'm sure he understands. Ask if he's busy and would he like to get together. At least get a cup of coffee or a glass of wine."

Peyton rolled her eyes. "Mom," she groaned.

She studied the small screen and tapped out a message. *Do you have time for coffee or something?*

She hit send and turned the phone so her mom could read it.

Her mother grinned her approval. "That was a friendly invitation. But you could have called him, made it more personal."

Her cell phone buzzed. She looked at the text from Jack. *I always have time for you. Gazebo for lunch?* She showed Mom.

"Guess that answers the most pressing question of the morning." Mom patted her on the shoulder. "Now, go pick out something pretty to wear."

Peyton settled into the dark-green leather wingback chair in her therapist's office. It was her favorite spot. She'd sat there once a week for almost three years. When she had divulged her secret to Kate and then to her parents, her mom found Jane, who was a rape survivor herself and used her experience in their sessions.

Jane, petite in stature, made up for it in her demeanor. She sat in an overstuffed floral chair complete with an oversized footstool. Peyton thought she should have a chair to match her diminutive size instead of it looking like there was room for at least two of her in it.

"So tell me, how is Owen? On the mend, I assume?" Jane gave her a serene smile.

Peyton relaxed. They always started with something easy to talk about. "He's a resilient kid. You'd never know he had surgery. It's actually hard to keep him still."

"I'm sure that makes you feel so much better."

Crossing her legs, Peyton smiled. "You have no idea. I keep thinking about what might have happened. The nurses and doctors were amazing. He was in excellent hands."

"I sense some hesitancy in your response."

Peyton marveled at how she picked up more on what hadn't been said than what had. "I'm having nightmares." Her heart rate increased. "He's sick and dies and I'm not there to save him."

"Why do you think that is?" Jane's gaze was kind but unflinching.

Peyton clenched her hands in her lap. "I keep reliving the phone call from Mom, when I was on the boat with Jack. I wasn't there when he needed me."

"This has less to do with Owen than you believe."

Peyton met her look. "I sound like a crazy mom, right?"

"You have been an extremely committed mother since the moment he was born. Along the way, you pushed Peyton, the woman and not the mother, aside."

"So I am an overprotective mother." She brushed an invisible speck of dust from her slacks. "Great."

Jane gave her an understanding smile. "I want you to think about what *you* need. Owen is growing up and you need to live a full life. What do you want for your future?"

She shrugged. "These last few weeks, I've felt guilty even thinking of leaving him to go on a date."

"Being a single parent doesn't mean your sole focus has to be your child. Show him by example how to fall in love with a good person. Fill your world with positive people."

"Do you mean like Jack?"

"You have a long history with him, and now you've found your way back together. Are you enjoying time spent with him?"

She could feel the corners of her mouth turn up. "Things are progressing."

Jane rubbed her hands together and grinned. "Oh, good. Tell me all about it."

Peyton laughed. "Since our romantic date got interrupted with a fast trip to the hospital, this morning I sent him a text and asked if he wanted to get together. We're going to have lunch at the winery."

"That's sounds nice, but what about after that?"

"It will be at the gazebo, which has views of the vineyard. It's a nice place to relax and talk. I'm going to suggest we have a do-over date on the boat. I want to pick up where we left off."

"And where were you?" Jane's smile reached her eyes.

Feeling the blush splash across her cheeks, Peyton said, "I'm ready to be intimate with Jack. We had come close two weeks ago, but the next time we're together, it's going to be a very special night."

Jane beamed. "I'm happy for you. I know there hasn't been a steady guy in your life since you were assaulted."

"No. I wasn't ready until I let Jack back into my life."

"And now you're ready?"

"Yes, but I did need a nudge from Mom to make plans with him today. I didn't want to leave Owen so soon."

"Your mom's right. Part of being a good mother is to be happy."

Peyton pushed her hair off her face. "I feel like the two of you are pushing me out of my comfort zone."

"Not pushing, Peyton. Giving you a firm shove. You're ready to spread your wings, so test them." Jane gave her a thoughtful look. "We've talked several times about your attentiveness to Owen as a coping mechanism for the past."

Peyton gazed out the window and laced her fingers together. "I want to be a great mom, and I think I've been the best I can considering this wasn't the path I chose. But I'm starting to see by spending time with Jack *and* Owen, I can be a mom and a woman who has needs and deserves a loving man in her life." Her mouth formed a small *O*. It was as if a light bulb just went off over her head like in a cartoon. "I've been using Owen as a speed bump."

"Interesting analogy."

"So how do I change that pattern?"

"Recognition of the issue is the first step toward making a change." Jane folded her hands in her lap. "You have a lunch date today with a handsome man, and it's a date *you* initiated."

"I do and did." Her eyes opened wide. "I've started to flatten my speed bump without even realizing it."

Jane grinned broadly. "So, did you pack a picnic?"

"Heck no." Peyton laughed. "I'm going to pick up lunch from the deli. I want to date him, not scare him off."

With a large paper bag in one hand and a small one in the other, Peyton struggled with the tasting room door. She had plenty of time to get lunch set up before Jack was supposed to meet her. She set the bags down on a table and flicked the switch that turned on the bar lights. The large bag ripped and one container tumbled onto the tabletop. She caught the potato salad container before it fell to the floor. Hopefully Jack was hungry; she had enough food for a small army, but sometimes he could eat like one.

The room was cool and she plunked down in the chair to think about her earlier epiphany. Dealing with a dose of unfounded guilt, she had been using Owen to slow things down with Jack. All she needed to do now was figure out why. Was she worried he would hurt her again, that he saw her as a damaged woman or had she never gotten over him and that was what scared her?

The sound of footsteps on the concrete floor in the warehouse caught her attention. She glanced toward the stairwell. Kate stuck her head in the room. "Peyton, is that you?"

She got up and flicked on another set of lights. "Just me." She gestured to the bags. "I'm having lunch with Jack in the gazebo."

Kate crossed the room and peeked in the bags. "I would have whipped up something for you."

"You can't cook for us all the time. Besides I'm great at picking up takeout; you know I hate to cook, and I'm not very good either."

"I'd be happy to give you pointers anytime."

She smiled at Kate. "Thanks, but it's fine. I manage."

"I'll take off. Have fun." Kate gave her a quick hug. "I like this look on your face. You're wearing happiness well."

*P*eyton grabbed a tray from behind the bar, loaded on the containers for one trip to the gazebo, and tossed the ripped bag in the garbage. She set the table in the gazebo with plates, silverware, and water glasses from the bistro. She had just finished when she heard a UTV approach. At the stroke of noon, Jack pulled up next to the tasting room door and killed the engine. Right on time.

With a huge grin, he jogged across the parking area and stepped inside the spacious wooden structure.

"Hi. You look pretty." He kissed her and held up his hands. "I'll be right back; I need to wash up."

She felt a warm glow flow through her. "I'll be here."

A few minutes later, Jack came back and pulled a chair close to her. "This is a nice treat. One I could get used to."

"Lunch in the gazebo?"

"No, seeing you more and more." He kissed her. "What's for lunch? I'm starved."

"I wasn't sure what you'd be hungry for, so I brought a little of everything."

He raised his eyebrows, his eyes darkened with desire.

She laughed at the double entendre. "Jack, stop." Butterflies bounced around her insides and a flush crept over her cheeks.

"I love that I can make you blush so easily. It's charming." He picked up his glass and took a sip of lemonade. "How was your morning?"

"Good. I saw my therapist."

"How did that go?"

"It was interesting." She was evasive, as she didn't want him to know that she had been using her son as her wingman. A smile tugged at her lips. "And enlightening."

"Well, it sounds like you got something out of it, which is good." His finger trailed down her jawline. "What prompted you to text me?"

She loved the way he touched her. Casual but intimate. "I woke up thinking about you. The last couple of weeks, I've been focused on Owen."

He placed a finger across her lips. "It's where you needed to be, and I'm not going anywhere."

She kissed his finger and took his hand. "I was thinking that we should have another date on the boat." She tipped her head. "If you're interested."

His eyes brightened. "Are you saying you want to pick up where we left off?"

Her stomach did a pleasant flip. The way he was looking at her caused her blood to warm. "That's the idea."

"Tonight?" The question was more of a statement.

"It's a date. Two in one day—I think that might be a new record for us."

"Maybe next we should plan three dates for tomorrow."

"I think that would just be an all-day event." She handed him a container. "We should enjoy this delicious-looking lunch before you need to get back to work."

*J*ack loved watching Peyton as they lingered over lunch. He still couldn't believe they had a second chance. At the time, he had hoped they could have a long-distance relationship but instead of giving him some time to deal with family issues, she never tried to connect—and neither had he.

Between bites of his BLT, he asked, "Hey, can I ask you something?"

"What's on your mind?" She wiped the corner of her mouth with a deep-purple cloth napkin and placed it in her lap.

"When we were dating before"—her face remained neutral—"and I had the opportunity to go to California, why did you break it off with me?"

She arched a brow. "Correction. You broke up with me." She jabbed a strawberry on her plate. "Do you remember when you convinced me to go to Columbia?"

"It had a great architecture school and I was in the business program."

"But it wasn't my first choice." She lowered her gaze and avoided his eyes. "We were going to be at school together—you were going to get your MBA and I was going in as a freshman. It was going to be so much fun. Then out of the blue, before I had even unpacked my dorm room, you announced you were leaving and going to California. I wanted to be able to talk to you. Before we could, you were gone and I was devastated."

Jack shook his head. "That's not how I remember it. I was tired of business courses, and Dad was always on my back. I wanted to get dirt on my hands, make a difference growing the grapes, not trying to figure out how to sell the finished product."

"I know I've asked you this before, but why didn't you talk to me?" Her eyes were filled with hurt from the past. He could see the lingering pain and uncertainty in them.

"It was an amazing opportunity, and if I took too long making a decision, it would have been withdrawn or Dad would have convinced me not to go."

"I'm not saying I would have said not to take it. But it wasn't like you applied and on the same day got the offer. It's a process. You could have said, 'Peyton, I'm thinking of going to California. What do you think?' But you made your decision and then told me. How would you have felt if I had done that to you?"

He was quiet for a moment. She was right. That had been uncool and he couldn't blame any of that on his dad. It was all on him. "I'm sorry. I assumed you'd be happy for me, but I didn't put myself in your shoes."

"Jack, at the time I was lost, at a huge college without a single friendly face. And I'm not exactly a social butterfly."

"I was pretty selfish back then." He placed a hand over hers.

"Yes, you were."

"Ouch. I deserve that, but in my defense…"

She cocked an eyebrow.

He held up his hand. "I did it to piss off my father. He

was pushing me to be a replica of Don and I wanted—no, I needed—to be my own person."

"Your dad always pushed your buttons. That didn't mean you should have taken off without talking to me. We were in a relationship." Her voice cracked. "Did it mean more to me than it did to you?"

His heart broke for what they had lost. "No. I was in love with you. I never meant to hurt you. If I had realized what I was doing, well, I wouldn't have." He squeezed her hand and was reminded how fragile things could be and that she had been hurt. How would she feel if she knew he had been married for a few months?

Tears glistened in her eyes and she blinked them away. "I couldn't bear it if you did something like that again. I'm not saying you need to discuss every detail of your life with me, but if it affects me, and now Owen too, just do me the courtesy of talking to me first before you change the course of all our lives, and promise me you'll always be honest."

"I will." He brushed away a tear that lingered on her cheek. "Can you forgive a young and stupid guy?"

"I already have. That's why we're here now." She rested her cheek in the palm of his hand.

He slid closer and put his arm around her. Their foreheads touched and they sat quietly.

Jack spoke softly. "I really am sorry."

She pulled back and looked at him with a somber expression. "That was a long time ago. If there's one thing I've learned over the last couple of years, it's that we can't change the past. All we can do, today and every day, is be our best."

"Have you put the mistakes of my youth in our past?"

"Yes." There was a husky warmth in her voice. "Now, about our date tonight…"

"Why don't you meet me at the marina at five thirty? That will give me enough time to wrap up the workday."

"Sounds like a date." Her voice and eyes highlighted her excitement.

Jack's cell phone rang. The name *Corine* was displayed across the front. He grabbed it from the table before Peyton saw it and slipped it into his pocket.

"Don't you want to answer that?" she asked.

"It's nothing important. I'll call them back." Had she seen the name on the display?

Anxious to divert her attention, he said, "I'm looking forward to tonight. I'll take care of everything since you brought this amazing lunch."

"I can't wait." Her kiss tasted like sweet lemons.

He slipped a hand around her waist, wanting her to be closer. "Neither can I."

Jack drove back to the field and pulled his cell phone out of his shirt pocket. Corine hadn't left a message. Should he call her back? He wished he had someone to talk to about this mess, but no one in the family knew he had been married and divorced. Normally he'd talk to Anna, but she was still in France. The time difference wasn't an issue; it was only eight over there. He paused and dialed.

Anna said, "Hi, Jack. Is everything okay?"

"Yeah, everyone's fine. I just wanted to say hello. It's been a while."

"Hello. But I know you and if I were to guess, you're sitting near one of the fields in the truck."

"Close. The UTV." He chuckled. "How's Colin?"

"Everything's good here. We'll be home at the end of August. I can't believe that's less than two months away."

"Good. I've missed working with you; it's not the same with Dad."

"I guess you'll appreciate me a little more now, huh, little brother?"

Her teasing lightened his mood. "While I've got you, I wanted to ask your advice about something."

"I'm listening."

"When I worked in Napa, there was a girl I was pretty serious about. I wasn't in love with her or anything, but I never told anyone back here and she's called me a few times saying she wants to meet."

"You never told Peyton about her, did you?"

He could hear the reproachful tone in her voice. "I never talked to anyone about her. We were only together about six months." Of which a couple of them were as a married couple, but he wasn't going to get into that on the phone.

"I think you should talk to your ex and find out what she wants and then tell Peyton. Don't go into this new relationship with any secrets."

"It was over before it began, sis." He watched as a hawk glided on the wind currents, looking for prey. It was how he felt about Corine calling him.

"Then there's no reason to avoid the woman, but the most important thing you have to do is talk to Peyton. Secrets have a way of coming out."

He knew Anna was right and this secret could destroy their new relationship.

"Thanks, Anna. You're right. I'll tell Peyton right after I talk to Corine."

"If you need something else, give me a call. Otherwise, we'll see you soon and be ready to put your dancing shoes on. There's an engagement party to plan."

"Yeah, I still can't believe you decided to get married during next year's harvest. Pretty bold for an enologist."

When she laughed, she sounded like the sister he remembered, full of life and very happy.

"Living in France the last year has taught me a few things, and one is to seize the day. The family can take one day and celebrate the start of a new branch on the family tree."

"You're right and I'll be the first one to toast to the happy couple."

"Thanks, Jack, and don't forget to take care of things in your life. I expect Peyton to be in your arms, dancing at our party."

"Thanks again, and maybe it'll give her an idea or two." He sat there, just taking in the view and the sounds of the vineyard after he and Anna had hung up.

He decided to call his ex-wife back. It went to voicemail.

$\mathcal{A}$ soft tap on the door interrupted Peyton as she was getting dressed for her date with Jack. "Mom? Can I come in?"

Peyton eased open the door. Owen was standing in the middle of the hallway.

"You look pretty." His face brightened. "Do we have a date with Jack tonight?"

"You don't." She brushed the hair out of his eyes. "I do."

"It's a grown-up thing?"

She turned Owen around in the doorway and pointed him toward the kitchen. "Yes, it's for grown-ups tonight."

He dragged the toes of his sneakers down the wood floor as he walked down the hall. Peyton frowned. "Pick up your feet, please." She closed the bathroom door and fixed a smudge of mascara on her eyelid. Now she was ready.

After retrieving her petal-pink leather handbag, she breezed into the kitchen, where Owen and Mom were making dinner. She kissed the top of his head. "Be good for Grammie."

Mom looked up. "Don't hurry home. Everything's under control."

"Thanks, Mom."

She only had to bring herself; Jack was taking care of everything else. Turning, she took one last look at Owen and Mom. She blew her son a kiss. He would be fine.

Peyton skipped lightly down the front steps. To her surprise, Jack had parked his truck in the driveway, effectively blocking her car. He leaned against the door all casual-like, dressed in a black T-shirt that hugged his six-pack abs and bulging biceps, and jeans that clung in all the right places too.

"Hey, you," she said as she closed the distance between them. "I thought I was meeting you at the marina."

"It's what I wanted you to think, but there was no way you were driving yourself to our very special night."

There went the butterfly parade again. She leaned in to give him a lingering kiss. *Oh my*, she thought. *He smells like the breeze on the lake and all male.* "You're sweet."

He wrapped his arm around her and pulled her in close. "Are you ready to go?"

"I think so." She hoped her voice didn't betray her nerves as she felt his heart. She knew what she wanted to happen, but it had been a long time since she had, even though they'd been well on their way the last time they had the boat to themselves.

"Perfect. Then let's take off before a certain someone catches us, to use his phrase, making goo-goo eyes again."

They stepped around the truck. He held the door open and helped her step up. Before he closed it, his eyes seemed to drink her in. She felt herself blush under his gaze. "You look gorgeous tonight."

Her mouth went dry. "Thank you."

She guessed the skort, simple short-sleeve floral-print top, and wedge sandals were dressy enough for a date on the water while still being functional. She could climb on and off the boat without baring all to the world.

She snorted just as Jack got in.

"What's so funny?"

"Nothing."

"Oh, come on. You can tell me. I know that you only snort occasionally, so something must have really touched your funny bone."

Peyton flashed him a grin. "Maybe."

"You can keep your secret for now." His dimples made an appearance. "But I have ways of making you talk."

With a light heart, Peyton laughed. "We shall see."

*J*ack parked at the marina. Peyton looked down the dock toward his boat slip. Their path was littered with rose petals. "Did you do this?"

He gave her a wink. "I wanted tonight to be special." She waited as Jack came around to her door and held out his hand. "Shall we?"

He said it just like the line from an old movie with Tom Hanks and Meg Ryan. She was excited to see what might be next.

They strolled down the dock and Peyton looked left and right, taking delight in picturing Jack dropping petals along the path. She hugged his arm to her body. "I wasn't expecting for tonight to be so romantic."

He gave her that knee-knocking smile again. "You ain't seen nothing yet."

It was in that moment she saw the twinkle lights strung from the top of the canopy, casting a soft glow over the deck. There were blankets tossed on both sofas and the table in the center was set for two. A bottle was chilling in the bucket stand and there was a cooler off to one side. As the final touch, sensual jazz was coming from the speakers.

"Jack," she breathed. "This is incredible."

She stepped onto the boat deck and took in each detail, right down to the small vase in the middle of the table filled with two red roses.

"I can't take credit for the food. Kate pitched in with that."

She smiled at him. "You told Kate?"

"I was running short on time and I needed a little help." He held up two fingers close together. "About this much. Wait." He took her in his arms and kissed her. "Now it's perfect."

Peyton felt her heart quicken, but then she had an attack of nerves. She looked around. "Should we have wine?" She pointed to the bottle.

"We may want to wait until we get away from the bustle of the marina."

Peyton looked up and saw people were smiling in their direction. "Excellent point."

Jack turned the key and the motor rumbled to life. He untied the moorings and in a few long strides took the wheel in one hand and the throttle in the other. "Join me?"

She crossed the boat deck and sat in the other seat.

"Do you want to drive?"

"Not tonight, but maybe the next time we go out, you can teach me?"

"I can do that."

As the boat trolled along, the wind wafted around her like a warm blanket. They picked up speed and skimmed over the open water. Even though it was midweek and people had been milling around the dock, there weren't many boats on the lake. The farther across the water they went, the more it seemed they were the only two people on earth.

Jack cut back on the throttle as he navigated the boat toward a small, secluded island. He pulled in close and killed the engine and then dropped anchor. "Is this what you had in mind?"

She glanced around and grinned. "It'll do."

"Come with me."

She took his outstretched hand and he guided her to one of the sofas. He then pulled the cork and poured them each a glass of wine.

"A blush?" She accepted the glass. "You're not a fan."

"Anna created this wine, and she had you in mind."

"Your sister, one of the best enologists in the country, thought of me? Why on earth would she do that?"

"Isn't it obvious?"

Peyton laughed. "Not to me."

"You blush. Often." Sliding his arm around her, he pulled her close and nuzzled her neck.

A shiver of desire raced down her back.

"Anna knew before I did that I had fallen in love with you for the second time. Crafting this wine was her way to show support for our second chance." He picked up the bottle and displayed the label.

"I'm—I'm speechless." She read, "*Peyton's Blush.*"

He put it back in the bucket.

"That might need some work." She laughed softly.

"You have your very own wine."

She brought the glass to her lips to taste it. "This is good—not overly sweet or too fruity." She took another small sip. "It's floral and bright."

He took the glass from her hand and set it aside. "Enough about wine."

"I agree." She laced her hands behind his neck and pulled him close. "Thank you for all of this. It was unexpected."

"I had a lot of fun planning."

She laid a finger across his lips. "Shh."

His mouth brushed hers. She sank into the kiss, taking —no, demanding more. She wanted to become one with him. She was astonished at the intensity of her emotions.

She placed her hands on his face and kissed his lips, tenderly and filled with every ounce of love bubbling up from her heart. "I never thought I would be this happy again."

"Are you sure you want to make love?" Jack searched her eyes.

"I've never been more sure of anything in my life."

His fingers traced the outline of her nose, sliding over her face, past her chin, and down her throat. His lips followed as she melted under his touch, lost in the sweet sensations he elicited with his fingers. Unwilling to be a passive participant, she let her hands roam over his broad back; his muscles seemed to strain against the fabric of his T-shirt. He was familiar and yet tonight his touch was new. This time, she was ready to love Jack, thoroughly and completely.

Before she eased him back on the deck, she pulled his

shirt off and tossed it aside. Her fingers traced the outline of each muscle, his collarbones, and rib cage. She was in control. Each time he moved under her caress, she changed where she touched him.

Peyton concentrated on his mouth. She outlined his lips with her finger. Finally, he matched her strokes and she sighed with pure pleasure. He ran his hands down her back to the hem of her top and stopped, as if questioning what he should do next.

"Yes," she breathed.

In one slow, languid motion, he slid his hand under and released the clasp on her bra. She pushed off his body just far enough that he could finish removing her top, and with it came the pink lace.

The soft glow of the candle and twinkle lights in the growing dusk were pinpricks. His voice was husky. "You're so beautiful."

Her hands skimmed his chest. She hesitated. He placed his hand over her, guiding. She released the button and zipper, and he pulled a foil packet from his jeans before tossing them aside. Her skort and panties were next.

One look at Jack was all she needed; her nerves ceased. She wrapped her arms around him.

They moved together as if they had been making love for years instead of this second first time. Each touch and shiver brought her closer to the peak of pleasure. Time lost all meaning. There was no need to rush as sensations rolled over her; she reveled in touching him. His mouth teased and tantalized all her sensitive parts. They came together, two hearts beating as one, and rode the slow waves of pleasure.

. . .

*A*fter, they lay quietly in each other's arms, listening to the water lapping against the boat. It was so peaceful. He smoothed back her hair and placed soft, tiny kisses from her forehead to her lips. This surely was heaven on earth. "Happy?"

"It feels like we're the only two people for miles."

He nibbled her lower lip. "We are."

She shivered despite the warmth of his body. He pulled a blanket over them. "Are you warm enough now?"

"I am." She snuggled closer. Tonight was turning out better than a dream.

His arms tightened around her. They watched as stars appeared in the inky sky. This was the most romantic night of her life. She sighed.

"Hungry?"

"For you or food?"

His eyebrow cocked. "Well?"

"You're incorrigible. But I could eat a little something." She sat cross-legged on the deck and pulled the blanket tighter.

Jack pulled his jeans on. Peyton watched as he padded across the deck and carried the cooler close to her. Then he picked up their glasses and the bottle and sat down next to her.

Peyton poured wine while Jack unpacked the cooler. Despite the blanket around her, she felt goose bumps race down her arms. He gave her a concerned look. "As much as I love seeing you wrapped in nothing but a blanket, maybe you should put something on."

He turned and picked up her clothes, which were scattered around the deck. He handed them to her, plucking her bra from the pile and held it up so he could get a better look.

"I'm a big fan of your undergarments."

"Thanks." Should she say she bought them specifically for tonight?

"New?" He turned his head slightly to look at her.

Heat flushed her cheeks. "Jack…" she began, and then laughed. "Yes, and I have other colors too."

He chuckled. "I can't wait to see them all."

He watched as she dressed in the candlelight. By the look on his face, he definitely liked what he saw. *It was good to feel free and not in the least bit self-conscious. It has been a long time since I've been comfortable in my skin.*

She dropped back to the blanket to pick up her glass and nibble on a cracker. Completely relaxed, she said, "I was thinking about this wine. Has anyone ever had a blend named after them before?"

"No. Just you." He reached out and wiped a crumb from the corner of her mouth. His touch caused her heart to skip. Would she always feel like this when he touched her? She certainly hoped so.

She reclined into the crook of his arm and sipped her wine. "This is nice."

He kissed her head. "Are you in a rush to get back?"

"No. Let's just enjoy the evening."

He raised his glass to her. "Who knows; maybe we'll watch the sun rise over the water."

She clinked her glass to his. "To the sunrise."

*A*fter an amazing evening of making love, she had fallen asleep in Jack's arms while they talked the night away. The sunrise had been spectacular. The first brush of dawn had the wisps of clouds bathed in a blue-gray hue, which gave way to a glow of orangey-peach on the horizon. As the sun climbed higher in the sky, the clouds shifted to lavender and then to puffs of white gliding across the sapphire blue, and the sun completed the transformation from peach to a warm yellow.

Reluctantly the couple weighed anchor and began a leisurely ride back to the dock. Peyton snuggled on Jack's lap in the captain's chair, his arms keeping her warm. "Jack?"

He nuzzled her neck. "Hmm."

"This was an incredible night."

His lips continued on their journey. "Uh-huh."

She laughed as the timbre of his response tickled her neck.

His lips followed the curve of her throat to her mouth. He murmured, "It's too bad it's morning already." His lips tantalized her.

"We should have thought ahead and taken the day off."

"Next time."

The closer they drew to the dock, the more Peyton wished they had more time together.

"Do you think real life will intrude on this moment?"

Jack turned her face so he was looking in her eyes. "Our life will only get better every day." He gave her a searching look. "And this isn't just about the two of us—that includes Owen."

He stopped before they reached the dock and kissed

her tenderly. A feeling of happiness settled over her. This was love.

"I will never look at this boat in quite the same way."

She had to laugh. "It'll put a smile on your face the next time we go fishing with Owen and the family."

He gently docked the boat. Peyton slipped from his lap and looked around. "What can I do to help?"

"Okay. I know you can help us cast off but to round out your prowess as an excellent deckhand, follow my lead." He picked up a line from the dock and looped it around the cleat. "And give it a good tug to secure it." He then moved to the front and waited for Peyton to grab the next line and repeat the procedure. "Good. Now always make sure the fenders are secure. This keeps the dock from damaging the boat as it moves with the water."

She nodded. "There's a lot of stuff to do with boats."

"Not so much."

"Why this kind and not one of the flat-bottomed boats?"

"I like the look and handling of the open bow. It's good for taking everyone out and spending the day on the lake. As the family expands, hopefully more of us will buy boats too. It'd be fun to all spend the day on the lake. But time will tell."

He hopped back aboard and gathered up the cooler and tucked the blankets in a tote bag. Everything looked tidy and he said, "Ready?"

She took the canvas bag from him and slipped her hand into his. "Can we stop for coffee on the way home?"

He chuckled. "You are a woman after my own heart."

She tugged on his hand. "Let's not wait too long before we take the boat out again, just the two of us."

His eyebrow arched. "Is tonight too soon?"

"Mom, what time is Jack coming to pick us up for the movie, and how do we watch it before it gets dark?" Owen glanced at the slowly dipping sun while they sat on the front porch. "Grammie said we sit in our car and watch it." His eyes were round and the grin that split his face caused Peyton to laugh.

"We are given a speaker that goes in the window, and then when it gets dark, the movie will be on a huge screen in front of us. It's really fun."

"Can we get snacks too, just like at a real movie place?"

"O, this *is* a real movie. But we can only go to the drive-in when it's summer. But if it was raining, we wouldn't be able to go either."

He clapped his hands together and hopped around in front of her. "I'm so excited."

"Me too, kiddo, and we're taking Jack's truck. You'll sit up front with us."

"So I'll be able to see, right?"

A sharp toot of a horn caused Owen to stop jumping around. "Mom, he's here." She was on his heels and laughed as he raced down the front steps. "Jack, are we leaving now for the movie?" He skidded to a stop next to the driver's side door.

*J*ack was chuckling. It was a good thing his window was down so he could answer Owen.

"Hi, buddy. Are you looking forward to the movies?"

"Uh-huh." His head bobbed. "Mommy said we're seeing a cartoon and then a nature movie." He held up two fingers. "Two of them. Have you ever seen two in the same night?"

"I have, but it's been a long time." He grinned broadly, his focus totally on Owen. Jack liked the one-on-one with the boy. He had recovered from surgery, but he'd missed the end of baseball season and his birthday party had to be postponed since he had appendicitis. He wouldn't be going to camp for another week, so there seemed to be a lot of pent-up energy in a four-foot-tall kid.

"Mom said I can sit up front with you to watch. Is that okay?"

"Absolutely." Jack opened the truck door. "Look. I already fixed the seat so when we get there, you'll be all set."

He helped Owen into the driver's seat so the boy could see the console was flipped up. He tipped his head to the side. "Can I bring my pillow?"

"Why?"

"I can sit on it."

"I have an idea. How about you sit in the middle of the seat and pretend we're at the drive-in?"

He scrambled up and sat back, lacing his hands behind his head.

Jack smothered a laugh. "Can you see out the windshield?"

Owen nodded and said, "Yup." He crossed his ankles and wiggled his bright-red sneaker-clad feet. "Can I ride up here too?"

"Sorry, kiddo. There are laws we have to follow. Until you're twelve, you have to ride in the back seat."

His smile dimmed for a millisecond. "It's okay. Mom said I'll be all grown up before she can blink."

"Isn't that the truth? You've grown a couple of inches just this spring."

"It's 'cause I eat all my vegetables. Even the yucky ones like broccoli."

"You should ask your mom if she'll put cheese on it. Everything is better with cheese."

"Okay." He held up his fingers and crossed them. "Maybe she won't make it again." He leaned toward Jack. "Grammie's dinner is better."

Jack twirled him to the ground. "Don't count on it. Moms love cooking veggies that are yucky."

Owen looked up as they climbed up the steps. "But cheese makes it better, right?"

Jack ruffled the boy's hair and laughed. His eyes fixed on Peyton, who watched them from the porch. "Hi there."

"Hi." She tipped her head up to accept a tender kiss.

Owen watched them with curiosity. "How come you kiss Mom every time you come over?"

Peyton covered her mouth with her hand. She didn't say a word.

"Well…" *How do you tell a seven-year-old boy that you're*

in love with his mom? "When you see your girlfriend, you kiss her hello."

"Is it kinda like when I go to camp or school, Mom kisses me goodbye?"

"She loves you and likes to kiss you hello and good-bye." *That was a relief—my first tough question and I aced it.*

"Hey, Jack. What about all the other times you kiss Mommy? Sometimes, I've seen you kissing her for no reason."

He swore he could hear Peyton snicker, but she still wasn't saying a word. "Well, you know, since she's my girlfriend and I really like her, I want to kiss her sometimes."

"Oh, I think kissing girls is gross unless they're Mom or Grammie."

"Owen, why don't you get your pillow so we can leave?"

He popped one shoulder up. "Okay, but I can see out the front." He skipped into the house, conversation forgotten.

"You couldn't jump in and rescue me?"

She let out a belly laugh. "I wish you could have seen your face. It was priceless when he just wouldn't accept your first answer and move on."

Jack pulled her to his chest and wrapped his arms around her. She kept her forearms against his body as her laughter rocked them both.

He dropped his mouth to hers and her laugh died. He let his lips roam over her lips until she moaned softly with pleasure. He wanted to kiss her until her knees grew weak. He pulled back and looked into her eyes.

Feigning innocence, he said, "What can I say? Your son put the idea of kissing you senseless in my head."

"Blaming a sweet little boy for your strong desire to kiss me?" She bit the corner of his lip with just enough force for his eyes to widen.

"What's that for?

She cocked her head to one side. "Because you're my boyfriend." With one final peck on his lips, she said, "I'll go check to see what's keeping Owen and we can go."

"Good. I thought we could take him to the playground and hopefully by the time we get snacks and go back to the truck, he'll be ready to settle in and watch the movie."

"Fair warning. He's going to fall asleep before the second movie's end credits roll."

"It's okay. As long as I can hold your hand, I'll be happy."

She arched an eyebrow. "You do remember there is a child between us."

"I know, but I'll figure it out."

With another playful laugh, she slipped away before he could wrap his arms around her again. He waited on the front porch, loving her easy, carefree smile. She was more and more like the Peyton he had fallen in love with all those years ago. They were becoming comfortable with each other again. But their relationship was different than it had been. He wondered…if they hadn't gone their separate ways all those years ago, would they be together now?

He had a flash of regret, but he pushed that aside. He had to share what had happened in California while they were apart at some point, but not tonight.

Peyton and Owen came out. He was carrying a pillow and a small blanket and his brown stuffed dog. Jack took the pillow and blanket. "Ready to go, buddy?"

He gave one nod. "Ready, Jack."

. . .

*P*eyton and Jack strolled hand in hand as Owen ran in front of them on their way to the big slide. It was one of Owen's favorite parts of any playground, and the taller, the better. He had two to choose from. The playground was empty, so he had it to himself.

"Mom, I'm going down this one first." He pointed to the small one, which was still pretty tall. On the opposite side of the area were slides and teeter-totters in smaller sizes for younger kids.

"Okay, but please be careful."

Jack tugged her toward the swings. "Come on; when was the last time you were on one?"

"Jack, I shouldn't." Her cheeks flushed pink.

"I'll push you. Just like I did when you and my sisters went to the town park."

"You mean when we were your shadow and you used to do it just to humor us?"

"No, you four girls were always into some kind of mischief. I went along to keep you all out of trouble."

She sat down on the swing, the toes of her sneakers kicking the sand. "Being the good altar boy?"

"I watch over the people I care about." He gave her a little push while he kept one eye on Owen.

A screech filled the air. "Whee!"

Jack remarked, "Sounds like that run was a good one."

"Wait until he goes down the huge slide. Then he'll really scream."

"He's quite the daredevil."

Peyton pointed to Owen as he climbed the ladder. "If I took my eye off him, he'd probably run down it instead of slide on his backside."

After a short while, an older woman approached them. She smiled as she watched Owen slide down with his arms up and hands waving toward his mother. "Your son is so adorable; he looks just like your husband."

Jack beamed. "He is a great kid, and fearless." He placed a hand on Peyton's shoulder. "He gets that from his mom."

"I love watching kids play. They're so carefree and full of life. Well, you have a lovely family. Enjoy your evening." The woman moved in the direction of the snack bar.

"I hope that didn't make you uncomfortable." Peyton slowed her swing by dragging the toe of her sneaker in the sand. She stood and motioned for Owen to take one final slide. He raced around the back and climbed the ladder again.

Jack's hand trailed down her arm. "It's nice. I get to take the credit for your son." He pecked her lips. "And I like it that others recognize we belong together, the three of us."

Another screech pierced the air. Peyton and Jack watched a flash known as Owen fly down the slide. He ran over and tugged Peyton's hand. "Did you see me, Jack? That was fun."

"I did. I liked the tall slide too when I was a kid."

He beamed with pride and stood a little taller. "Can I have a hot dog and some peanut butter M&M's and can we come here again? It's been a blast!"

"Owen, I'm sure there is a magic word in your vocabulary." She shook her head.

"Please." His deep brown eyes looked between her and Jack.

Jack placed his hand on the boy's shoulder and turned

him toward the snack stand. "I'm going to get popcorn too, just in case you want to share."

"With lots of butter. That's the only way, right, Mom?"

"Oh no. If you two start ganging up on me, I'm done for." She squeezed Jack's hand.

"Don't worry, Mommy. I'll always be on your side."

She leaned over and kissed his cheek. "Thanks, little man."

He plopped one on her cheek too. With eyes shining, he said, "You can have half of my hot dog too."

Her heart melted just a little. He was such a sweet boy. She looked at Jack. The two men in her life made her insides squishy. She kept her eye on Jack as she said, "Thank you, O."

22

Jack jumped out of bed, eager to get to the winery. The last few weeks had been busy with Peyton and Owen. They had gone fishing, biking, and even to a minor-league ball game. They were growing closer every day and he could see them spending even more time together. Last night they had gone to the drive-in again and it had been as much fun this time as it had been the first time, even though Owen fell asleep halfway through the second movie. They had waited until it was over before driving back to Peyton's place.

He threw on a lightweight shirt and work pants, grabbed a quick bite, and filled his thermos with iced coffee. He rushed out of the house and then back in; he'd forgotten his cell phone. When he glanced down, he saw a text from Peyton. During the night, she had sent him a message: *XO*

He grinned. He liked knowing she was thinking about him. Maybe if he got everything done early today, he could take the boat out tonight with Peyton and Owen on board. And he was looking forward to planning another romantic date too. He glanced up and saw ominous clouds were forming. He would need Plan B.

As he drove to the winery, he called his sister, Liza. She'd know what was fun to do with kids. Over the truck speaker, his sister's phone rang. After the fifth ring, she answered, sounding frazzled.

"Hey, sis, what's going on over there?"

"Hi, Jack. The usual. Fighting over breakfast cereal, spilled milk, and who gets to choose what chair to sit in."

His shoulders sagged. It had been like this for Liza ever since the funeral. His sweet, lovable nephews were acting like little monsters half the time. He made a split-second decision. "I was calling to see if I could take the boys off your hands tonight. Peyton and I are taking Owen out for some fun. I was thinking about the diner for an early dinner and maybe we'd go bowling or something to get rid of some excess energy."

"That's really kind of you, but things aren't that bad." But in the next breath, she snapped, "Boys, quiet. I'm on the phone with Uncle Jack."

"No, really. You'd be helping me out. Owen would have fun too. Most of Owen's school friends have scattered for the summer and Peyton says this will help him be with friends. What do you say? Can I come around five and take them off your hands for a couple of hours?" He waited a half beat. "I'm sure there must be something you'd like to do with a few hours of downtime."

"Well… I could spend some time in the garden. The weeds seem to have taken over when I wasn't looking. I'd like to get something out of the tomatoes this year."

"Then it's settled. Tell the boys they need to be extra helpful around the house today and I'll see you later."

"Thanks, Jack." He could hear the relief in her voice.

"Don't mention it." He chuckled. "On second thought, tell Mom."

"Are you buttering her up?"

"It never hurts to have credit in the Bank of Mom."

Jack heard her yell for paper towels as the phone line went dead. He couldn't imagine how hard this was for her. Losing Steve and being both mother and father to active boys. Shaking off the melancholy that descended over him, he dialed Peyton. It didn't even seem as if it had rung when he heard her voice.

"Good morning, handsome."

He could feel the smile fill his face. "Hello, gorgeous. How did you sleep?"

"Extremely well."

"Do you have ears near you?"

She laughed. Jack liked the sound of it, light and care-free. "I do."

"Well then, just listen and you can either jump at the chance to spend time with me tonight or bow out."

Before he could tell her the plan, she said, "Yes!"

He couldn't help but laugh. "But you don't even know the details."

"It doesn't matter." She laughed again. "Well, it might since I need to know what to wear."

"If you're up for it, I'm picking up Johnny and George for dinner at Rose's Diner, then bowling. I wanted to know if you and Owen will join us."

"That sounds like fun. But let me check with Owen."

He could hear her ask and then a very loud, "Cool!"

She said, "I'm sure you could hear him."

"I think the entire town could. I told Liza I'd pick the

boys up at five. Do you want me to swing by your place before or after?"

"I'd like to see Liza, and I should be out of work by three, so come by here. We'll go out to her place together. I've been wanting to call her to see if she'd like to go for a pedicure or something girly with me."

"If you two make plans, I'll take the boys."

"All three of them?"

"Yeah. How hard could it be?"

Peyton let out a hearty laugh. "Hold off on that until after tonight. I'll see you after I finish up in the tasting room and get ready for a date with four of the best-looking guys in Crescent Lake. Even if three of the four are less than four feet tall."

She really was the best woman for him. Jack grinned. Tonight was going to be fun.

*

Jack picked up Peyton and Owen just after four. Once Owen was belted into his booster in the back seat of the truck, Jack turned to look at Peyton. He ran a hand through his short blond hair. "How do parents do this all the time? I'm nervous and we haven't even picked up the boys yet." He brushed her cheek with his hand and looked into her eyes.

"Practice. Oh, before I forget, a woman named Corine called the tasting room today looking for you. She said you were old friends with her husband when you lived on the West Coast."

He kept his voice neutral although his heart was in his throat and said, "Did she say anything else?"

"She wanted me to tell you she's still working on a gift for her husband."

"Thanks for letting me know."

Before they could talk further, Owen groaned, "Can we pick up Johnny and George now?"

Over his shoulder, he said, "On our way." He caught Owen's attention in his rearview mirror. "Are you a good bowler?"

"I'm the best," the boy announced proudly. "Just ask Mom."

"Owen." Peyton held back a laugh and turned in her seat. "I don't think you've ever bowled before. Have you?"

He looked at her. His brown eyes grew serious. "Mommy, you said I can do anything great. Remember?"

"I do, but I meant things you've done before or practiced."

"I think Mommy should have the boys on her team. She's gonna need help. Did you know Grammie said Mommy should have been named Grace?"

Jack gave a snort and glanced her way. "She did, did she?"

"Yup. I like Mom's name. It's pretty." He turned to look out the window. "Don't you?"

Peyton listened as her son's innocent remarks seemed to make Jack's smile grow even wider. He reached over and took her hand, just out of sight of Owen. "I think your mommy's name is very pretty." Under his breath, loud enough for Peyton's ears only, he added, "Just like the rest of her."

"Oh, Jack." It still amazed her that he looked at her *that* way.

"I know you're athletic since you're a killer at softball, but you never did say—can you bowl?"

She laughed. "Not well. My score is usually lucky to crack fifty, let alone three hundred."

"At least you know your goal." He couldn't help but tease her, and it was just one of the things she loved about him. Love. The idea of loving Jack made her heart swell.

"I used to go with your sisters when we were in high school. On Saturday night, it was the thing to do."

"If you bowl like Tessa or Anna, Owen and I have this all locked up."

"Is that a challenge I hear, Jackson?"

"Oh, bringing out the full name." He laughed out loud. "Care to place a wager on this little game? All in good fun, of course."

"What do you have in mind?" She looked at him from the corner of her eye, chin thrust upward. Clearly, he'd sparked her competitive spirit.

Jack stroked his chin and then a slow grin slid across his face. "The winner gets the date of their choice."

Her eyes narrowed. "How would that work?"

"As an example, say you wanted to go to the ballet. I would take you without any attempts to change your mind to go to a heavy metal concert, which I happen to know you hate. And if the date is on the other foot, well, you need to arrange an evening I would really like. Maybe take me to a pro sports game." He slowed the truck to pull into Liza's driveway. Up ahead, there was a restored Corvette.

"Leo's here. I wonder what's going on?"

"Do you think he and Liza want to join us tonight?"

"I don't think so. She wanted to work in her garden, and since it's not raining, she'll be knee-deep in dirt before we make it to the road." He glanced at her. "Don't change the subject. Do we have a deal?"

She waited until he parked and turned off the truck. Sticking out her hand, she shook his. "You've got yourself a bet." She hung on tight. "But no cheating, Price."

He feigned shock. "Me? Never."

"Ha. Remember, I know you better than you know yourself." She pointed to her eyes and then to his. "I'm watching you."

"Mom, are you and Jack ever gonna get out of the truck?" Owen popped his seat belt and leaned forward between the seats. "Huh?"

Jack unhooked his seat belt. "Ready when you are, kiddo."

Owen pushed open the door and leaped out onto the ground, taking off at a dead run. Jack turned to her. "Ready?"

She paused as she opened her door and looked over her shoulder. "The question is, are you?"

"With you by my side, I can conquer the world."

*J*ack held the kitchen door for Peyton after Owen had charged ahead. It made him smile to see the three boys were the best of buddies. Peyton stepped in front of him. He caught the subtle scent of flowers; he wasn't sure if it was her perfume or body wash, but it smelled nice. Just enough to tantalize his senses without overwhelming him.

Liza greeted both of them with a hug and a strained smile. "Since it rained all day, the boys are full of pent-up energy. Are you sure you want to take them tonight? They're definitely going to be a handful."

Peyton flashed her a brilliant smile. "Are you kidding? You're doing us a favor. Owen needs kids around more often and the bonus is they get along like brothers."

Liza snorted. "That's not always a good thing."

As soon as she said that, Jack's attention was diverted by high-pitched screeches coming from the family room. In a few short steps, he rounded the corner and discovered the three little guys had Leo pinned to the ground. As he tickled them, the kids squealed.

In a deep, booming voice, Jack said, "What's going on in here?"

In unison, Johnny and George yelled, "Uncle Jack!"

Leo cracked a grin. "Just having some fun to get them a little more wound up before you take off."

"That's nice of you." Jack grabbed the back of his nephews' shorts and pulled them off his youngest brother. "Get ready to go, boys."

Owen and the boys hurried from the room without a backward glance, leaving Jack and Leo.

Leo said, "It's been a tough day. Liza is worn out."

Jack gave him a hand up from the floor. "Is that why you're here?"

"I had a feeling she needed reinforcements. Mom called to tell me she found Liza crying when she dropped by earlier today."

"Where were the boys?"

"Watching a movie."

Jack rubbed a hand over his eyes. He glanced over his shoulder to see if Peyton and Liza were still near the kitchen counter. Satisfied they were alone, he asked, "What's the plan now?"

"I'm taking Liza out to dinner, maybe Sawyers. Just to let her be an adult and not Super Mom."

"You're a good brother." The sounds of excited boys stopped him from going any farther. "I gotta go."

"We should get out to the kitchen before the rug rats drive themselves to the diner."

Jack clapped Leo on the back and chuckled as he patted his jeans pocket. "Little brother, I'm one step ahead of them. I've got the keys right here."

As they entered the kitchen, Liza was kissing her boys' cheeks. "Are you going to be good for Uncle Jack and Peyton?"

The boys grinned.

Johnny said, "We will, Mommy. Promise."

George crossed his hand over his heart and Johnny tugged on his brother's arm. "Come on."

Jack ruffled the boys' hair and smiled at Liza. Then his gaze came to rest on Peyton. He grinned. "I think we're ready to hit the road."

He pulled open the door and looked at Liza. "Don't worry about a thing. And if we get home before you, we'll put the kids to bed." He pointed to Leo. "He's buying you dinner tonight. So order something expensive."

Jack winked at his brother and ushered the boys and Peyton out the door. She flashed him a questioning look, but he'd fill her in later.

etween three very active little boys and the sugar rush from the strawberry milkshakes they had to have with dinner, Peyton was pleased to see Jack take their bouncing off the proverbial wall in stride.

They walked into the bowling alley. The music was thumping down near the lanes, but at the counter it wasn't as bad; at least she could hear the kids talking. The air smelled like old shoes and sweaty feet to her. At the other end, the pinball machines emitted clacks and dings to get the attention of people. It was early and there were a few lanes occupied with other families. "Jack, let's get a lane with bumpers."

Johnny looked up at her with a very serious expression for a seven-year-old. "Peyton, we don't need bumpers. We're big kids now."

Jack knelt down and whispered in the boy's ear. She couldn't hear what he said but watched Johnny nod, still wearing the serious look on his face.

"Okay, Uncle Jack." Johnny flashed her an angelic smile. "I'm gonna be on your team."

Jack grinned and held up his hands. "Innocent."

She held out her hands to Jack's nephews. "Let's go get our shoes while Uncle Jack and Owen take care of getting our lanes."

Owen tagged along with Jack. She watched them go. Every time they were together, she melted inside just a little. Jack was amazing with her son.

She looked down and grinned at the boys. "We have to get bowling balls, right?"

George grinned and pulled his hand away. "I want a red ball."

She chuckled. "The right color is very important."

"Peyton." George gave her a sidelong look. "Mommy says you're good for Uncle Jack."

Curiosity piqued, she said, "Really?"

"Uh-huh. Uncle Jack smiles all the time now."

She let her gaze slide to Jack and Owen, who were waiting for their turn at the high counter. "That's nice to hear."

Not to be outdone, Johnny chimed in next. "Mimi says it's too bad you and—" He gave George a shove. "Don't step on my foot."

She swallowed her laugh. "Boys." She placed a hand on their shoulders. She wanted to ask what else was said, but she couldn't drill the kids.

George poked him. "Mommy and Mimi talk about you all the time."

Peyton had a flash of worry. What did Sherry think? Was she concerned about her and Jack rekindling their relationship? Instantly, old insecurities reared their ugly head. Unsure how to respond, she was grateful when Jack and Owen rejoined them.

Jack ushered the boys and Peyton the last few steps to

the shoe rental. She told the girl behind the counter the sizes; thank goodness Liza had mentioned what they'd need.

Jack said, "We're in lanes ten and eleven, and yes, they have bumpers. I'm not taking any chances of you beating me tonight. I need all the help I can get." He brushed Peyton's cheek tenderly with the back of his hand. "I'm not sure if I want to win or lose."

She could feel warmth flood her cheeks. "Either way, we're both winners."

He gave her a wink. A hint of amusement flickered in his sexy hazel eyes.

The wail of a little boy brought her back to the present. Jack stepped in and resolved the new crisis. Finally, smiles filled three young faces and Peyton glanced over their heads at Jack. She mouthed *thank you.* Thank heavens he did get the bumpers—it was one way to avoid tears and squabbling between the kids.

The night had been a huge success. Everyone bowled well. On the ride back to Liza's, the boys had fallen sound asleep within minutes. Peyton looked over the seat and then at Jack. She slid her hand across the console and took his. "I'm guessing everyone had fun."

He lightly squeezed her hand. "I had a blast watching you and the boys. It was so funny when Johnny was teaching you how to bowl." He brought her hand to his lips and grazed her knuckles. "Thanks for being such a good sport."

"I had fun, and so did Owen. It's good for him to be with the kids."

"It's good for the boys too. And Liza."

"Yeah, you still haven't told me what was going on with Leo. Is everything okay?"

"He was just being a good brother. Asking Liza to help him with a girl problem was his way of getting her mind on something else." He nodded toward the boys. "They've been giving her a hard time."

"I'm sorry to hear that. Leo's a good guy and he's sweet. How is she doing emotionally?"

"It's day by day, but I think it's a little easier in some respect with the kids home from school. She has company, but then they act up, which is perfectly normal, but she has to deal with it alone. That has to be hard too."

"She's doing a great job with the events she's planned and as the liaison for the winery with wedding planners and other parties."

Jack nodded. "She's very detail-oriented, and Kate is very supportive, helping to fill in gaps about catering too." He caressed Peyton's hand. "You know better than most of us how tough being a single parent can be." He smiled her way. The lights from the dashboard highlighted his strong jawline and deep dimples. She was a goner when it came to those dimples. "You haven't said where you'd like to go on your special date."

Peyton laughed quietly. "Are you sorry the boys and I won the last game?"

Even though the kids were snoring softly and they couldn't hear the conversation, he lowered his voice. "I would lose all over again to know I have the chance to have you to myself. Maybe we could try that new Greek place on the lake."

She continued to look at him. "Before we make definite

plans, the boys said something tonight that made me wonder."

"What's that?"

"I'm not sure your mother is happy we're dating."

His brow shot up. "What? That's crazy—Mom loves you. She always has."

"They said that Liza and your mom talk about us. A lot."

"Did they spill any details?"

She shook her head. "No."

"Now, don't start worrying. My entire family loves you." He slowed the truck as he turned into Liza's drive-way. "They can see how happy I am." He parked the truck but left it running.

"I just don't want them to think I'm going to cause you any problems." She looked toward the house. All the lights were blazing, welcoming them.

"Now I'm confused. What kind of problems?"

She let out a deep sigh. Before she could answer, the boys began to stir. The lack of motion must have woken them. "We can talk about it later."

He wouldn't let go of her hand. She looked into his eyes as he said, "Yes, we should talk about it when we're alone."

The back door opened and Liza appeared in the doorway and waved.

"We'd better get the kids inside." Peyton pulled her hand from his and pushed open her door.

Jack made short work of unbuckling the boys. Johnny held Peyton's hand as the three boys stumbled toward the house. He put both car seats in Liza's van before following them inside, where the boys were giving Liza and Leo the blow-by-blow of the night.

"Sounds like you guys had a lot of fun. What do you say to Uncle Jack and Peyton?"

"Thank you, Uncle Jack. Thank you, Peyton." Johnny and George rushed forward and wrapped their arms around her midsection, squeezing for all they were worth. Then they did the same to Jack.

"Mommy," George said, "can Owen have a sleepover with us tonight?"

Peyton said, "Oh, boys, we can do it another time. I'm sure your mommy would like us to plan in advance."

Liza's head snapped up. "Actually, that's a great idea."

The boys took off up the stairs toward the bedrooms before Peyton could agree or disagree. Owen came racing back and gave her a hard and fast hug. "Bye, Mom!"

She managed to briefly kiss his head before he took off. "Owen, make sure you listen to Liza."

A muffled "I will!" was all she heard.

She looked at Liza. "You don't need to keep Owen tonight—we can do it another time."

"To be honest, it would really help me out. They haven't been out of school long, but the boys are tired of not having anyone else to play with besides each other and they're going to camp next week with Owen." She leaned against the counter. "If Owen's here, it might stop the constant bickering they've been doing almost daily for the last week. I've got clothes Owen can wear, so nothing to worry about there, either."

Peyton could hear the weariness in her voice. "Then it's settled. Just let me know when you want me to pick him up."

"I have a better idea." Liza's face lit up. "I'm going to have an impromptu family cookout tomorrow night. You and Jack can come, along with whoever else is free, and then you can retrieve your son." The gold flecks in her eyes showed signs of life.

"We'd love to come. Shoot me a text and let me know what to bring." Peyton glanced at Jack. "Sorry. I didn't mean to speak for you too."

He took her hand. "Liza, we'll be here at five. Is it okay if we ask Mary and Ken too?"

Peyton opened her mouth, but Jack flashed her a quick look. She closed it again. She got it. Jack was trying to fill his sister's house with people who cared about her and the boys. She suspected this would be another first without Steve.

"The more, the merrier." Liza grabbed a pen and paper. "I've got lists to make."

Leo, who had remained quiet during the rapid-paced plans, said, "Sis, I'm free tomorrow too. I'll pick up chips and ice."

She gave him a playful shove. "Taking the easy way out, are you?"

"Heck yeah." He playfully poked her in the ribs. "Thanks for letting me bend your ear tonight."

She stood on tiptoes and kissed her brother's cheek. "Thanks for just being you."

Jack tugged Peyton's hand. "We're outta here. Leo, are you coming?"

"You go ahead. I'm going to check on the boys one last time."

Jack said, "See you all tomorrow." He and Peyton stepped out into the cool night air. She gave a slight shiver and he slipped his arm around her waist and held her close. "Now, before I take you home, we're going to talk about those issues you mentioned."

She glanced at him and then looked toward the truck. "It's nothing. Really."

"I saw the look on your face, and it's important to talk about anything that might be bothering you. So, we'll have a glass of wine and chat?"

Peyton leaned her body into his. "That sounds nice."

On the drive from Liza's into town, Jack had been unusually quiet. "Penny for your thoughts?" Peyton said as Jack pulled into a parking place on South Street in front of Sawyers.

"They're not worth that much." He was thinking how to tell Peyton about Corine. He hadn't heard from her in a while, so he was sure by now she had taken the hint that he wasn't interested in rehashing old times, but he still needed to be honest with Peyton.

"Is this okay? I thought it might be nice to relax and have a drink." He peered through the windshield and up at the sky. A few stars were starting to peek out. "It's cleared up, so we should be able to sit outside on the patio." He reached behind his seat and pulled out a fleece. "I grabbed this for you too."

Peyton laughed. "You just happen to be driving around with a fleece in my size?"

"Not just any fleece." He unfolded it and held it up. "Your purple CLW fleece. I grabbed it from behind the bar and I'll return it in the morning."

Her head tipped to one side. "You do think of everything."

"I try." He paused, leaned across the center console, and wrapped his arm around her. He murmured, "Now, this is what I've been thinking about doing all night." He lowered his mouth to hers, drinking in her sweet, subtle scent that was oh, so Peyton. His lips followed the curve of her jaw and nuzzled behind her ear. She giggled like a schoolgirl as he reclaimed her lips. Jack could stay like this, just kissing her breathless all night.

She eased back. "I thought you were buying me a drink."

His brain woke up. They had to talk about whatever she thought were their issues. The only issue he had was that he couldn't be with her as much as he wanted. He pecked her lips. "Let's go inside." His hand slid down her arm and he kissed her hand. He pushed open his door. "Ready?"

She picked up her shoulder bag from the floor and looped the jacket through the handles. "Yup." They strolled down the sidewalk.

"I used to come in and sit at the bar when you were hostessing, just so I could see you."

"You did not." She gave him a playful punch on the arm. "If I remember correctly, you had just moved into your apartment and said you weren't going to cook after working a long day." She looped her arm through his. "You'd sit at one end of the bar and order a cheeseburger, almost mooing, a large tossed salad with blue cheese dressing, and the beer of the day."

His brow shot up. "You remember my order?"

Peyton laughed softly. "There are many things about you I will never forget."

He was stunned that she recalled such an insignificant detail.

Jack opened the door and told the host they were going to the bar. A short, thin man was behind the bar. He was wiping the highly polished oak top. Alan Waters, the owner and an old family friend, called out a greeting from behind the bar. "Jack, Peyton, long time no see." He placed two napkins on the bar in front of a couple of empty stools. "What can I get for you?"

Jack looked at Peyton. "What would you like?"

"A glass of Pinot Noir?"

"Al, how about CLW's Pinot from last year, if you have any open."

Alan turned and said over his shoulder, "Sorry, I don't. Want the Sand Creek Pinot?" He held up an open bottle.

Jack nodded and picked up their glasses. "Is it okay if we go out back?"

"Of course. Switch on the firepit too, or I can come out and do it for you."

Peyton smiled. "I can take care of that; it hasn't been that long since I worked here."

Alan wiped his hands on the bar towel. "If you ever want to come back, Peyton, just say the word. I've always got a hostess job for you."

"Thanks Al, but I'm pretty busy at the winery. Now that Kate's opened the bistro, the tasting room has us more hectic than ever."

Jack felt himself beam with pride. "Peyton's being modest. This girl could sell wine to a teetotaler."

Alan nodded. "I can believe that." He pointed to the side door. "You guys enjoy."

Jack and Peyton closed the door behind them and shut out the busy restaurant noise. They had the patio to themselves. She uncovered the gas firepit and he dragged over an Adirondack chair built for two and a matching table from under the overhang. He moved the glasses and bottle to the table.

The fire softly whooshed to life and she sat down next to Jack, taking the glass from his outstretched hand. His fingers lingered on hers. "Do you need your fleece?"

"No. I'm warm enough."

He enjoyed watching as she slowly swirled the deep ruby red wine in the glass. The little spot between her eyebrows wrinkled in concentration. She was savoring the aroma of the wine before taking her first taste. She pursed her lush kissable lips and sipped.

"How is it?"

"Smooth. It has notes of cherry and I want to say… raspberries." She took another taste, savoring the liquid. "Max does blend a good wine; this is delicious."

Jack held the glass to his nose. She was right: cherry and berries.

"I'm glad Tessa bought the winery and it's back on track, to say nothing of the fact she and Max fell in love and are now living happily ever after." She took a sip and watched the flames dance.

"We didn't come here to talk about my sister, her husband, and their company." Jack laced his fingers with hers. "Before we talk about what's on your mind, I wanted to tell you about Corine. When I was in California, I was in a relationship for about six months. It wasn't serious, but she's called a couple of times. I wanted you to know it meant nothing then or now."

"Jack, we all have a past." She toyed with her glass. She turned in the chair so she could see his face. "Thank you for telling me, but I do have something else to talk about."

He sat up, set his glass aside, and eased sideways in the chair.

"I can't help but wonder if you should keep Owen and me at arm's length."

He could feel his face scrunch up. "I'm not following you. Why would I want to put distance between us?"

"To protect you." Or was she protecting herself from exposing her vulnerable side to Jack for a second time?

"Sweetheart, can you be more direct?" He wanted to pull her into his arms, but on a deeper level, he knew she had to get this off her chest and put it to rest forever.

"Will Owen be a constant reminder to you about what happened to me?" She lifted her head, her eyes bright with unshed tears.

He put her glass aside and held her hands. "Sweetheart…" They were ice cold. Rubbing them together with his, Jack said softly, "Look at me."

Peyton averted her eyes.

"Please."

Slowly, her eyes met his.

"I want you to hear what I'm about to say and never for one single second forget these words." He gave her a look that was intense and unflinching. "I love you, Peyton. I have loved you for longer than you realize. Every day, it deepens and my heart expands a little more than the day before. I love Owen. I would lay down my life to protect either of you from anything or anyone."

He watched as her eyes grew wide. She blinked and the tears that hovered in her lower lashes slipped down her cheeks. "You love us?"

He withdrew one hand and, using his thumb, wiped her face. He smiled. "Yes. I do."

"But what about—"

He cut her off. "I know what you're going to ask and you have nothing, absolutely nothing to worry about. There is not one person in my family who doesn't see how happy I am with you. And believe me, in this family, you can't hide anything, especially if you wanted to. And Owen is your son. That's all anyone needs to know."

Peyton bent forward. She whispered, "I love you too, Jackson, with all my heart."

He groaned. "Now I know I'm in trouble." He gathered her in his arms and said, "This is the real deal, Peyton. I have never felt about anyone the way I feel about you."

"Me either."

He kissed her lips and then said, "Is it too soon to tell you this is the 'grow old with me' kind of love?"

She placed a finger across his lips. "Can we table that part of this conversation for a little while?"

He chuckled as his heart thudded in his chest. "We can wait as long as you need. On one condition."

"Oh yeah?" Her voice held that sweet teasing tone that drove him wild. "And what's that?"

"You tell me what you want to do on our next romantic date."

A slow, sexy smile filled her face. "As long as I spend it alone with you, every night is special."

He was surprised. Out of all the possibilities she could have asked for, she had said something so sweet. "Then I'll plan something amazing."

She pulled him in for a kiss and shivered.

"Are you cold?"

"No." A devilish look came into her eyes.

He would love her always. His kiss was his unspoken promise.

•　•　•

*J*ack and Peyton strolled to the truck, arms intertwined.

He kissed the top of her head. "Remember, you can depend on me for anything and everything."

"I know, Jack. Trust me, I know."

The drive to Peyton's house went by fast, but when he pulled into her driveway, she noticed he kept the engine running as if it were a signal. She cupped his cheek in her hand and pulled him in for a tender good-night kiss. "I had fun tonight."

"Me too. Let's have our special date night very soon. I can't wait to be alone with you again."

Her heart fluttered. She was already looking forward to it. "Definitely." Her lips hovered over his. "Good night, and text me when you get home."

"I'll walk you up."

She grinned. "That means we'll end up sitting on the porch and neither of us will get any sleep."

He gave her a slow come-with-me smile. "Not a bad way to spend the rest of the night."

She gave him one long, lingering kiss and then said, "That should hold you for a few hours."

She hopped out of the truck and ran up the stairs, blowing him a kiss from the doorway. She smiled into the darkness as he drove away. Oh, how she loved that man.

25

———

*S*ome days, everything just seemed to fall into place. It had been over a month since Jack and Peyton had taken the boys bowling and today Jack watched Owen jumping on and off the swing and zipping down the slide in the backyard at the Briens' house. Peyton had her feet up and was enjoying a glass of wine while he manned the grill. Ken and Mary were coming out to join the party. Mary was carrying a tray of sliced vegetables and Ken had a bowl of what looked like potato salad. There was nothing like an impromptu family get-together.

Jack wanted to get Ken and Mary alone for a few minutes. As if sensing something, Peyton smiled at Jack and then looked at Owen. "Young man, sit your butt on the slide—you're not going to run down it."

Mary took the tongs from his hands. "Why don't you join Peyton and I'll watch the chicken?"

He glanced at Ken. He dropped his voice low. "Actually, I wanted to talk to you and your husband. Alone."

Her eyes sparkled with curiosity. "Talk to Ken. He'll fill me in later." She nodded toward the house. "Go on now."

Jack turned. "Ken, Mary's asked if we can go look for something for her in the kitchen."

A flash of surprise slipped over his face until he saw Mary surreptitiously place a finger to her lips. "Oh, right. Yeah."

Peyton began to get up. "I'll help you, Dad."

A bead of sweat trickled down Jack's spine. He was really doing this. "You sit and relax. I'll help your dad."

Before she could get up, Jack followed Ken inside and firmly shut the door behind him.

"Let's go out to the front porch."

Ken chuckled under his breath. "This is going to be interesting."

Jack was nervous. They stepped on the front porch and Ken closed the door behind them, effectively blocking their conversation from Peyton. Ken sat down in a wicker chair and patted the arm of its companion. "Have a seat and tell me what's on your mind."

He paced in front of the chairs. Clasping his hands together, his knuckles went white.

"Jack, you're acting like you're picking my daughter up for a first date."

"Well, I've never done this before."

Ken folded his arms over his chest and leaned back. A smile tugged at the corners of his mouth. Was he enjoying Jack's discomfort? "Go on."

The man was not making this conversation any easier. Jack cleared his throat. "I had wanted to talk to you *and* Mary, but I didn't see any way to get the two of you alone without your daughter getting suspicious." He swallowed hard. "I'm in love with Peyton."

"We know you are. It's as plain as the sun in the sky."

"And I'd like you to know I plan to ask her to marry me and to adopt Owen."

Now Ken leaned forward, his eyes steady on Jack. "I know you'll be a good husband to my daughter, but do you love my grandson as a father loves his son?"

Nodding, Jack said, "I do. He's a terrific kid and I think of him as mine already. I want us to have a couple more kids, if that's what Peyton wants too. You know I come from a big family and I've always wanted to have lots of kids."

Ken leaned back and crossed his legs. With a slow smile, he said, "I'm glad to hear you say that."

"Does this mean you'll be happy for us?" Jack held his breath. He was determined to marry Peyton. But he really wanted her parents to be happy too.

Ken chuckled and shook his head. "Of course we will. Mary and I can see how much you love Peyton and Owen. We'll be proud to call you our son."

Jack could feel his face relax into a grin. "Great. I don't know when I'll propose, but can you keep this between us and Mary for now?"

"Absolutely, and thanks for giving us a heads-up." He opened the front door but before walking inside the house, he said, "Have you bought the ring?"

"Not yet. That's my next step."

"I'm sure Mary can help you with the size. That way, it will be perfect for Peyton the moment you propose."

"That's a great idea. Thanks."

Ken clapped him on the back. "We men need to stick together."

He grinned. He couldn't wait to buy the perfect ring and pop the question.

• • •

*T*he family was sitting at the picnic table when Owen said, "Hey, Jack, do you want to go with me and Mom when I meet my teacher and see my classroom before school starts up?"

"That sounds great, champ. Are you looking forward to school?"

"Yup, and I'll get to see all my friends and tell them all about fishing and stuff we did this summer."

He had barbeque sauce smeared across his cheeks, and Peyton pointed to his napkin. "Wipe your face, please."

"Mom said I can get a new book bag too. I'm gonna get Spider-Man."

Jack smiled. "Would you mind if I tagged along for your back-to-school shopping trip? Maybe we can go out to dinner at that pizza place with the arcade afterward."

His eyes got big. "That'd be great. Right, Mom?"

"It does sound like fun." She took a sip of water. "Jack, after dinner, how about we run over to your place and I can take a look at those curtains for you?"

He gave her a quizzical look. Then he winked. "That's a good idea. We could."

Her mom said, "Why don't just the two of you go? Owen can stay with us."

Peyton mouthed *Thank you.* She wanted to spend a little alone time with Jack since they had been kind of busy the last few weeks. Maybe they could sit by the firepit, have a glass of wine, and see where the rest of the night took them.

When Jack and Peyton arrived at his house, the sun was beginning to set. A stack of large flattened cardboard boxes leaned up against the side of the garage, so she figured he must be starting to decorate more rooms. She noticed the new porch swing he had installed and a large planter with scraggly red and pink geraniums on the top step. The porch gave the house a focal point. She loved the old, rambling farmhouse; it had a lot of potential and Jack had barely scratched its surface. It was the kind of house she'd love to live in, and Owen would want to explore the woods out back. At the rate she was socking money away for a house, who knew, maybe she'd be able to find a deal like this when it was time for her to purchase her first home.

"It's looking good, but what's up with the boxes?"

He held out his hand. "Come with me and I'll show you." They walked in through the tidy but outdated kitchen and he opened the patio door.

She lingered in the doorway, looking back over her shoulder. "This really is a great space."

He leaned against the doorjamb. "What would you do to make it functional and a space for a family to gather?"

She let go of his hand and crossed to the sink, taking in the room. "I'd replace all the cabinets and add a center island with stools on the other side for a breakfast bar and install a small sink in it for meal prep." She gestured to the stove and refrigerator. "Next, I'd move the fridge so there is a triangle pattern and get it away from the heat of the stove. With the additional space, add a six-burner gas range. The cabinets should be maple and the uppers, glass fronts. Granite countertops, but in a light color so they don't make the room dark. Last but not least, I'd have oak floors, durable but warmer than tile."

He teased, "All that off the top of your head?"

She crossed the room and gave him a lopsided grin. "It's my dream kitchen. But since you are in desperate need of a kitchen makeover, I'll let you borrow any of those ideas. Besides, when I buy a house, it'll be years before I get to do something as grand."

He nodded thoughtfully. "I like the suggestions." He steered her to the door. "Now, weren't you curious to know what was delivered in those big boxes?"

She looked into his eyes. "Am I going to like it?"

"I hope so. I bought everything with you in mind."

She stepped through the door and onto the slate. "You fixed the patio."

He took her hand and gave her a smile. "I didn't want anyone to trip and get hurt."

That's when she saw a large seating area with a love seat, a chaise lounge and four side chairs, and a copper firepit in the middle of it all.

"What do you think?"

"It's perfect, but I'm confused."

He kissed her lips tenderly. "We've had several wonderful nights around a fire this summer, and I wanted to create a space for us here."

"It's beautiful. Thank you." She brushed his arm.

"The only downside is that the canopy hasn't arrived yet." He nuzzled the nape of her neck.

"It's going to be a star-filled night; I don't think we need to worry about rain or sun." She tilted her face up and brushed his lips with hers as he pulled her closer. She stepped back and took his hand.

"We should try out the love seat." Her voice was soft and husky. Desire hovered in his hazel eyes.

A come-closer smile slid over his face. "I couldn't agree with you more."

Peyton slipped her arm around his waist and guided him forward. All she wanted was to be in his arms. "Come with me."

In the early morning hours, Peyton lay wrapped in Jack's arms. Sometimes she still had to remind herself this was her reality and not a dream. His arms snuggled her closer in the king-sized bed. The windows stood open and the cool morning air wafted over them.

"Good morning, beautiful." He nuzzled her neck. "Sleep well?"

She couldn't control a sigh of contentment that escaped her lips. "Like a log. You?"

"I always sleep great with you by my side."

Somewhere in his house, a clock chimed seven. "I have to get up. We're taking Owen school shopping later today."

"Just five more minutes?" His breath was warm against her skin.

She wriggled from his arms and slipped from the bed. "You're in charge of coffee."

She picked up her clothes from the floor as she wandered into the master bath. He had installed the new door, but it didn't have a knob yet. She pulled it halfway and finger-combed her hair into place. The upside of having chin-length hair was she could do that and it would still look decent.

She hovered in the doorway. Jack had made the bed, and from the sounds drifting up the stairs, he was making coffee.

"Hey, Jack," she called down the stairs.

He appeared at the bottom step. "Yes, ma'am." He looked like a man who had slept very well.

"Any chance you have an extra toothbrush?"

"As a matter of fact, I picked up a few things for you. There's a bag on the dresser. Help yourself."

"Thanks. I don't care what your sisters say. You're a sweetie pie."

His laughter drifted up the stairs.

When she entered the kitchen, he looked over his shoulder. "Coffee's ready and I'm making toast."

"Thanks." She fixed them each a cup and kissed his cheek. "You know, if you'd rather not go shopping with us today, you can skip it. I can say you have work to do. Owen will understand."

"Would you prefer I didn't tag along?" The toast popped up and he smeared it with peanut butter and jelly. It was one of her favorite quick breakfasts.

"I'm sure it's not exactly top ten things a single guy wants to do on a beautiful day."

He swept her in his arms and focused on her, then said, "Any opportunity I get to spend with you and Owen is always at the very top of my list. Besides, I promised pizza, and I never go back on my word."

"O's birthday party is next week; do you want to come over for dinner and have birthday cake with us? I'm going to do a kids' party on Monday. Sort of a back to school and birthday party rolled into one."

"His birthday was a couple of months ago."

"With the appendicitis I delayed it."

"In that case do you need help kid wrangling?"

"Thanks, but Mom and Liza are helping out. And I don't know if you're ready for ten kids all sugared up."

"If you change your mind, let me know, but I'm all in for school shopping."

She laughed. "You've been forewarned. School shopping with a seven-year-old boy is not in my top ten, but it is something that has to be done."

He handed her a mug of coffee. "Sounds like this calls for lots of caffeine."

She gave him a quick kiss. "That's an understatement."

$\mathcal{Y}$esterday had been fun shopping for school supplies with Jack and Owen. Peyton wasn't sure who had more fun: her son or her guy. She smiled as she counted inventory. With a good weather forecast for the weekend, the winery should be very busy. Lily had been a huge help all summer and the weekends were easier with her on board; she was a good hire.

The door opened and a pretty woman with short dark hair and skin like porcelain came into the room. She was about Peyton's age but she was impeccably dressed, right down to her Gucci sandals. Her eyes roamed the room, taking in the space, and a smile played across her lips.

"Hello. Can I help you?" Peyton said as she stepped from behind the bar. "We're not open for tastings today but if you wanted to buy some bottles, I'd be happy to help."

"Thank you. This is my first time to Crescent Lake Winery although I've heard a lot about it and it's exactly how I pictured it, right down to the burgundy door to the tasting room." She stuck out her hand. "I'm Corine Price and you are?"

Peyton was confused. Did she just say Price? "Peyton Brien, manager of the tasting room."

The woman gave her a broad smile. "I've heard a lot about you. It almost feels like I know you."

"I'm sorry. You said your last name was Price?" What the hell had happened in Napa?

"Yes, I'm Jack's ex-wife." Her smile faded. "Well, I was sort of his wife."

Peyton's mouth dropped open and she snapped it shut. "Jack? Married?"

"Well, not really. We haven't seen each other in over seven years. I've been trying to get in touch with him and thought it would be best to come to the Finger Lakes." She reached out a steadying hand to Peyton. "Are you okay? You're very pale."

"What? Yes, I'm, I'm fine." She stumbled back to the bar. She needed a glass of water. Corine followed her.

"By your reaction, I'm going to guess you've never heard about me?"

She shook her head. "Yes and no." She turned on the tap and filled a glass of water and drank it down in several large gulps. "Jack's in the fields, but I can call him if you want to wait."

Her blood roared in her ears and she couldn't believe she was standing in her place of work, talking with her boyfriend's ex-wife, one she hadn't known he had. What the hell was going on? Was she in the Twilight Zone or something? It was obvious he had lied to her about Napa and what had happened while he was there. All this time, she believed he had been working through his issues with Sam and instead he had gotten married, and why hadn't anyone in the family ever said anything? Had they all been sworn to secrecy, to not tell the girl he had dumped when he left? How could he have been married and she not know it? She was a big fool; he hadn't changed at all. Life revolved around what Jack wanted or needed at any given time.

Steadying her voice, she said, "I'll call Jack." She gestured to a stool. "Feel free to have a seat. Depending on where he is, it might take a while for him to get in."

"Thank you, Peyton."

She grabbed her cell and walked into the storage room before she dialed. "Hi, gorgeous." His rich deep voice caused her anger to spike.

"Jack, you need to come to the tasting room right away."

"Peyton, what's wrong?"

"Your ex-wife is waiting for you."

"What are you talking about?"

"Corine Price is sitting at my bar and I suggest you get over here, now. It seems there is something she needs to discuss with you." She didn't wait for him to say anything more, just hit the end button. She jammed the phone in the back pocket of her jeans.

Taking a few deep, calming breaths, she forced herself to return to the tasting room. She maintained an expressionless face. "Corine, he'll be here soon."

"Thank you, Peyton. I'm sorry if this has come as a shock to you." Corine did look genuinely sorry.

She held up a hand. "You have nothing to apologize for." She blinked away tears of anger and hurt. "I need to check on something in the bistro. Will you excuse me for a few minutes?"

"Certainly. You don't need to keep an eye on me. I'll be

fine while I wait for Jack."

Peyton walked out of the room with her head held high, but her heart was dragging on the cement floor. She pushed open the swinging door to the kitchen, expecting it to be empty, and was taken aback when she discovered Kate sitting at a counter with a stack of cookbooks spread out around her.

"I didn't expect to see you today." Her voice was flat.

"What's wrong? You look like you've seen a ghost." Kate pushed out a stool. "Sit."

Peyton did as she was asked and hung her head. "You could say I've seen a ghost. One from Jack's past, and who knows, maybe his present."

"What are you talking about? You're not making a lot of sense."

"Jack's ex-wife Corine is sitting at the bar in the tasting room right now."

She gave a snort. "Jack's not married. At least not yet."

Peyton gestured to the door. "Go look for yourself. She's stunning, from the perfect golden highlights in her hair right down to her Gucci sandals and handbag."

Kate hurried to the kitchen door and was back in a flash. "Wow. She's beautiful—and she says she was married to our Jack?"

"Not only that, but she says she knows about me and the winery." Peyton narrowed her eyes. "You've never heard about her before?"

Kate shook her head. "No. I swear, and it's not something I would have kept from you. I can't believe Don didn't tell me."

"If you didn't know, do you think Jack could have kept it from Don too?"

"I wonder if he kept it from everyone. You know in the

Price family, there are no secrets."

"I need to get back out front. I can't just leave her sitting there. It's rude." Peyton got off the stool and Kate gave her a hard hug.

"I'm going to track down Don and see what I can find out. Do you want to come over later?"

"Thanks, but no." Her heart ached. He had done it again.

"If you change your mind, the door's always open."

Peyton touched her arm but didn't respond. She walked back into the bar and hoped Corine wouldn't feel the need to ask her questions she didn't know how or want to answer.

Jack couldn't drive the UTV fast enough. He hit the ruts in the gravel road and clutched the steering wheel with both hands. The minutes seemed like an eternity as he made the trip in from the back field. What the hell was Corine doing here and announcing she was his ex-wife? And why come here now?

What must Peyton be thinking? He slammed the steering wheel with his fist. How stupid could he be? He should have told her when he had the opportunity. Had he just torpedoed their future? He groaned. How was he going to fix this?

The first thing was to talk to Corine. Then he'd have to face his family, and how was he going to explain that he had been married, even for a short time, and never breathed a word about it to anyone?

He skidded to a stop in front of the warehouse, tossed his ball cap on the seat, and strode to the door. He took half a second before he walked inside. It had been years since he had seen Corine and he had never expected to see her here.

She was sitting at the bar, asking questions about the season. Peyton responded with basic answers about the winery and the types of wines she thought were best-sellers, and all the while it must be killing her to be pleasant. He admired her. The scene was surreal and not something he had ever expected to witness in his life. He stuck his hands in his pockets and walked into the room.

"Hello," he said generically.

Peyton's eyes were flat and unreadable. "I'll give you two some privacy." She didn't look at either of them.

"Wait," Jack pleaded and took a step toward her. "This isn't what you think. I need to explain."

She held up a hand, which was more like an invisible shield. "There is nothing to explain." She gave Corine a short nod. "Goodbye." The tasting room door closed behind her with a resounding thud.

Jack held out a hand to her after she turned. His heart just walked out the door and there was nothing he could do at the moment, even if all he wanted to do was run after her. Instead, he turned his attention to Corine.

"What are you doing here?" His tone of voice sounded harsh even to his ears.

"It's nice to see you too, Jack." She looked at the closed door. "I'm curious. Peyton had no idea we were married?"

"She knew we were involved but what we had wasn't a marriage." In truth, he hadn't considered himself really married, not in the sense like his parents.

"She's in love with you, and from the forlorn expression on your face, you're still in love with her too. Is this why you didn't want me to come here?"

"You and I both agreed from the beginning that no one would know it was a marriage in name only. I wanted to protect you and we were both angry with our families and thought it was a good way to show them we could handle our own problems. Then we realized the stupidity in it and got divorced after a couple of months. What was there to tell?"

"You love her. That's the reason you should have told her everything about us." She toyed with the glass of water in front of her. "She needs to know I'm not a threat to your relationship. That we're friends."

Jack took a step closer to the bar. "What do you mean, and is that why you've been calling and texting me?"

She held up her left hand, revealing a huge solitaire diamond ring on her finger. "Congratulations. That's quite the rock."

"Thank you. I'm very happy and Greg is a wonderful man, but there's an obstacle standing in our way."

"Okay, still not sure why you're here."

"Greg and I thought I needed closure from our past and to thank you for being a good friend and protecting me when I felt alone and vulnerable, when I had nowhere to turn. I never meant to make things difficult for you or upset Peyton, and if I had thought, I wouldn't announced myself as a Price. I've used your name as a shield for so long, it's hard to let it go. But I'm ready to marry Greg and start a new life and I only want you to be happy."

He nodded. "I can see his point. And you're happy?"

Her eyes shone with a happiness that couldn't be dimmed. "I am, but there is one little hiccup. Our divorce papers were never filed, so in the eyes of the law, we're still married, and this was discovered only when I had to give a copy of our paperwork to my minister. We need to both sign this in front of a notary and once it clears the courts, we can officially be unmarried. My lawyer's office set up expedited handling for all the cases affected."

"I thought you took care of the paperwork." He rolled his eyes but when he thought back, maybe he should have followed up to make sure everything had been finalized.

"I know what you're thinking, that I flaked, but it was the paralegal at the lawyer's office. Remember she was super pregnant?"

"No, I never went to the office."

"Well, she went into labor and apparently a ton of paperwork never was finalized." She held her palms up toward the ceiling. "So we're still married and if you had actually talked to me instead of cutting me off, we wouldn't be in this situation." She pointed to the door. "You're going to have some explaining to do. If there's anything I can do to help, just ask."

That was an understatement. "Thanks. I appreciate that, but now what? We sign the papers and you fly west for your idyllic life?"

"I'd like to have dinner with you and Peyton and anyone else in your family you'd like to invite. On me, too. But, Jack, I have to ask. Are things good here now? Are you happy being home?"

He nodded. "I am, and I want to have a future with Peyton."

"I'm glad. Do you want to go today? Or you could meet me tomorrow at the First National Bank in town. Once we sign them, you'll have a copy and we can both move on with our lives." She touched his hand, her voice gentle. "Which means you can find a way to make things right with Peyton."

"I think we should skip dinner, but tomorrow is better.

Will nine o'clock work for you?" He crossed his arms over his chest. "And you'll take care of everything else?"

"I will, and Jack, for what it's worth, I can see why you never got over her. Even from the limited time I was with her, I can see Peyton's quite a woman."

"Did she say something?"

"No. It was just a vibe, but you do have some groveling to do if you want to keep her in your life."

That was an understatement. She was his next conversation after his family.

Corine stood up and pushed back the stool. "If you need a friendly ear who knows the whole story of us, I'm staying at The Grapevine B & B in town."

"I appreciate that, but I'll handle it. I'm sure once I explain what happened, we'll get back on track."

"I'll see you tomorrow and good luck with everyone."

Corine left without looking back. At least this time he didn't have the sinking feeling he had failed, but unlike all those years ago, he knew what he wanted for his future. His cell phone rang and he pulled it out, praying it was Peyton. Instead, it was Don.

He might just as well get this over with. Nothing happened at CLW that Don didn't know about.

"Hey, Don. I'm on my way up." He walked toward the back stairwell.

"Good. It sounds like we have something important to discuss."

Jack's only response was to stick the phone in his pocket. How was he going to tell his family about his marriage and subsequent divorce? He climbed the stairs with heavy steps. More important: How was he going to explain it to Peyton?

Jack pulled into Peyton's driveway and clutched the steering wheel. She hadn't returned any of his calls or texts for the last two days. The divorce papers were signed and Corine was back in California. All that was left was to explain this mess to Peyton. It might be easier since he had already talked to his family and although they didn't understand why he had kept it from them, they were being supportive.

How could he explain to Peyton that his marriage meant nothing; it had been his choice, but he had needed to feel a part of something, and his desire to be a good friend overrode good sense. Deep down, since he hadn't told anyone in the family, he had known it was the wrong thing to do, and even after they had moved on, Jack had wanted to keep it that way.

He looked at his phone again, rereading her text asking him to come by so they could talk. His heart thudded in his chest and his stomach was in knots. Ken's truck was gone and he was disappointed Owen hadn't come bopping through the door to greet him with his wide grin and wave. The house was unusually quiet.

He climbed the stairs and tapped on the screen door. He breathed a sigh of relief when he saw Peyton standing in the hall and asking him to come in.

She was dressed in a pink tee and white jean shorts. Her hair was pulled off her face with a headband. Her eyes were filled with hurt and he knew it was his fault.

"Hi."

Without answering, she turned and walked into the kitchen. "Mom and Dad took Owen to the diner so we have the house to ourselves." She leaned against the counter and her eyes searched his. "I don't want Owen to overhear our conversation."

She was distant. That didn't bode well for their relationship. He longed to cup her face in his hands and kiss her lips, but he didn't. Her eyes were wary and he wasn't going to add pressure to the evening by trying to pretend they didn't have a huge problem to resolve. He was grateful she had given him the chance to talk at all. He could only hope what he was about to tell her would make some kind of sense.

"Thank you for agreeing to talk."

"I love you, Jack, but you've hurt me more than I can tell you." She took a step back. "Do you want something to drink?"

"Beer would be good." He was relieved. Offering a beverage wasn't necessarily a good sign but just her normal response when someone was in her home and he wouldn't be leaving in the next thirty seconds or so.

She grabbed two bottles and twisted the tops off before handing him one. "Let's sit on the deck."

He followed her outside. Citronella torches blazed in

the dusk to ward off thirsty bugs. She took a seat in a deck chair and he sat across from her. He wanted to be able to look at her when he told her everything.

"Thanks."

She took a sip. "Did you talk to your family?"

He gave her a half nod. "Yes, and it helped me to understand the whys of what happened, but Mom didn't excuse what I did. She's hurt too." He pulled on his beer. It didn't settle his nerves. He set the bottle on the side table. "I don't know where to start."

Quietly she said, "At the beginning."

He bent forward and clasped his hands together. Peyton appeared to be completely relaxed; however, she chewed the corner of her lip, so he knew she was anything but calm.

"When I went to Napa to work at the vineyard, I discovered a certificate program which focused on new ways to grow grapes organically. I was interested in how to make changes at CLW to prove to my father that I could handle running that part of the business, so I enrolled. Being in the field was my passion, and I knew if I didn't make some immediate and drastic changes to my life, I'd be pigeonholed into what my father wanted my life to be, and I couldn't stand that. In California, I was free from a desk or making sales calls. I wasn't cut out for that."

He felt better talking about the curriculum. He smiled. "The program was amazing—the instructor cared about the environment, and I was with people who were looking down the road to the future, not just for the next couple of years of harvest. I mean how to do it better long term."

She watched him but didn't interrupt. Which, in some ways, made this harder.

"In one of the courses, I met a girl. Corine. She was

quiet, almost shy, but very nice. She was local and worked at one of the larger wineries. We became friends, and soon her group of friends welcomed me into their circle. We spent most of our non-school and working hours hanging out. She was dating some guy at the time and nobody liked him, especially her family. They are pretty well off and the guy was a jerk. We all thought so."

"Jack, I'm not sure why this is relevant to Corine showing up and saying she was a Price." He could see the sadness in her eyes.

"I'm trying to explain everything."

She sipped her beer as if needing something to do for a brief moment.

He took that as a sign to continue. "Corine's boyfriend was a class A jerk, always making mean comments to her, and one night he told her she had better marry him or she'd be sorry. At first, we thought he was joking, but then we started to see a darker side. I thought he saw her as a bank account and he could intimidate her into agreeing."

Peyton's eyes grew wide.

"Corine didn't know what to do or how to get rid of him. At this point, he accused her of having her eye on some other guy."

"Did she? Not that it makes it right to act like an ass."

With a shake of his head, Jack said, "No, but she didn't want to date him anymore."

"Were you the guy he thought she was interested in?"

"Not exactly." Inwardly, he cringed. He didn't want to say the words, but there was no choice. Peyton would never stay in a long-term relationship with him if he wasn't truthful. Honesty was the foundation for all long-lasting marriages. "Corine was convinced there was only one way to get him out of her life, and that was to get married to someone else."

Peyton's mouth fell open and her eyes became like saucers. "Please don't tell me you thought that was a great idea." She smacked the middle of her forehead with her hand. "Of course you did. That's how you ended up married."

He looked at the floor and when his eyes met hers, he could see tears of anger and hurt. "We got married before a justice of the peace with two of her best friends as witnesses. When it was over, we made the decision to only tell the ex and a few of her very close friends to create the illusion of a happy couple. We agreed not to tell our families."

She stammered, "You *what*?"

"Right from the beginning, I think we both knew it wasn't the best idea and we didn't have the maturity to think of a different solution, like tell her parents she was being bullied. The marriage certificate was just a piece of paper."

"And a name. Your name." Peyton jumped to her feet and turned to the backyard. Then she swung around.

He couldn't look at her while those five words hung in the air. An oppressive silence weighed down on them.

Her face twisted. "How could you not make sure everything was finalized?"

He heard the accusation in her voice and he agreed with her that he had been stupid. "After a few months, her ex had left town and we filed for the divorce. I signed the paperwork and forgot about it. Apparently, after she dropped off the documents at her family's lawyer, something happened and it never got filed with the court. She only found out when she went to get a marriage license. A couple of months ago, she called and I didn't give her a chance to talk. I kept cutting her off since I didn't want to think about the past. I was focused on a future with you."

Peyton paced the length of the deck and back again. "Why would you do something so harebrained as to marry her? People break up all the time and they move on."

"I was protecting a friend from a dangerous situation the only way I knew how. She was convinced he would never leave her alone. We agreed it was the only solution."

Peyton smacked her hand on the railing and winced. "You lied to me all this time. I can't believe you didn't tell me you were married, especially when we've talked about the past. We covered all of that and during those conversations, you never thought to say *I made another mistake…*" He could hear the anger mixed with hurt in her voice. It was a powerful combination.

"Peyton, I didn't tell anyone. Less than a handful of people knew, and my family certainly didn't." He got up and stood beside her and took her hand. "I thought I was doing the right thing."

She jerked it away. "That's right. Jack to the rescue. Is that what you've been doing with me? Because if it is, I don't need to be rescued." She didn't attempt to disguise her anger.

"It's not like that and you know it. I love you and have since we were kids. What's between us is real."

With a snort, she said, "Right. If it was, why on earth wouldn't you tell me? Would you have ever told me if Corine hadn't come to Crescent Lake?" She held up a hand

and looked away. "Don't answer that since I'm pretty sure I know the answer."

"I would never have withheld that from you."

"Then when would you have told me?" She took one giant step away from him. "You've had over seven years to say, *By the way, I married a girl but divorced her and don't worry. It didn't mean anything.*"

He ran a hand over his face. "Peyton. It's not like we were dating at the time."

"But we had been dating and you left. I have to know if we hadn't broken up, would you have married her anyway and not told me?" Her voice was flat but her eyes softened. "Did you ever love her?"

"Not the way you mean. She was my friend and I'm not sorry I helped her."

"While I was studying and working my butt off in college, you were out having a great time with your new friends *and* getting married." She waved her hands in the air when he tried to hold them. "No. You don't get to be all lovey-dovey right now. We've been dating for a few months and you should have told me."

He understood why she kept repeating this and he wished he could say he was just kidding and he hadn't really been married.

"And to not tell your family about the marriage? All I can say is wow."

He clenched and unclenched his fists. "It was water under the bridge by the time I came home. Why bother telling them anything? Besides, you know how my family feels about marriage. Look at my parents, Don, and Tessa, and Anna, and even Liza. When a Price commits to one person, they love them with all their hearts and will do anything for their partner." He touched her arm and waited until she looked up. "You are the only woman I've ever loved."

She heard the emphasis he put on his last sentence but she turned away. She didn't want to look at the man she loved and have him see her cry. Her shoulders slumped. "You need to leave."

"Not until we clear the air." He put his hands on her arms.

The warmth of his hands took away the chill that had stolen through her. She wanted to lean back into his chest so he could wrap her in his embrace. But she remained stoic. "I can't do this anymore. Just go."

"Peyton, please. There is more we need to talk about."

She could hear the sadness in his voice. It broke her heart, but she couldn't cave in to his needs. Not now.

With a slow shake of her head, she whispered, "Go."

For what seemed like an eternity, she knew Jack stood behind her. He hadn't moved. She wouldn't relent even though she longed to.

Finally, he took a step back. "I'll call you later."

She didn't acknowledge him, and when she heard the truck's engine rumble, she turned to look at where he had stood moments before. Her heart was hemorrhaging. *How could you, Jack? How could you not be honest with me, and how could you do this to us?*

2 8

The last week had been hell but Peyton had been all in mom mode with Owen's birthday party, and he loved his new bright-blue bike. But he was disappointed Jack hadn't come to his party and kept asking where he was. She just said he had to work; things were busy at the winery. So far, she was able to distract him, but that wouldn't last much longer.

She longed to talk to Jack, but at the same time, she didn't want to talk to him. He called, texted, and left bouquets of flowers on the bar for her every day she worked. He even left a present for Owen, but she hadn't given it to him, not yet. Lily and Tony knew something was going on, but to their credit, they never said a word. On top of it all, Owen was now asking when they could go fishing again on Jack's boat.

Don had called to check and see how she was doing since she learned about Corine. He'd been point-blank and asked if she was thinking of leaving CLW. That had come as a shock since there was no way she was letting her personal situation derail her career. Don told her she had a future with the Price family business for as long as she wanted.

She stood in front of the tasting room door and dug into her bag for the keys while juggling her to-go coffee mug and a hanger with her freshly laundered work shirt. She looked up as tires crunched in the driveway and raised her hand in greeting.

Lily got out of her car. "Hi, Peyton."

"Hi." She noticed Lily was dressed in the winery logo polo shirt, crisp khaki-colored capris, and tan ballet flats. She was ready for a busy workday.

Lily took the hanger. "Let me help."

Peyton jingled the keys and forced a smile. "Found them."

She turned the lock and pushed open the door. Lily reached in and flicked on the overhead lights. The sun streamed into the room, bathing the center display of wineglasses, books, and other items, all wine-related, in a brilliant light. Peyton marveled at how much had changed for her in the last couple of years. Her role in the business had grown; she had good friends, and up until a week ago, an amazing boyfriend.

Lily took the hanger and walked toward the bar. "I'll hang up your shirt and then get set up for the day."

"Thanks." Peyton set her coffee on the bar and turned on the LED lights underneath. They were bright enough to see all the supplies. "Tell me how it's going with Beth. Is our marketing guru overwhelming you yet?"

Lily popped out from the back. Her grin was wide. "Amazing. I've learned so much about wine and pairing it with different foods to create appeal to lots of different demographics and how you need to understand the basics before you can influence a customer to purchase. I mean, I knew about marketing, but to really reach a customer and make an impact, you need to understand the wine too."

Peyton knew more was coming since Lily's enthusiasm bubbled up and over like champagne.

"Did you know there are wines that even a beer drinker might like?"

"Really?" Peyton gave her an indulgent nod. "And I do."

"Yeah, and that champagne is from a region in France and we have sparkling wine here, but it can't be called champagne."

"I did, and I can see that you've been learning a lot from the ground up."

"There was so much I had no idea about; I was naïve, in fact. It's like I'm a kid being given a brand-new book that holds the secrets to a new world. This is going to be the best job ever."

Peyton held back a chuckle and Lily's very serious expression fell.

"What's the problem then?" Peyton asked.

"This isn't permanent, so when the tasting room slows down, I'll be out of a job."

"You never know. The company is expanding, so something might open up."

"Well, worrying about what might happen won't get the inventory done or us ready to open." Lily picked up the clipboard and pen and hurried down the hall to the climate-controlled storeroom.

Peyton made a mental note to check in with Don to see if there was a place for Lily long term. She was an excellent worker and Peyton remembered what it was like to be young and starting out. It reaffirmed her decision to support the girl. Everyone deserved a chance.

She double-checked the shelves to make sure there was enough glassware. Next was the dishwasher, which she set up to be able to run glasses if needed. Most people liked to buy the glass, but there were always some left behind.

She opened the door to the storage room and called to Lily, "Can you bring out a case of crackers? We're out."

"You got it, boss."

The afternoon was a whirlwind of people and another big sales day. Not a record-setter for a Thursday, but definitely a good day, and for part of the shift, Peyton had stood back to see how Lily handled things. She was doing great and her confidence was growing.

After the tasting room closed, Peyton loaded the dishwasher for a run. She noticed a tall, handsome blond man walking in her direction. "Jack, how long have you been standing there?"

"Not long." In two short strides, he was standing in front of her. "Too long."

Her heart skipped and she longed to lean into his body for a long, slow, sensual kiss that would rock her to her toes.

The look in his eyes sent a jolt of electricity to her heart. He touched her hand. "Can we talk?"

Someone cleared his throat. Jack stepped back and they looked up.

"Don. We didn't hear you come in." Peyton didn't move away from Jack, but she did force a smile. She was uncomfortable with Don walking in on them. She wanted to keep their disagreement private. It was embarrassing for everyone to know that even she hadn't been aware of Corine.

"What's up, bro?"

"I got a call from Anna, and she and Colin will definitely be home next week even though they're a couple months behind schedule while she worked on that new blend. And as you know, Mom loves to have a reason to host a family dinner. Just thought you'd want a heads-up."

His brow arched. "Thanks."

Don's gaze slid between the two of them. "Good day for the tasting room, Peyton?"

She breathed a little easier now that the conversation had shifted to work. "It's been steady."

"Good." He gave her a warm smile, reminding her of the talk they had. No matter what happened between her and Jack, she had a place here.

"Thanks, Don."

"See you both later." He left the way he came.

Peyton looked around the room. "I don't think we should have a personal conversation in here. Anyone can walk in, and I really don't want the entire family to know any more of our business than they already do."

"Will you take a ride through the vineyard with me?"

Torn, she looked at her watch, calculating how much time she had before needing to get home. "I have an hour to spare."

*H*e didn't like the clipped tone in her voice, but he would take what he could get at this point. She hadn't spoken to him or returned his calls or texts since they had talked about California. He extended his hand, but she didn't take it. They walked out the back to where his two-seater UTV was parked.

They went down the drive at a slow speed. Jack lifted his hand in greeting to several of his guys, who were on their way out of the fields for the day.

"How's Owen?" He glanced her way. She was looking straight ahead.

"He's good. He loves school."

"Is he going to try out for soccer this fall? I hear the coaches are solid." He wanted to keep the conversation light until they were farther away from the buildings.

"It's up to him. I'm sure once he knows which of his friends are playing, he may decide to join the team. I'm pretty sure he knows that Johnny and George are playing, so he's leaning in that direction." She folded her hands in her lap as her shoulders relaxed a little.

Jack took this as a good sign. "I've missed you."

She didn't respond verbally but her chest heaved and her breath caught.

He slowed even more and turned down a grass-covered path. "I wanted to take you someplace that's important to me."

She didn't respond. Jeez, she was making this hard on him.

He took a deep breath. Everything would work out.

They hit a rut hard and he reached out a steadying hand to keep her secure in her seat. She flashed him a grateful smile.

"We're almost there." He took one final turn and slowed to a stop. They were surrounded by a newly cleared field.

She squinted. "What's all this?"

He leaned over the steering wheel and let his gaze run from left to right. He smiled. "The future."

"Jack, I've seen fields before; what's so special about this spot? And the more important question is what does it have to do with me?"

Ouch, that stung. He held up a hand. "Hear me out. I

should have told you when we first started dating again about what had happened in Napa with Corine. I don't regret helping her, but I should have found a better way to do it, and my biggest regret was not being completely honest with you. I'm hoping you can forgive me. I promise from today and for the future, I will never keep anything from you."

"Are you still married to her?"

"No. She confirmed the paperwork was filed and her lawyer pushed it through since she had a wedding to plan. She is in love with a good man and they're starting a new life together."

"Why didn't you tell me this the other night?"

"You didn't give me the opportunity—you asked me to leave."

She was quiet but then asked, "Does she know about me? That we were dating?"

Jack turned in his seat so he could face her. "She knew about you from the first time we met. You always popped up in conversation. She knew I loved you then and always would."

Her smile softened.

"My friends out there couldn't believe you didn't come with me to Napa, and more than one of them said I was a fool to have left you behind. I'm pretty sure they thought they knew you from all that I had said."

Her smiled faded a bit. "I'm still angry that you kept it from me. You know every detail about my life. I have zero secrets from you, and if we're going to have a future, you have to promise that you will not keep anything from me again. No matter how awful you might think it is. I will not settle for less than a one-hundred-percent open and honest relationship."

He slid the short distance across the bench seat until they were thigh to thigh. He could feel her warmth flood his veins. "I didn't talk about the marriage thing because I wanted to be able to say I married once and she is the love of my life." He kissed the palm of her hand. "You are the love of my life."

Her gaze was unflinching. "But being involved and getting married, even if it was in name only, are two very different things."

"I was wrong and I'm sorry."

She blinked away tears and pressed her body into his. He could feel her heart pounding in her chest until his heart beat in concert. With their arms around each other, they held on tight. Not speaking, just letting the moment wash away any remaining hurt. Yes, he had hurt Peyton by withholding the absolute truth, but he had also hurt himself. This last week had been so much worse than the last time they broke up. This time, he could have lost her forever. It was not a risk he was willing to take again.

"Tell me again why we're here?"

Jack kept one arm around her shoulders and turned them so they could look at the field. "There is a tradition in my family. When a Price thinks about getting married, a parcel of CLW land is given to us. This is where we can plant a variety of grapevines of our choosing. The goal is to ensure the vineyard for future generations." His arm swept the land in front of them. "Last year, I received this parcel of land from Dad. I guess he knew I was ready to put down roots. Someday I want to plant a variety of grapes that will represent my contribution to the family legacy. When it's producing, the yield will be around thirteen hundred bottles. It will be a CLW wine, but a special blend that we will develop with Anna's help."

"What a sweet idea. Does everyone have a section too?"

"They do. Dad's blend is Ruby, the red wine that is served chilled or can be used in sangria—it's Mom's favorite—and Don's grapes should be ready this year, Liza's next, and Anna has to decide what variety she and Colin want to plant. It takes a couple of good growing seasons to have a decent harvest. It's a tradition my grandfather Donald started for my grandmother, and we're the third generation to do it."

With a laugh, she said, "I hope your dad doesn't run out of land. There are a lot of Price kids and grandkids coming along behind them. And what about Tessa and Max?"

"Funny you should ask; I was just talking to them about it, and they have forty acres that haven't been planted yet. They want to plant some vines there and here and create a new brand, Crescent Creek, as a way to honor both vineyards. But don't say anything yet. They want to tell the family once they have the details worked out."

"Sam will go nuts over that idea. But will that mean more land is needed for the new venture?"

"Not to worry. Dad will just buy more land if he runs low. This is one of his favorite things to think about: the living legacy of Crescent Lake Winery."

"I'll look forward to tasting your wine someday."

He turned her face to look at him. "I hope to blend this wine with you."

His lips brushed hers, which led into an all-consuming, breathless kiss.

She looked up at him through her long dark lashes. "How about we start over with a date tomorrow night?"

"I'll pick you up at five." He sealed it with another kiss.

The next night, Peyton was ready at ten to five and waiting for Jack on the front porch. He had been able to secure tickets for the last event of the season at Vine Music, an outdoor venue. It had always been one of her favorite concerts of the year: music soundtracks played under the stars. Jack said all she needed to do was look beautiful and he'd take care of the rest. In a small way, it felt like old times; he used to do sweet things for her from time to time when they were dating.

She heard his truck before she saw him. Of course, Owen came charging through the door and was literally bouncing up and down. Peyton held out a hand to restrain him. "Wait until Jack turns the truck off before you run down the stairs."

As soon as the engine was off, Owen raced down the steps. "Jack, wanna see my new school sneakers?"

Jack picked Owen up with one arm and carried him up the stairs. "You bet I do."

The boy slipped an arm around his neck. "Mom said you've been working extra hard 'cause you got a lot to do.

Is that why we haven't gone fishing and you missed my birthday party?"

"I'm sorry, buddy. I have had a lot going on, but I promise that's behind us and how about we celebrate your birthday again with a day on the boat fishing, okay?" When he reached the top step, he set Owen down and kissed Peyton hello. His eyes sparkled. "I need to see these spiffy sneakers before we can go."

"I heard."

Owen took Jack's hand. "Come on in my room."

Peyton trailed behind them, listening to Owen tell Jack everything he thought was important that had happened over the last week. She couldn't help but smile. Those two made quite a pair.

After Jack admired the bag, sneakers, and every new shirt she had bought, she said, "Owen, it's time for us to go. We have tickets to a concert."

"When are we gonna go on the boat again and have a family date and my do-over birthday?"

"There's a half day of school on Wednesday," Peyton volunteered.

Jack said, "How about we plan to go as soon as you get off the bus?"

"Yes." Owen grinned. "And I'll put the worm on the hook for you, Mom."

She held up a hand. "You two can fish. I'll just watch, okay?" She kissed the top of his head and said, "Be good for your grandparents."

"I will." Owen hugged Jack around his midsection. "Bye, Jack."

Jack took her hand as they strolled down the stairs to the truck. "Now it's time for us. I packed the cooler with a gourmet picnic, and for the record, I made it myself, complete with wine and dessert. All day I've been looking forward to lounging on a blanket with you and listening to music."

"Sounds romantic." She couldn't take her eyes off him tonight. There was something about his crooked smile that had her wondering what else he might have up his sleeve.

They drove down the road. "Oh, before I forget. I talked to Anna earlier."

"She called to make sure I asked you to come to dinner at my parents' Thursday night at six thirty. She wants to catch up and it won't be a late night because the kiddos have school."

"I'm sure it will be good for you all to get together." She watched the road as they turned to head out of town.

"You're coming too."

"It's a family thing—you don't need me and Owen intruding."

He pulled her close. "You're my family; you have to come. It's in the rule book."

She wrinkled her nose. "I didn't get my copy."

"I'll fix that later."

"In that case we'll come." She pulled her hand away. "I need to call Sherry and see what she'd like me to bring."

Jack groaned. "She's going to say you and Owen. You know that's how she is."

Giving him a side-eye, she said, "The polite thing to do is ask."

He held up his hand in defeat. "By all means, call Mom."

She pulled her cell phone from her bag and dialed his parents' house. Sherry answered on the second ring. After confirming that Sherry didn't want her to bring anything, Peyton thanked her for the invitation.

"Your mother is something else." She slipped the phone into her purse. "Looks like we're going to dinner empty-handed."

He brushed his lips across the back of her hand. "Now, where were we?"

She laughed. "You're driving."

His eyes filled with desire. "You are an amazing woman and I love you. I want us to have lots more of these nights just the two of us."

"Me too." She pecked his cheek. "And I love you too."

*J*ack wrapped his arms around Peyton as she sat between his legs and leaned against his chest. He could smell her lavender shampoo. The night air was markedly cooler than he had expected, but he'd keep her toasty warm. She hummed along with the music playing, and he was content.

She tilted her head back to drink in the stars. "Tonight is perfect. It's like you had the magic touch with every-thing: the stars, the music, and the food."

"It's called being in love."

She burst out laughing. "You're so corny." She continued to laugh but confessed, "But I love it."

She turned to face him and pushed him backward on the blanket and leaned over his body.

He said, "You know what? I love you too and we have a bright future."

She pecked his lips. "There's nothing from the past that lingers. It's just you and me."

He tapped her nose. "And Owen."

Her lips twitched and she said, "Like I'd ever forget my second love."

He opened his eyes wider. "And who, may I ask, was your first?"

She came in close, her lips almost touching his. "You're my first and my last."

He wrapped his arms around her and he wished the love in his heart could be sent through his kiss. "You're my one and only, Peyton. Forever."

A short time later, she was in the crook of his arm, lying back, looking at the stars. In her heart, she had known Jack did what he thought was best for a friend, and part of her admired him for it. Maybe one of these days, she'd get another chance to talk to Corine, but if not, it didn't matter. The foundation of her relationship with Jack had been grafted a long time ago.

She rested her arm across his midsection. "You know, you make a great rock."

He kissed her temple, and for her ears only said, "Like Gibraltar, baby."

As they drove home from the concert, Peyton sat close to Jack. He had pushed the center console up and his arm rested on her shoulders. She yawned.

"Tired?"

"Uh-huh. In a good way. Tonight was just what we needed. The two of us alone."

"Along with ten thousand other music lovers."

She placed her hand on his thigh. "Everyone was lost in their own world, like tiny bubbles of happiness."

He looked at her out of the corner of his eye. "I love how you see the world. You really do wish the very best for everyone."

"Life is hard enough without adding the burden of

sadness to it. I have Jane to thank for helping me see the glass will be half full if that's what I want."

"Can your glass be almost full?"

She grew quiet for a moment. "I guess it is. I never really thought about it, but I've dealt with crappy stuff and survived. I'm luckier than some; I have an amazing son, my family, friends, and you." She kissed his cheek. "One of these days, I'm going to have a home of my own with Owen."

He wanted to ask her if there was a place in her home for him, but he didn't want to give away what he was planning for his next big surprise. If she wasn't ready, he'd wait.

She caressed his leg. "What do you see for your future?"

"House, kids, a couple of dogs, and who knows, maybe a bigger boat if there's a boatload of kids."

She gave a snort. "Your wife will have a say in that, but I'm glad you think you're so funny. You might want to hang on to your big house then, if you're going to have a lot of kids."

"Maybe the future Mrs. Price would want to buy a house together."

She didn't look at him, but she smiled. "Anyone would love your house, and together it will become a home."

He pulled into her driveway and turned off the engine. They walked slowly up the porch steps. Standing on tiptoes, she kissed him good night. "I'm going to spend some time with my son tomorrow night." She gave him a look from under her lashes. "Care to come over? I just might have the fixings for s'mores, and then we can snuggle by a toasty fire because it's supposed to be chilly. I'll do my best to keep you warm."

"Now there's an offer I can't refuse." He flashed a grin. "But I have a better idea. How about if we start at your place and end the night at mine. This way, we can spend some time with Owen and have some one-on-one time for us too."

She flicked her hand in the direction of his truck. "Good plan. Come over around seven."

"You don't have to ask me twice. But before I go, I need a kiss to keep me warm for the long, lonely drive home."

She wrapped her arms around his neck. "How's this?" Their lips met for a mind-blowing kiss.

30

A few nights later, Jack waited for Peyton in his backyard. The fire he had started had flames dancing and licking at the logs. Blue and orange mixed with yellow to cast a soft glow over the patio. It was romantic. He had set up a chiller bucket behind the sofa and placed a bottle of sparkling wine in it along with two glasses, just out of sight unless you were looking for it. It was Crescent Lake's best vintage and he had squirreled a bottle away for this very special night.

The door slid open and she stepped out, carrying a throw in her arms. Her eyes sparkled as she held it up. "In case we get chilly."

He chuckled. "I won't let you get cold."

She arched an eyebrow. "Ya never know."

She curled up next to him on the dark-green cushions. They sank into them and stretched out their legs on the small wicker table in front of them, the firepit just beyond that. He put his arm around her, holding her close. She spread the throw over their legs. "Isn't this nice?"

He had to admit it was, but not because of the blanket.

"I should have put some music on." He turned and scanned the darkness. "But I like sitting in the quiet with you." The crickets and peepers chirped in the distance. "Well, almost silent."

She sighed. "Life doesn't get much better than this."

He had rehearsed what he wanted to say half a dozen times on the ride to her parents' house, but now he was tongue-tied. How should he start? Should he just say *marry me*? With a forgone conclusion that she'd say yes? No, that wasn't how he wanted the love of his life to remember this moment.

"Warm enough?"

She looked up. Her finger traced his jawline. "Are you okay? We've established we're both warm enough."

"You are so beautiful." He caught her hand and kissed the underside of her wrist. "I am the luckiest guy in the world to be here with you right now."

Her eyes narrowed. "What's gotten into you tonight?"

"Nothing." He kissed the tip of her nose. "I just want you to know how important you are to me."

"Sweetheart, I feel the same."

He loved that term of endearment. She didn't use it often, which made it more special. Jack eased Peyton to a sitting position. In one smooth motion, he dropped to his knee and took her hand. Her mouth fell open and her eyes grew wide.

He tapped her chin to close her mouth and placed a finger across her lips. Reaching into his shirt pocket, he withdrew an engagement ring.

The firelight reflected off the facets of the pear-shaped diamond solitaire. He heard the sharp intake of her breath.

"I know we've had some rough days, but I've loved you since we were kids and I've waited a long time for this day to come. I can honestly say I can't imagine my life without you. You know, only one time I didn't plan ahead and it caused you pain, and now I'll never do anything without a plan, but this time, I want us to plan the future together. As a family, with Owen."

She wiped the tears from her cheeks with the back of her hand.

Holding the ring a little higher at the tip of her finger, he said in a clear, deliberate voice, "Peyton Brien, will you marry me?"

She was stunned and elated at the same time. She nodded and breathed, "Yes, Jack."

He pushed the ring onto her finger.

"Yes!" She flung her arms around his neck and crushed her lips to his. She knew tears filled his eyes. He was a tenderhearted man who was bowled over as to what one simple but powerful word could do to the both of them.

He gave her a searing kiss and then pulled back. Taking her hand, he pressed his lips to her finger. "It's official. We're getting married."

Showering his face with kisses, she laughed, unable to contain her joy. She held up her hand. "Jack, this is the most beautiful ring I have ever seen." She gave him a quizzical look. "How did you know the right size?"

"A very sweet mother helped me."

Her eyes widened again. "Mine?" She felt the grin spread across her face.

"I talked to your parents before I bought the ring."

She struggled not to laugh out loud. "You went old-school?"

"Well, not quite. But I can tell you I was relieved when your parents told me they were happy for us."

"You're two for two."

His eyes glimmered with happiness. "Well, not quite."

"What do you mean?"

"In the morning, I want to ask Owen if he'd be okay with us becoming a family."

Her hand flew to her mouth as a lump rose in her throat. Peyton couldn't believe her ears. "You want to ask Owen if we can be a family?" Fresh tears sprung to her eyes. "Now *that* is the sweetest thing you've ever said."

"Love, I have one more important question for you." He got up off his knee and sat next to her. Taking both her hands in his, he got close and kissed her tenderly on the lips. "If you agree, and Owen too, I want to adopt him. Legally, he'll be my son. I promise you I already love him like he's my flesh and blood. But it would mean the world to me for the three of us and whoever else may come along to share the same last name."

Her head dipped and then she looked him deep in the eyes. "I know you love him. Have you thought about what your family might think?"

Confusion flashed across his face. He said, "I don't understand."

"Well, you know because of—"

Jack interrupted her and placed a finger lightly over her lips. "Peyton, my family loves him, and when we make the announcement tomorrow at dinner that we're becoming a family, he will be a Price forever. It's not DNA that makes a family. It's love."

"Wow." She sat back. That one statement alone packed a powerful punch.

He searched her eyes. "Does that mean I can adopt him?"

"I'd be honored for you to be my son's father—and any other children we will have." She rested her forehead against his. She didn't want to break the spell.

"I have one more surprise for you." He tipped her chin up.

A small laugh escaped her lips. "I don't know if I can handle anything more."

He reached behind the love seat and pulled out the bottle of sparkling wine and two glasses. "We need to toast to our future."

"It's like icing on a cake." She clapped her hands together. "Wedding cake."

He popped the cork and poured two glasses. He raised a glass, but Peyton said, "Can I make the toast?"

He gave a half nod.

"I've known you for most of my life. I'm so thankful you had the patience and love to wait until we were both ready to begin a new life." She clinked his glass. "You are my hero and my love. I can't wait to spend the rest of our years together."

"Peyton, you are and were worth the wait."

In the early morning sun, Peyton and Jack walked hand in hand up the porch steps to her parents' house. She squeezed tight; she was excited and nervous to tell Owen. She paused at the door and touched his cheek. "Ready?"

Jack nodded. "I'm more than ready. I can't wait to hear what he says. Hopefully he's as excited as we are."

They walked in the front door. The house was quiet. She could smell fresh perked coffee. "Let's go out on the deck."

"Good idea." He slid the glass door open, and before long, she could hear Owen call her name.

She called to him, "We're out back."

The sliding door whooshed open and the little boy hopped onto the deck with a thud. "Hey, Jack. Did you come for breakfast?"

"I did, but first I wanted to talk to you."

"Did you hear that, Mom? Jack came to talk to me."

She got up from the chair. "I'm going to get some coffee. Owen, hot cocoa?"

He nodded and plopped down next to Jack and started to talk about their next fishing trip.

"I'll be right back."

Jack would wait for her for the important part of the conversation. She left them to talk about bait and fishing lures. She filled three mugs and went outside just as Owen was saying he was ready to catch a super big fish.

Holding back her laughter, she passed Jack his coffee and Owen his cocoa. She perched on the arm of the chair next to her fiancé and looked at him over the rim of the mug as she took her first sip.

"Owen, I was hoping we could talk for a couple of minutes about something important."

He slurped the cocoa and said over the next slurp, "Sure."

"You know that we've been spending a lot of time together."

The boy nodded. "We have a lot of fun, right, Jack?"

"We do. Which made me think about what it would be like if we could spend all our time together."

Owen just looked at him. She had a flash of panic. What if he wasn't ready for them to take the next step?

"I'd really like to marry your mom, and if it's okay with you, I'd like to be your dad."

His eyes grew wide. "You want to be *my* daddy, like for real?"

"If that's okay with you." Jack glanced at Peyton, and she gave him an encouraging nod.

"Is Mommy's and my name going to be different from you? 'Cause most kids in my school have the same name as their daddy."

"I'd really like for the three of us to have the same last name. We'd all be Price." Peyton watched as the coffee sloshed in Jack's mug, betraying his nerves. "What do you think? Should we get married?"

She held her breath.

"Yeah, that'd be really neat." Owen jumped up from the chair and threw his arms around Jack's neck. He looked at Peyton. "Can I tell Grammie and Grampy that we're getting married and Jack's going to be my dad?"

She was thrilled with his reaction. "How about instead you tell them we're going to have a celebration breakfast and I'll cook."

Jack stood and pulled her up and pecked her lips. "How about I cook and you can help."

"Can I help too? 'Cause that's what families do, help each other, right?"

He grinned at the boy who would be his son. "That's what our family does. We'll meet you inside."

Owen raced into the house, leaving the door open and calling out for his grandparents. Jack pulled her into his arms. "That went smoothly."

"You've made me very happy. And when we have

dinner at your parents', he'll tell the entire family our news the moment we walk through the door. Oh, shoot, but that will take away from Anna and Colin's homecoming. I'll talk to Owen and tell him we'll have to wait to make the big announcement."

"Are you kidding? Anna will be thrilled and it'll be all the more reason to celebrate. But if it makes you feel better, I'll talk to her ahead of time."

She hugged him around his waist. "That's a better idea and if she has any hesitation, I'll talk to Owen."

Arms around each other, they strolled to the back door. Jack kissed her cheek. "I'll let Mom know there will be two more for dinner. We can't celebrate our engagement and upcoming wedding without your parents."

Peyton brushed his lips with hers. "I love you, Jackson Price."

3 1

Owen raced up the walkway when they got to Sam and Sherry's house for dinner. Peyton's parents were a few steps behind her and Jack. Her hand clasped his, hiding her engagement ring. Jack really wanted to do a grand announcement. Hopefully Owen could keep the news under wraps until everyone in the family arrived.

However, that hope was short-lived when the moment he burst through the front door, he shouted out, "Mr. P, Mrs. P, come quick!"

He rounded the corner to the large spacious kitchen and dining area and ran smack-dab into Sam, who steadied Owen and then looked over his head to the four adults trailing him. "Owen, what's all the excitement about?"

"Me, Jack, and Mommy are gettin' married!"

Sherry threw the towel she had been holding onto the counter and rushed around to scoop Owen into her arms and then hugged Peyton and Jack.

"This is wonderful news." She kissed Owen's cheek and then Peyton's. "Jack, why didn't you tell us? We'd

267

have been prepared." Her smile pulled in Mary and Ken. "After all these years, we're going to be officially family."

Mary held up a basket. "I brought the bubbly."

Sherry set Owen on the floor and hugged Peyton again. "I'm so happy for you"—she patted her son's cheek—"and Jack." She tugged at Peyton's hand. "Let me see the ring."

Peyton held up her hand and wiggled her fingers. She flashed Jack a smile. "Isn't it beautiful?"

Sherry admired it. "Simply stunning, and it suits you perfectly. Elegant but understated."

Sam set out a dozen glasses on the counter. Within minutes, Tessa and Max, Anna with Colin, and Leo wandered in, followed by Liza and the boys with Don, Kate pushing the double stroller, and Ben as the stragglers. Sherry poured glasses of apple juice for the boys into plastic wineglasses. With everyone talking at once, offering congratulations to the happy couple, the chatter was deafening. Peyton wouldn't have it any other way. A sharp whistle brought the noise level down a few decibels.

Sam pulled himself up to his full height, matching his three sons. He waited until the last of the glasses were passed out. His eyes roamed over the group and his grin stretched from ear to ear. "I'd like to propose a toast to Jack, Peyton, and Owen." His eyes found the little boy standing with his grandchildren. "Today, Sherry and I are the luckiest parents alive, with the exception of Ken and Mary. We are expanding our family not by one, but four. Peyton and Owen, Ken and Mary, welcome to the Price family."

Glasses clinked and a chorus of congratulations for Peyton, Jack, and Owen echoed around the room.

Ken said, "If I may offer a toast."

Sam held up his glass.

Dad stepped forward. He smiled at Owen, Jack, and finally Peyton. "Jack came to me and said he planned on marrying my little girl and wanted to be a father to my grandson. Without a second thought, I told him Mary and I were thrilled. For quite some time, I've been watching Jack with them, and without a doubt, they were meant to be a family."

Peyton could tell her father was getting choked up. She was about to interject when Mom said, "Jack, you may be a Price, but you're about to become a Brien too."

Liza piped up, "Does this mean I get to be your wedding planner?"

Peyton laughed. "We wouldn't have anyone else." She looked at Jack. "Before anyone asks, we haven't set the date yet and we have a lot of decisions to make, and there is another wedding that we should all focus on first." Her smile reached Anna and Colin.

Crossing the room, Anna pulled her into a hug. "Welcome to the family and"—she looked at Jack—"it's about time."

Kate put her hand up. "I've got dibs on making the wedding cake."

"That's an awful lot to ask."

Kate's face fell just a little. "I'm making Anna's."

Peyton said quickly, "Can it be chocolate?"

With a laugh, Kate said, "I'll make anything you want." She picked up Ben, who was tugging at the hem of her top. She gave him a squeeze. "Try not to pick the hottest day of the year."

"I was thinking cooler temps. Maybe a spring wedding next year." She grinned at Jack. "But I need to consult with my fiancé first."

He pulled her to his side and kissed the side of her head. "Whatever my bride wants, she can have."

"Since that seems to be settled…" Sherry waved everyone toward the table. "Dinner's ready."

inner was the usual boisterous affair, children anxiously wanting to go play or have dessert first and *then* play. Wine flowed like water. Peyton soaked up every moment of the insanity. And her parents seemed to be enjoying themselves too.

Jack leaned back while he toyed with his wineglass. He wanted Anna and Colin to know how happy he was that they were home.

"Colin, when do you go back to work?"

"Next week. We're going to take some time and clean out my house before putting it on the market."

"Do you need help moving anything to Anna's place?"

Colin took Anna's hand. "We've hired a moving company. With the family preparing for the upcoming harvest, it just made sense." He gave his future bride a smile.

Anna said, "Hey, family." She waited until all eyes were on them. "We wanted to tell everyone when we were together, but we've decided to push our wedding off until next year."

Peyton leaned forward in her chair. "Is it because we announced our engagement?"

"Not at all. We made the decision while we were in France. We've spent so much time away from our families and it might sound a little selfish, but we'd like to have an engagement party, plan a beautiful wedding, and just enjoy the process of preparing for our special day."

Colin kissed her cheek. "Also, this way I can build up more vacation time and whisk my bride away on a fabulous honeymoon."

Peyton gave Jack a worried look, one which he knew well. He could almost read her mind. "Anna, are you guys being straight with us? You already had this planned?"

"Definitely. That was the main reason we wanted to have the family get together, so we could tell everyone before plans went into overdrive." She gave Peyton and Jack a reassuring smile. "I really want to enjoy all the festive stuff with our family and friends. And now it's even better since Peyton and I can talk weddings all we want."

"Did you set your date?" Peyton asked.

Anna smiled broadly. "It'll be in the fall. Once we confirm the location, you and Jack will be the first to know so you can plan around us."

Sherry came over and perched on the chair next to Peyton. "Two weddings in one year. We have so much to celebrate."

"Mom, did you ever think your family would grow this much?"

Her eyes scanned the room. "Only in my dreams. When your father and I got married and we wanted to have kids, I had hoped we'd have lots of grandchildren, and finally we have our first granddaughter and four, no five grandsons." She squeezed Peyton in a one-armed hug. "Hopefully we'll have a few more in the coming years, and I've already told Sam that if we have to add on to the house to hold holidays, then we will." She wiped a tear from her cheek. "I am one of the luckiest women in Crescent Lake." Her smile included Mary.

"Mrs. P." Owen had come over to the group. "May I have a glass of water?"

She stood up. "Owen, from now on, I'd like you to call me Mimi, since I'm your grandmother, and Mr. P is your Poppi."

Owen looked at Peyton and then Jack. "Is it okay, Mom?" And then it seemed to hit him. "Am I gonna be related to everybody? Like, I have cousins and aunts and uncles too?"

Jack laughed. "Son, we're one huge family now."

Owen jumped up and shot his fist in the air. "Yes!"

The adults laughed and he said, "Mimi"—color flushed his cheeks—"may I please have a glass of water?"

She held out her hand. "Come with me."

Peyton placed her hand over her heart and smiled as her son held her future mother-in-law's hand.

*L*ater that night, Peyton and Jack sat on the front porch at her parents' home. Owen had been tucked into bed, and Mary and Ken had gone inside, leaving the happy couple to enjoy some time alone.

"What a day." Peyton snuggled closer to Jack. He was so warm and she loved to be close. "It's so good that Anna's home. I can't wait to hear all about France."

"She looks happy. Some of that is Colin, but I think she's happy to be home."

"It was sweet of your parents to recognize Owen as a grandchild. I swear he was walking on air after your mom asked him to call her Mimi."

"It was comical when he announced to the boys that they were cousins."

She snickered. "Ben was funny when he declared they needed more girl cousins. I thought your mom was going to fall off her chair, she was laughing so hard, like we could go to the store and get more girls in the family."

"I wouldn't mind giving him a sister, especially if she looks like her mother. Do you think Owen would like to be a big brother?"

"Are you kidding? He's getting the life he always asked me to have. A dad, cousins, aunts and uncles, and more grandparents. I think your mom was right. This is the life I could only have dreamed of." She tipped her face up and invited him to kiss her. "Thank you for making my dreams come true."

"There is one thing I'd like to talk to you about. It's about you buying a house."

She half turned in the chair. "I was thinking about the money I've been saving for a down payment. What if we took that and put it into the kitchen remodel at your place? I know I'm not much of a cook but maybe I'd be inspired to learn."

"Or we can sell my house and buy something together and start our life as a family with a home that has just our history." He brushed her hair back. "It doesn't matter where we live as long as we're together, so it's your choice."

"Then I choose to finish the remodel at what is currently your home and make it our forever home on one condition."

"Name it."

"If I never learn to cook edible dinners, you won't hold it against me."

He chuckled. "Darlin', the only thing I'm ever going to hold against you is me." And to prove his point, he pulled her close and wrapped his arms around her. "Just like this."

"You say the sweetest things."

He looked deep into her brown eyes. They grew wide. He was overwhelmed with how much he loved this woman. "You don't have to worry. If you can dial a phone, there's always takeout."

He kissed her through her laughter.

She sighed. "Oh, Jack."

The Following Spring

Jack walked around the outside of the house. It was no longer just an empty shell—now it was a home where he was going to live with his family. Today he, Peyton, and Owen would officially become a family. He couldn't wait to share this home with his bride and son.

Peyton had been busy packing and getting ready for the wedding, and was happy to turn over the kitchen project to Jack. It had been completed in record time. The painters freshened up the main rooms too, in neutral shades. As a surprise for his bride, he hired a landscape designer to plant a butterfly garden in the backyard. Even the swing set with an extra big slide was installed and ready for his son.

Jack had spent the last several nights, with help from Don, Leo, Max, and Colin, painting Owen's bedroom and setting up the new furniture to get it ready in time. The big move was scheduled for the day after he and Peyton returned from their honeymoon.

But today was the day he'd longed for. He would marry the woman he loved. He could picture carrying Peyton through the dark-green door and over the threshold later tonight. They'd spend their first night as husband and wife here before heading to Turks and Caicos.

His cell phone rang in his back pocket. It was her special ringtone. He smiled and said, "Good morning, my beautiful bride."

"Good morning, my handsome groom."

He could hear the smile and happiness in her voice. "I was just admiring our new front door."

She dropped her voice to a hush. "Did you and the guys finish the junior area?"

"All set. I hope he likes it. The guys had a blast adding their special accents. For Leo, it was muscle cars and Don and Colin, sports memorabilia, and Max added a chemistry set."

"That was really sweet of them." Jack heard Mary's voice in the background, but he couldn't tell what she was saying. "Jack, I gotta go. Time for the hairdresser."

"Have fun. I'll be the guy in the dark-gray tux at the end of the aisle."

Her laugh was musical. "I'll be the girl in the white dress. I love you, Jack."

Peyton felt like she floated on air down the hallway. She stopped to peek into Owen's room. "Hey, kiddo. I'm going to get my hair done. Be good for Grampy." He grinned. The gap in his front teeth made her pause. Time was going by lightning fast. "You sure are a cute kid, you know that?"

"Ah, Mom." A flush of pink dotted his cheeks. He got that from her.

"Grampy's going to give you lunch, and then when I get home, I'll help you with your bow tie."

"Can't Grampy and I go over to Poppi Price's house with all the other guys?"

"Ask Grampy, but I'm sure he'll be okay with that."

Owen did a fist pump and said, "Yes!"

With a shake of her head, Peyton went in search of her dad. He was reading the newspaper in the family room and appeared to be the picture of calm. "Hey, I just checked on Owen. He wants to go over to Sam's and have you two hang out with the guys."

"That's not a bad idea. I'm sure the kids are there and he'd be occupied."

"Thanks, Dad." She turned to leave and then stopped. "Jack makes me very happy."

He stretched out his hand to her and got up. "I'm glad, honey." He took her hand and gave her one last kiss. His voice was thick with unshed, happy tears. "We'll meet you at the church."

He left the room and she did a slow three-sixty turn. All the pictures on the walls documented her life from the first time Mom had carried her into this house. Pictures of Owen lined the walls too. Today she was going to be walking out the door, and her home would be with Jack and Owen, a new life.

Mom called, "Peyton, come on! We're going to be late."

Taking one final look, she smiled. "Coming."

Cars dotted the church parking lot. Peyton took her small tote bag from the back of the car, and Mom picked up the garment bag that was lying over the back seat in her SUV. They walked in through the back door of the church, pausing in the hallway. Controlled chaos was in full swing.

Liza looked beautiful in an aubergine-colored gown with short sleeves and a ruched front. She clutched her clipboard to her chest and pointed to an empty box on the table. "Where are the boutonnieres for the groom and the groomsmen?"

A girl from the florist handed her a flat white box and pulled the lid off.

Liza smiled. "Let's get those across the hall, please. Mom, would you find the photographer and have her take a picture of you pinning Jack's on? Oh, and Owen's too. That'll make a cute picture."

"Consider it done." Sherry flashed Peyton a reassuring smile. "Don't worry; I'll make sure they're ready."

"Thanks, Sherry."

Kate wore a long sheath the same color as Liza's. It had a square neckline, which enhanced her tall, slender frame. She had taken charge of the tote and garment bag and gestured for Peyton to follow her into the adjoining room. "I have everything set up in here, including a plate of sliced fruit and cheese in case you want to nibble on something."

Tessa piped up, "Don't forget the bubbly!" Her gown graced one shoulder and featured a sweeping skirt.

Anna beamed and swished her long skirt. It flowed below a rounded neckline. "Do we look like you had hoped?"

Peyton swallowed the lump in her throat. These

women were sisters to her. They had all worked together so today would be something she would remember for the rest of her life. "Better!"

Mom touched her arm. Her eyes were bright. "It's time to get the bride dressed."

Kate nodded. "It is. Peyton, the next time this gaggle of girls sees you, you'll be ready to take a long walk down a short aisle."

Peyton's dress was a long creamy white gown that had three-quarter-length lace sleeves and a floral lace overlay with a full sweeping skirt and a long train. The sweetheart neckline would show off the Brien family aquamarine necklace perfectly.

She tossed aside her yoga pants and button-up shirt. Kate and Mom held the dress so she could step into it. The zipper was on the side, and once secured, Peyton smoothed the fitted bodice and positioned the emerald-cut gem above her heart. Kate set her matching pumps on the floor and Peyton stepped into them.

Mom held her veil up. "Peyton, can you sit while I double-check the comb in your hair?"

Instead, she kicked off her shoes. Mother and daughter were now the same height.

Her mom secured the comb in her hair, and Peyton swept her bangs out of her eyes with a spritz of hairspray. She checked her makeup one last time and then slowly turned to Kate and Mom. "How do I look?"

Peyton's mom placed a hand over her heart. Tears glistened in her eyes. "Radiant, in love, and very happy."

Peyton hugged Mom. "I'm good"—she laughed—"except for my shoes."

Kate said, "I'll check with Liza to see if we're ready to start this party."

"Thanks, Kate."

After she left, mother and daughter had a few moments alone. She handed Peyton a small cream-colored hanky. The embroidered flowers in one corner were dark purple. "Here's another something old. It was my grandmother's."

Peyton tucked it up her sleeve on the underside of her arm. "I can never thank you enough for all you've done for me," she began. "I hope that someday I'll be a mom as amazing as you."

"You already are." She kissed Peyton's cheeks. "No one deserves to be happy more than you."

"Don't make me cry," she whispered. "I don't have time to fix my makeup."

"You have a hanky," Mom reminded her with a tear-filled smile.

Kate poked her head in. "Peyton, we're all set if you are."

She stepped into her shoes and accepted the cascading deep-purple and white rose bouquet from Kate. "You go ahead. I'm right behind you."

Kate and Mom stepped through the door. She pressed her hand to her stomach in hopes of calming the butterflies dancing inside. With one last look in the mirror, she was ready.

Peyton stood next to Dad, who looked exceedingly handsome in his dark-gray tuxedo. He wiped his eyes and looked straight ahead. Liza had ushered everyone out into the vestibule and the organ was playing the wedding march. One by one, the Price women walked down the aisle.

In a happy twist, Owen had asked if he could escort his grandmothers to their seats. Once they were down the aisle, it was Kate's turn. When she reached the altar, the music changed. The guests stood up and Dad offered the crook of his arm to Peyton. He gave her a heartfelt smile.

"Are you ready?"

She kissed his cheek. His aftershave teased her nose. "Yes, Dad. I am."

She took her first halting step. Her eyes sought Jack and found his. The aisle seemed to be too short. Her blood was humming and her heart flipped.

Jack was absolutely heart-stoppingly handsome. The dark-gray tuxedo was molded to his tall, lean, muscular frame. A lavender rose in his lapel drew her gaze to his smile and those dimples. Her knees grew weak just looking at them.

He held out a hand as she took her final steps toward him. Dad placed her hand in his and waited as they turned to take their first step to the altar. Owen stood on the altar, looking adorable in his matching tux and flower. He stood tall, so much like Jack. He waved to Peyton and grinned. "Hi, Mom."

She blew him a kiss. He pretended to catch it and put it in his pocket. Where had he learned that? Her not-so-little man was full of surprises.

The pastor asked the congregation to be seated. He smiled at the couple. Before he could begin, Jack leaned toward her and said, "You are so beautiful."

"You look pretty handsome yourself."

As the pastor moved through the ceremony, Peyton's eyes kept drifting to Jack. She couldn't believe this day had finally come. She was marrying the best man she knew, and the only man for her.

"Now, we've come to a point in the ceremony where we're going to light the unity candle. But we're doing things a little differently. As you may have noticed, we have three tall tapers and in the center is the unity candle." Pastor smiled at Owen. "Are you ready?"

Owen stepped in between his mom and Jack. "Yes, sir." His voice carried in the small chapel.

Peyton took a lit candle and handed it to Owen, and then she took her candle and Jack took his. Three tall white tapers glowed.

"Today we join together one woman, one man, and one son to create a family."

Together Peyton, Jack, and Owen blended the flames and the unity candle burned bright. Applause filled the church.

"It's my pleasure to introduce, for the first time, Jackson, Peyton, and Owen Price!"

Jack leaned over and pulled Peyton into a sizzling but quick kiss, and then he pulled Owen close with one arm and slid the other around Peyton's waist. Holding his bride and son close to him, they turned to face their family and friends.

Owen did a fist bump with Jack and proudly announced for all to hear, "I've got a mom *and* a dad!"

Peyton looked at Jack. Before they kissed again, she whispered to him, "All my dreams have come true."

The End

Thank you for reading Jack and Peytons's story. I hope you enjoyed the story. If you did, please help other readers find this book: **Please leave a review now!**

Join Lucinda's Newsletter today to be notified about upcoming releases and specials just for you, my newsletter subscribers.

Keep reading for a sneak peek of:
Vintage, Book 4 in the Crescent Lake Winery
Available October 2021
Featuring loyal Leo Price and the talented Stephanie
James

AND DON'T FORGET TO PRE-ORDER

For the love of hotrods and heart throbs…

Leo Price loves classic cars. He opened a successful, classic car restoration company and skipped working in the family wine business in the Finger Lakes. But more important to him than business, is family, primarily his twin sister and her two sons. A wrench is thrown into his life when he meets the beautiful Stephanie James and as a bonus, she knows how to keep an engine running.

On the worst day of her life Stephanie discovers Leo and his two nephews in her car restoration shop. It wasn't bad enough she had just become an orphan but the kids knocked over a display and broke a very special car model. A sweet memory of when she had built it with her dad. Returning to the small town of Black River for six months she needs to put the business on a steady path and return to her life on the West Coast.

When Steph realizes someone is stealing from her business

*it could threaten her plans to keep her father's legacy
alive. And then there's Leo, dating him gives her ideas
about what life might be like if she stayed or is it possible
he'd leave his roots in the valley and follow her?*

*Thank you again for reading Blush, book 3 in the Crescent
Lake Winery.*

I hope you enjoyed the story. If you did, please help other readers find this book:

This book is lendable. Send it to a friend you think might like it so she can discover me too.
Help other people find this book by writing a review.

Sign up for my newsletter by contacting me at http://www.lucindarace.com.

Like my Facebook page: https://facebook.com/lucindaraceauthor.

Join the Friends who like Lucida Race's reader group on Facebook at:

https://www.facebook.com/groups/1659098381010817/?ref=br_rs

Between Here and Heaven

Lost and Found

The Journey Home

The Last First Kiss

Ready to Soar

Love in the Looking Glass

Magic in the Rain

ABOUT THE AUTHOR

Lucinda Race is a lifelong fan of romantic fiction. As a girl, she spent hours reading and dreaming of one day becoming a writer. As her life twisted and turned, she found herself writing nonfiction articles, but she still longed to turn to her true passion: novels. After developing the storyline for the Loudon Series, it was time to start living her dream. Clicking computer keys, she has published nine books.

Lucinda lives with her husband Rick and two little pups, Jasper and Griffin, in the rolling hills of Western Massachusetts. Her writing is contemporary, fresh, and engaging.

Visit her at:
www.facebook.com/lucindaraceauthor
Twitter @lucindarace
Instagram @lucindaraceauthor
www.lucindarace.com
Lucinda@lucindarace.com